THE
TYPHON EXPANSE

Townsville Speculative
Fiction

The Typhon Expanse
Copyright © 2017 Townsville Writers and Publishers Centre

ISBN 978-0-6480462-2-6

Created by Terry Mullins
Edited by Jarryd Luke
Formatted by Lana Pecherczyk
Cover design by Michael Huddlestone and Michelle Mullins

Publisher's Note: This is a work of fiction.
Names, characters, places, and incidents are a product of the author's imagination. Locales and public names are sometimes used for atmospheric purposes. Any resemblance to actual people, living or dead, or to businesses, companies, events, institutions, or locales is completely coincidental.

Serenade Publishing
www.serenadepublishing.com

TABLE OF CONTENTS

FOREWORD

Over a year ago, a group of writers decided one night to write an anthology. I don't think any of us realized at the time that this would entail over fourteen months of writing, editing, rewriting, editing, arguing, artwork and still more editing. What we have created was not done for the purpose of profit (although that would be nice) but to give all of us experience in creating and publishing a book.

The group in question is the Townsville Speculative Fiction Group (TSFG), and it is an offshoot of a larger body, the Townsville Writers and Publishers Centre (TWPC). We are a group of writers, ranging in number from six to twelve persons, from many different walks of life, aging from 18 and up. We have different view and likes, but one thing we have in common is the desire to write fiction that others would want to read. Speculative fiction covers science fiction, fantasy and horror genres and each of us has our favourite.

To introduce myself, I am Terry Mullins, and I am basically a university tutor. However my real love is science fiction, and I decided, at the age of forty nine, that I wanted to be a science fiction writer when I grew up. And to aid this, I started to write a novel, set in a vast nebula called the Typhon Expanse, so named due to the shape of the nebula resembling a tentacled monster. (Free points to those who know where Typhon comes from). Now of course real life kept interfering, finishing degrees, work and other boring things, so I am still writing it. But I had created a time line of how the universe I created came to the point it was at. A nice long timeline, with many references to events not fully explained. If you are interested the time line is located at the end of the book. So I offered this world to the other writers in the group as the basis of a shared world anthology.

The Typhon Expanse is a space opera setting with two large powers (the oppressive Terran Union and the multi-specied Outworld Alliance, facing off with each other in a war of survival. But the stories of this anthology are not about that conflict. That is a story for another time. These are stories set for the most part in the Terran union, showing in part how it came to be the way it is. The Terran Union is my nightmare vision about the way things could develop in the future, considering the many issues facing the world today.

Each writer here brings something unique to this world. There are horror stories, and suspense stories, political intrigue and character development pieces. Even comedy. Each story has added flavour and texture to this universe. We hope you enjoy.

FIAWOL

Terry Mullins

GHOSTS OF THE PAST
By William Elliot

Author's note: *An over-analyser with a creative side, by day I solve problems and manage stuff. As a writer, I like to escape reality, but not too far. I gravitate towards urban fantasy, melding the real world with the unreal. For the Typhon Expanse, I took a plunge into the Scifi universe. I cheated, though, picking events from the timeline in the near future so I could use today's real issues as a launching pad into the nightmare that might be. So, my apologies to the hard core Scifi readers, because at its core, Ghosts of the Past is a real world thriller.*

Robert looked at the text again, his hands shaking so badly he almost dropped the phone.

No, please, God no.

Wracked by indecision, he took a step toward the door, stopped, turned around, took a half step and turned again. His heart was thumping hard in his chest and he was having trouble breathing. All he wanted to do was curl up into a ball and shut the world out, but his body wouldn't let him. His limbs demanded action, but they didn't know where to go, what to do. Groaning like a wounded animal, he raised his hands to his head only to fling them down again.

Think, damn it. Stop and think.

Deep breaths. One, two, three… Don't look at the text. Just think.

His heart was racing and he was still breathing hard, but at least his brain was working. Think first, then act. That was his mantra. Think first. Every problem had a rational solution.

Except his body didn't want to analyse. It was screaming for flight, making it hard to think. Intellectually he knew it was just the adrenaline flooding his body, but he felt physically sick. He was starting to sweat now and could taste the bile in his throat.

Robert barely made it to the restroom in time.

'Hey boss, have a look at this.'

John sipped his coffee as he drifted over and peered over the tech's shoulder. It was security footage of one of the labs and someone appeared to be in one hell of a hurry.

He took another sip. 'Can you track him and put together a montage of where he goes.'

'Sure boss.'

Robert burst through the front door and ran to the garage. This was what he had feared. This is why they had left, what they had escaped. It had to be them. He should have known he could never escape, never be safe. He had wanted to believe, though. For the kids' sake, he had wanted to believe.

'Dad, are you okay?'

He swung around, eyes wild, containers strewn across the garage floor. Tiisha! Damn, he had forgotten Tiisha would be home. He grabbed hold of the shelf to hide the shaking and ignored the mess he had created. Swallowing the hard lump of fear in his throat, he said, 'I'm fine honey, just looking for a few things.'

He saw the frown on her forehead and the quizzical look on her face. 'Where's your brother, sweety. Where's Alan?'

Tiisha shrugged. 'Dunno.'

She was lying. There had been fleeting hesitation, and she broke eye contact just before she shrugged. It was subtle, but he knew her signs well. Almost as telling was the lack of sarcasm at the mention of her brother. She knew.

Tiisha folded her arms and compressed her lips. *Bugger*, she knew he knew she was lying.

He shut down the automatic response forming on his lips. Calling her out was bound to get her back up. This was not the time for an argument with a pig-headed 17-year-old. He needed to get moving.

Hands still gripping tightly to the shelf he tried to soften his voice. To his ear it came out shaky and pleading: 'Please Tiisha, I need to talk to him. It's important'.

Tiisha looked at him, her dark eyes impenetrable. He could tell she was weighing up the implications, how much trouble she would bring on herself with her answer. She paused for a few moments then shrugged. 'Fuck it. I'm not going to protect the little shit. He's at Michael's. He's been there like every day this week.'

Robert felt the tension drain out as he released the breath he hadn't known he'd been holding. He was so relieved he let the profanity slide. 'Stay here, lock the door and don't open it for anyone but me. And don't answer your phone for anyone but me. I'll be back with Alan as soon as I can.'

Hands still shaking, he quickly stuffed a few supplies into a backpack and raced out the door. He had no idea what he intended to do. At the moment he was relying on instinct. The important thing was to keep moving. Every fibre of his being was telling him that time was of the essence.

John watched the screen intently. *What the hell was that about?* In all the years he had known Robert, he had never seen him act like that before.

Still looking at the screen, John absently addressed the tech, 'Has anyone tried to contact him.'

'No response to all calls and messages.'

There could be a dozen reasons why Robert ran out of the facility. He probably just had some sort of family emergency. Still…

John could feel the muscles across his chest and shoulders tighten, the tension working its way up his neck to his jaw.

Something wasn't right here, best take a closer look. Eyes still glued to the screen, voice a little tense, he started issuing orders. 'I want to know where he is right now. Someone go to his house. And check his phone. I want a list of every call, every text and every site he visited in the last 24 hours. Start from the time he left his office and work back.'

He continued to stare at the now blank screen, mouth set in a tight line and jaw clenched so tight it hurt. There was something building here. He had no idea what, but he had a bad feeling in the pit of his stomach.

He downed a couple of Panadol with a swig of coffee. He could feel the start of a headache coming on. It was the damn tension in his jaw. He needed to relax. Let the guys do their job. Go through the standard drills and let the facts tell the story.

Robert tried to form a plan on his way to Michael's house, but he kept getting distracted. He still couldn't stop his hands shaking, and every time he even thought about the text his stomach convulsed. He had already had to pull over twice to dry retch. Worse still, his mind kept replaying last night, trying to tell him something he couldn't quite grasp.

'You disgrace your family.'

'And you're an asshole.'

Alan looked at his father, 'Are you to simply sit back and allow this.'

Robert sighed. 'Yes I am Alan. This is your fight, not mine.'

Alan pushed his chair back hard, the legs scraping roughly on the timber floor, leaving scratch marks. He threw his napkin onto the table. Jaw hard, eyes flashing, he yelled, 'This whole family is a disgrace. Even my own father embarrasses me.'

Tiisha couldn't help herself, face frozen in a sneer and her voice tart. 'Whatever happened to respect thy father, asshole?'

Alan looked at this father, rebellion in his eyes. 'My father lost all respect when he abandoned his people.'

It stung, but Robert let it go. After Alan had stormed off, he sighed and looked at Tiisha, 'Why do you bait him so?'

Tiisha held his gaze, fire in her eyes and venom in her words. 'Because he deserves it with his medieval beliefs. We will never be accepted as long as zealots try to drag us back to such beliefs.'

She followed her brother, storming out of the room, only with no damage to the floor. In Tiisha's case it was more for show than anything. She had a temper all right, but she was far more controlled than Alan. When Tiisha played the drama queen it was usually calculated.

Robert pulled off into a car park, narrowly avoiding the curb. It took all his strength to put the car in park and kill the ignition. He hugged himself and whimpered, head against the control panel. *Surely not. Surely not Alan.*

He tried to block it out. Tried to deny it, but his stupid, over-analytical mind wouldn't let him. He had been betrayed by his own son.

Robert looked at the text, tears streaming down his face. One simple word – 'traitor' – from a number beyond the grave. It still stung, still made his guts clench. Now, though, there was anger mixed with the fear. Anger at Alan, anger at himself, but mostly anger at her. Even after all this time she still tormented him.

Every young man needs a cause to glory in, whispered in that soft, velvety voice that had made him tingle every time he heard it. There was nothing glorious in her cause, though.

Young men and their stupid causes. He had hoped to spare his children from that, the legacy of their ancestry. He had sacrificed much to ensure they grew up half a world away from the horrors of their homeland. He should have known he could never truly cut the tether. He knew Alan searched for his own identity and gloried in the fairy tales of his homeland. He had ignored it, though, convinced himself that it was only a phase. One that Alan would grow out of soon.

***

Easing himself into a chair, John grimaced. The painkillers were keeping the headache to a faint throb, but his back was playing up now. It was the legacy of five years as a grunt in the war. He was a big man. Not so much tall – though at 6'2" he was far from short – but broad across the shoulders and chest, with legs the size of tree trunks. Humping the section machine gun had been easy in his early thirties. Now, just over a decade later his knees and back were stuffed.

John jammed a cushion between his back and the chair to force him to sit upright and took a sip of coffee. It was strong, black and bitter, just what the doctor ordered. The only thing missing was a shot of scotch. Later perhaps. Right now, though, it was time to review the evidence and see what had turned up.

He had already reviewed the tape put together by the tech staff this afternoon three times, each time picking up more details. The tape told him that Robert had arrived at work at his normal time of 0830 and gone through his normal daily routine, taking a morning tea break at 1030 and then his lunch break at 1300. At 1345 he returned to the lab until 1600 when he took another break. On each break he checked his telephony device or teldee, which was normal enough. Smart devices were banned in the labs for security reasons, but allowed in the cafeteria and courtyard. It was common practice for staff to check their teldees, which could be stored in small lockers just outside the high-security perimeter, during breaks.

It was Robert's reaction when he checked his at 1606 that was unusual.

After looking at his teldee, Robert became visibly agitated, raced to the restrooms, where he vomited, and then left the complex, taking nothing with him. A subsequent check of Robert's internet history showed that while he had been in the lab he had received the usual social media crap. There was nothing that should have elicited Robert's extreme response, even though much of the shit on social media nowadays was nauseating.

Voice and text records had taken a little longer, and had only just come through via email. John opened the attachment and stopped cold. There were no missed calls or voice messages, but there was one text message. John had no idea what the message was, only that it had arrived at 1558 from a particular number. It was the latter that had caught his attention. The number was a fake; 10-digit cell phone numbers hadn't been used for almost a decade. It also appeared to originate from a public-access hub downtown, making it untraceable.

Eyes wide and hands shaking, John slowly put down his coffee so he didn't spill any. He gripped the table with both hands to steady himself as the room started to spin. A chill ran down his spine and settled deep in his gut. He swallowed the lump in his throat and stared at the report.

He knew that number. It was engraved into his memory. In 2017, he was part of a special combat team that spent six months tracking the ghost who used it across Europe, always two steps behind.

What the hell was Robert mixed up in?

Robert wiped the tears on his sleeve and blew his nose. He had to keep going. He didn't need to reason with Alan, he just needed to get him out of the house. They could butt heads as much as Alan liked later, once he was safe. The important thing was to get away. He had a contingency plan for that, one that had been in place for years. With trembling hands he pulled the pistol out of his backpack and placed it on the seat beside him before slowly pulling out of the carpark. It was an old-fashioned projectile weapon that used bullets, an antique from the war.

Next John checked the surveillance report. It took him three attempts to open the email because his hands were shaking. Not surprisingly it was a blank. Robert's house was already empty and his vehicle gone. Their one hope was that he hadn't changed cars, a big if given the revelations so far this evening. The cops were looking for it now.

John got up, stretched his back and limped to the window. It was cool inside the climate-controlled complex, but it would still be sweltering outside, even at this time of night. Fossil fuels might be a thing of the past, but climate change had already started to bite before the world went totally green. For Sydney that meant blistering summers were the norm. Hot and dry, just like the war. He leant against the glass, feeling the heat outside.

For John, the war ended in August 2017 with a deafening roar and then nothingness. His team had tracked the Ghost to a warehouse in Bonn. Finally, they had him. John was pumped and looking forward to taking the bastard down. The German special ops boys had just executed a full breach when the whole facility went up, booby-trapped with enough high explosives to flatten a city block. He had been shielded by an armoured personnel carrier. The rest of the team weren't so lucky.

He'd heard the Ghost had finally been caught a couple of months later, but was never sure. That was the problem with special ops, you had to be active to know what was going on. He could have checked, he still had contacts, but by that time he didn't care. After months of rehab he was focused on looking forward, not back. Anything that reminded him of what he had lost was too painful.

It wasn't long after that he started working security here. Robert started not long after, working as a junior research assistant. He could and did pass for English. He was born and educated in England after his parents were posted to the UK on a diplomatic mission. He remained at boarding school after they left and stayed on to complete university at Oxford. It was his UK connections that got him through the security clearance process. That and the fact that none of the checks raised any red flags. He had also worked hard at making sure no one ever had any reason to question his allegiances.

Robert might have English citizenship, but he wasn't always English. Nor was his late wife. They met in England and married in England, but she was born in his parents' homeland and died there during the war. A country whose only claim to fame was as the birthplace of the terror axis.

John grimaced as he looked out the window. He was tired and sore. All he wanted to do was go home, have that scotch and go to bed. He couldn't, though. There was a little voice inside his head telling him he had to see this one through, personally.

Robert parked down the street and walk slowly toward Michael's house, hidden from the glow globes by the massive trees that lined the street. He had never been here before and imagined it would look magnificent in the daylight. At this time of night, foreboding would be a better description.

By the time he reached the house, sweat ran down his back and his light shirt was plastered to his chest. His hands still trembled and his mouth was dry and metallic. His knees felt so weak he could barely make it up the drive. He desperately wanted to turn around and run. The only thing that kept him going was Alan. If he fled, Alan was a good as dead.

Robert paused on the doorstep, gathering his courage. It didn't amount to much, but it would have to do. He had no idea what to expect and was completely unprepared for anything anyway. Please, let it just be young men fantasising about things they didn't understand.

He tried the door handle and it opened in his grasp, the door swinging silently inward. He tentatively crossed the threshold, holding the pistol in his shaking hands. He resisted the urge to call out, instead walking as quietly as possible through the foyer. Off to the left he heard the sound of a holovision, so he headed in that direction, toward what he assumed was the lounge, his sneakered feet silent on the tiled floor.

The sound of his own breathing boomed in his ears. He

placed his free hand on the wall as he peered around the lounge entry. The first thing he saw was a huge holovision at the far end of the room. As he inched his head farther into the room a five-seater, two-piece lounge arranged around a coffee table came into view at the near end. His knees buckled and the pistol dropped from his fingers, smashing loudly on the tiled floor.

Robert collapsed against the wall. The two men on the couch didn't move, their eyes fixed to the ceiling, a neat hole in each man's forehead. They were young, probably a few years older than Alan.

John was distracted from his memories by the soft chime of his terminal. A new messaged had arrived from systems audit. He eased himself into his seat again with a grimace and opened it. He still had the jitters but now it was mostly from too much caffeine. He took a deep breath to clear his head and looked at the report.

It was a systems breach escalation report. Hackers were constantly trying to crack their system. Most didn't even know who they were targeting, just that it was a government system. Getting past government firewalls without getting caught amounted to a lot a credibility in the hacker world. The fact that 99 per cent failed to even get past the outer perimeter just made them try harder.

The outer perimeter of this system was a fake, made to look just like a standard government firewall. Rather than being greeted with success, the less than one per cent of hackers talented enough to get through its multiple layers found themselves facing a much harder, much more sophisticated perimeter. They also found themselves electronically snared by an automated counter-hack that had started when they penetrated the first layer of the outer perimeter.

In all John's years at the agency, only six hackers had managed to penetrate any of the layers of the inner perimeter. Five of those where foreign intelligence agencies and the sixth a 15-year-old kid. The kid had almost made it all the way, so John gave him a scholarship. He now worked for John and was one of the reasons government computer security was so damn good.

This report was odd. John frowned as he read it. Someone had sliced through the outer, fake perimeter like butter and then just disappeared. The counter-hack had failed because it was too brief. The only reason it was even tagged for escalation was because the hacker made it to the inner perimeter. It was annotated with 'breach failed – for review, non-urgent'.

John felt his jaw harden and bile rise in his throat. *Non-urgent, my ass.* He forwarded the report to the head of systems audit, punching in a short, terse note to look into it further as a matter of urgency. He then sent a text to make sure. He knew he was being a little harsh. The breach report would have been auto generated and then reviewed by a junior tech. It was escalated to ensure it was double checked by more senior staff. He didn't care, though. He was on edge and feeling like shit. Anything out of the ordinary warranted scrutiny at the moment.

His communicator beeped with a new text: 'on it'.

Robert joined Katiisha on the small balcony. 'Come inside, it's cold out here'.

She tore her gaze from the distance dockyard and looked at him with intense dark eyes. Always impenetrable, they could hide fierce love for their children or hatred for her enemies. That was Katiisha, focused, passionate and fierce in all things.

She gave him a smile. 'It'll warm up soon'.

He frowned, not understanding what she meant, but worried it wouldn't be good. He had been worrying a lot lately. For the past few months Katiisha had been driven, ignoring him as she dragged them across Europe. She claimed it was only to allow him to focus on his work, but at times he felt she was disappointed in him. She was always surrounded by other men. Men who fawned over her, like moths attracted to the flame of her cause.

She turned from him, looking back to the dock and pointing to a distant warehouse. 'Watch, watch the beginning of our victory'. Robert heard the edge in her voice and felt his stomach sink. He wanted to turn toward her, to ask what she meant. But he knew better, and kept his gaze firmly focused on the warehouse.

The explosion shook the whole hotel. Robert's head spun. He gripped the balcony, knuckles white, legs weak. The world slowed and he watched in slow motion as Katiisha calmly turned and walked inside, drawing a pistol from her wrap. Her voice sounded like it was at the end of a long tunnel, muted and distorted: 'Traitor'. He heard the soft thwop of the silencer and turned in time to see the man drop, a single hole in his forehead. He couldn't even remember the man's name.

She turned to him, her delicate features hard. If anything it made her look even more stunning and gave her a presence far larger than her diminutive frame. Her voice was hard and clipped: 'Get the children, we're leaving'.

John took an antacid to help with the reflux. He'd have an ulcer before tonight was over. He went to the coffee pot and paused. He was already suffering from caffeine overload. He looked at the water cooler instead. *Fuck it*. He poured himself another coffee and took a long sip as his Teldee rang.

'Michael here John. I've got some bad news and some good news. The good news is that we traced that hack. The bad news is that they penetrated the inner perimeter.'

John was glad he chose the coffee. He sat down before his knees gave out on him and kept his voice as neutral and business-like as possible. 'Go on.'

Michael's voice was a little high pitched and shaky. He sounded both apologetic and awed at the same time. 'The hack didn't fail at all. It opened a tunnel through the outer perimeter for one of our field units. The field unit didn't raise any alarms because it was a trusted device.'

John's head was starting to spin. 'Hold up a minute. Why would they need to do that?'

Michael slowed down a bit. 'Sorry, should have explained that bit. Our field units require a trusted terminal *and* a trusted communications device as a security measure. The communicator is matched to the field agent, but not the terminal. Any trusted user can log on once the connection is made.'

John ran his free hand through his thinning hair. He knew what was coming next.

'We think the tunnel was needed because they had the terminal but not the communicator. The field agent assigned the terminal hasn't checked in for 24 hours but isn't officially overdue yet. We are trying to contact him by alternate means.'

John's throat was dry and his voice raspy. 'Who logged in.'

Michael's response sounded like a shot. 'Robert Ondine.'

John rubbed his temples. His head was throbbing again. 'How long and what did he do?'

'They were in for 14 minutes, just long enough to download two folders of data from Ondine's home drive. We've accessed the back-ups, but it'll need a chemist to understand it. Looks to be something he was working on in his own time.'

'Thanks Mike', John mumbled, palm cradling his forehead, 'Let me know if you find anything more.'

It couldn't be her. It couldn't be Katiisha. She was dead, executed as a terrorist after he betrayed her.

Robert forced himself to pick up the gun and keep moving.

He found Alan out back, face down on the rear deck. Robert dropped to his knees. He ran his hands down his face and sobbed, an anguished cry escaping his lips. He gently lifted Alan and hugged him, sobbing,

He was still there, frozen in place, lost to the world and

cradling his son when the security forces arrived.

'What have we got?'

John leant his big frame against the wall, his fleshy face sagging with fatigue. He was sick of sitting. It was past midnight and the day just kept on giving. He was preparing to interview Robert, but didn't hold high hopes. Robert still responded to basic requests, but that was about it. He wasn't surprised.

'Looks pretty open and shut. They found Ondine at the scene, murder weapon beside him with his prints and DNA all over it.'

The local investigator was irritating and a little too keen to wrap this up. John's tone was clipped. 'Motive.'

'The hack. Your own geeks traced the source to the house they found Ondine in. He went to great pains to protect that information, storing it on a secure government system. It must have been valuable. He must have lost it when he found out it had been stolen.'

John wasn't buying it. The timeline didn't gel for him. He also couldn't believe the hacker had been that sloppy given the sophistication of the hack. No, something was still in play here.

He grunted and opened the door to the interview room, fresh coffee in hand.

Robert looked up as John slid the folder across the desk. John looked tired. Robert didn't feel tired anymore. He didn't feel anything now. It was like his mind was wrapped in cotton wool.

The folder was filled with pages from his work computer. He didn't have to read them, he knew what they were.

John tried to sound gruff and menacing, but he just sounded tired. 'What are they?'

Robert glanced down to the folder and back to John. He blinked, his face slack but for a faint smile. 'I call them Robert's folly.'

John frowned and tapped his fingers on the table. 'What the

hell does that mean?'

Robert smiled again. He wasn't smiling at John, though. He was smiling at Katiisha, beautiful, fierce, mad Katiisha. His voice was soft and lilting. 'It started as my PhD thesis but became my life's work, vapour clouds for airborne delivery of medicines and inoculations on a mass scale in poor, developing nations. It's how I met my wife, Katiisha. She was so taken by my vision, so supportive. At least that's what I thought at the time.'

'What happened?' John's voice was softer now, almost gentle.

'She got angry with me because I couldn't… wouldn't make it work. She wanted clouds that drifted over large areas and persisted for days, but not for medicines. Once I stopped my work, she deserted us. That's why I really betrayed her, because she deserted us.'

'What happened to Katiisha, Robert?'

'They killed her. Not because she deserted us, because she was a terrorist. She's come back, though. Just like the ghost they said she was.'

John froze, eyes wide and the hairs on the back of his neck rising. His hands started to tremble. 'Why, Robert. Why has she returned?'

Robert's face lit up to match his dreamy smile. 'I finally managed to make it work.'

Tiisha read the text from her father again. He had sent it last night, before he was captured. It was just one word, 'Why.' She was both surprised and pleased. She liked the fact that he knew, even though he didn't really get it. He never had. It didn't matter, though. It was too late for him to do anything about it, even if they believed him. Things were moving way too fast.

She went back to her laptop, the one she had used to meticulously hack her father's account, and opened a custom-made application. With a single mouse click she changed the world.

***

Robert blinked and looked at the stark, white walls. Everything he had done, all his sacrifices, had been for nothing. He had betrayed his own wife to stop a holocaust beyond imagination, yet it would still happen.

He should have stopped. He should have destroyed all his notes and turned his back on it. He didn't, though. His pride wouldn't let him. That and his love. He did it for her, so he could finally tell her he had succeeded. So she would love him again.

Little Tiisha was so much like her mother. The same dark, intense eyes. The same delicate features. The same fierce heart, but so much more measured. Calculating! That's what Tiisha was.

Tiisha was going to do something horrible. He should tell them, but he couldn't forsake her. He had been little more than a pawn in her plans, a distraction to buy time. She had used him, and killed her own brother, yet as perverse as it sounded, he was proud of her, what she had done. Horrified, yet proud. And he had a strong feeling she was only just getting started.

The seatbelt sign went out with a soft ding. Tiisha connected to the inflight server and brought up the news. Her lips curled into a smile as he read. Her gleaming, dark eyes drinking in the images of destruction gracing the small screen.

At midnight Greenwich Mean Time on 28 August 2029, coordinated nuclear, chemical and biological attacks were launched around the globe, including Sydney. Clouds of nerve gas, far more toxic than any previously encountered, still linger over the cities of Madrid, Sydney **and** Tokyo, covering thousands of square kilometres. The terrorist organisation known as Reclaim Earth, thought to have been destroyed in the terror wars, has claimed responsibility. Early estimates put the death toll at 10 million.

The authorities were off chasing terrorists, wasting their time running down false leads. It wasn't about religion, or culture or politics, though. It was about the earth, saving the earth from the parasitic human race. And the war had only just begun. Tiisha started humming Lilly Allen's *F**k U* to herself as she closed the news app and started orchestrating phase two. She was in such a good mood.

SUNRAYSIA
By Chris Picone

Author's note: I'm a 30 year old student, although I've spent most of my time in construction & mining. The inspiration for Sunraysia came from a video interview I once saw about a Jewish WWII survivor. He talked about the time his family had gone to the cemetery to bury a recently deceased family member, when shooting suddenly started. The man played dead as the rest of his family was cut down before his eyes. He managed to see one of the shooters, who he recognised as being his neighbour and a close family friend of the last twenty years. The interview finished then, and it left me thinking – what now? He can't just go back home. I then placed my story on an orbital farming colony, for no other reason than that I thought that would make an interesting backdrop.

Jamal held a hand up, shading his eyes from the sun as he watched the unmanned tenders launch from Garuda 9, their mother ship. They departed one after the other, roughly five minutes apart, which was about how long it took the ground crews to unload them. Garuda 9 loomed in the atmosphere above, far too big to land on this little rock. It was one of Europa's massive cargo ships that serviced the orbital colonies surrounding Earth, providing them with food, building materials, tools, and other supplies. Endlessly it cycled, going from colony to colony and returning to Earth only to resupply and begin the journey all over again. The round trip took about a week. It seemed silly at first, the concept of shipping food to a farming colony but, as the joke went, one would quickly grow tired of eating potatoes otherwise. Besides, the colony had to get their produce back to Earth somehow. The ground crews refilled the tenders as quickly as they unloaded them, sending the fruits of their labour back to the much bigger rock that many of them still called home.

A bead of sweat dripped into Jamal's eye, stinging slightly and making him acutely aware of his discomfort. His face felt like it was burning and he wondered how long he had been standing up here. The colonies were alternatively closer to and farther from the sun than Earth, which meant very hot days and very cold nights on the surface. The colony's climate controllers attempted to regulate the atmospheric conditions to suit the produce rather than the inhabitants, making the surface un-comfortable at the best of times and the colonists avoided it as a result. All except for the farmers who were, oddly enough for a farming colony, the minority of the colonist population. But the Garuda deliveries were about the most exciting thing that happened on a farming colony, and many of the colonists clambered from their holes in the ground every week just to see it.

Jamal wiped the sweat from his brow and reluctantly turned his back on the Garuda and its little worker ants. He was standing in the centre of the orbital ring, on a dirt track that separated two extensive fields of wheat-grain. The huge walls of the ring that marked the boundary of the station's atmo-sphere rose seemingly out of nowhere only a hundred metres or so on either side of where he was standing, at the edge of the grain fields. A square of yellow-and-red handrail with a little rolled steel roof jutted up from the ground a couple of hundred metres in front of him. The handrails had been painted so garishly in order to prevent the harvesters from driving over the manholes that led to the underground cities. The paint was vestigial now; the manholes were surrounded by sheds and silos, but the paint had been maintained in the same kind of tradition as barber poles. Jamal walked between the rails and lifted a little hatch that had the word *Sunraysia* imprinted on it – the colony's name – revealing a ladder that descended into the ground beneath. Only six feet of soil separated the surface from the underground city.

'Thought I'd find you here,' a voice called up as Jamal started climbing down the ladder.

'What can I do for you Tim?' Jamal asked, recognising Tim's squeaky voice immediately. He paused to lock the manhole.

'Don't you ever get sick of watching the Garudas?' Tim asked.

Jamal made sure Tim was out of the way before dropping the last few feet to the floor below. The lighting was poor in this section of the tunnel but Tim was so pale he practically glowed in the dark.

Jamal rolled his eyes. 'Don't you ever get sick of asking me that?' he retorted.

'Want to come around tonight for dinner?' Tim asked.

'That depends, who's cooking?'

'Ma. It's Garuda night, so fish, salad, and fruit for dessert,' Tim said, referring to the most popular night of the culinary week, the only time (relatively) fresh food was available.

'And you wonder why I never get sick of watching the Garudas?' Jamal joked.

'Oh, Bourke wanted to see you about something. Did you leave your tools in the ventilation shaft again?' Tim told him.

'I'm never going to live that down, am I?'

'Not until someone else does something sillier,' Tim answered amicably.

The pair headed toward 'the mall', which served as the business and retail district for the city and was where the food supplies from the Garudas could be purchased. The ladder was at a tunnel junction, splitting south to the residencies and north to the services district, distribution centres, and the mall. The tunnel itself was not particularly long, only extending a couple of kilometres in either direction. You could easily walk from one end to the other in less than an hour. The cities themselves were dotted all over the ring, with rolling hills marking the boundaries as the ground had to be raised to accommodate the living and working spaces beneath.

The climate was much more comfortable down here. The ventilation system drew in oxygenated air from the surface and pumped it around the city while the re-circulators filtered the air for impurities and extracted carbon monoxide and dioxide, which were released into the atmosphere out of tall stacks on the surface. The confined space made it easy to control temperature but it also meant there was an ever-present risk of running into pockets of dead air. Like the time when Jamal had notoriously left his tool bag in one of the ventilation shafts after servicing one of the extraction fans. The bag itself had caught in the fan, jamming it, but not before launching several of his tools down the shaft and into one of the filters like missiles. It had happened right before Jamal's 'weekend', his down day in between swapping from night to day shift, and so the error had gone unnoticed until an electrician tried to access a control panel in one of the rarely used service rooms and promptly passed out from asphyxiation. Luckily, the electricians always worked in pairs and his partner had rescued him before any permanent damage had been done. That whole section of the ventilation had had to be shut down to retrieve the tools and rectify the problem. Jamal's name was engraved on the tools that were extracted from the filter. That was a year ago. Tim was Jamal's apprentice, and was not likely to let the story go in a hurry.

'Good evening, Mr. Baker. It's lovely to see you, won't you please come in and take a seat', Tim's dad said with a thick Indian accent as he answered the door. Jamal stepped inside, bowing his head toward the brown-skinned man as he passed the threshold.

'Jamaaal!' Ma greeted Jamal as he came out of the narrow hallway into the kitchen. She bustled her way past steaming pots and pans to embrace him in a deep bear hug. Ma was a heavy-set Italian woman, and it never ceased to amaze Jamal how she could move around so quickly in the narrow confines of the tight living quarters without bumping everything. Jamal was much smaller but he was more like the proverbial bull in the china shop. He returned the hug, then went to take a seat before he could break anything. Tim's family's quarters were littered with trinkets: here a plaque of Christ hanging from his crucifix, there a gaudy statue of Vishnu. Tim was already sitting in the far corner of the dining room. Jamal had to squeeze into his seat as the dining table had already been extracted from where it folded into the wall and was dressed for dinner.

'How are you, Mrs Harshavardan?' Jamal asked politely.

'Oh Jamal, you know not to call me that,' Tim's mum said crossly. She was one of those women who was everyone's mother, and expected everyone to call her Ma accordingly. 'You know Alan only calls you that because he can't pronounce your name,' she continued, deliberately using the English approximation of her husband's name.

Alan smiled happily in response then went into the kitchen to help his wife, only to be ushered straight back out.

'Out!' Ma admonished. 'You will only get in my way, go and say your prayers or something.' Jamal and Tim laughed as Ma thrust a broom after Alan.

'Very well,' Alan said in his thick accent. He took a small folded-up mat from its place on the shelving in the main room and dutifully walked down the narrow hallway into his makeshift prayer room. Jamal had asked about it once. It was really the storeroom, but Alan and Ma had long since come to a compromise, Ma keeping her cooking tools, sauces and other bits and pieces restricted to the shelving on either side of the room, concealed by curtains. The back wall of shelving had been pulled out and replaced with a little shrine. Alan was a fervent follower of Hinduism. Ma was theoretically Catholic but food was her true religion.

Oddly for his upbringing, Tim was a Secularist. He borrowed

ideals from both his parents' religions as well as others, but committed to none of them. Tim was of American stock. As fortune would have it, Ma – everyone's mother – was barren. She could not bear the thought of going through life without children and so she and Alan had adopted Tim at a young age. They had planned to adopt more children until they had a bustling family but Alan's business had suffered a turn and their wealth vanished almost overnight. That was how they ended up all the way out on this rock in the middle of nowhere.

Jamal was a Secularist as well, but he had no idea what his ethnicity was; his parents firmly believed in liberation through non-identification. That is to say, the absence of labels. Even his last name wasn't real. His parents had changed their family name deliberately, to the most innocuous thing they could think of. Jamal couldn't even point at the continent he came from; he had been raised to see himself only as a Terran, born on Earth. He looked more like Alan's son than Tim ever would; his browned skin shared a slight golden hue, darker than Ma's olive complexion but lighter than the dark-skinned men and women he knew to be of African descent. They also had similar features. Certainly he was treated as if he was their second son. Jamal's parents had lived next door to Alan and Ma, and so Tim and Alan had spent a lot of time playing together. Jamal's parents had seven other sons and daughters and so they rarely noticed when Jamal was missing. It wasn't that his parents neglected him, it was just that they were busy. Ma really had been like a mother to him, and he felt closer to Tim than he did to most of his blood-brothers and sisters, one of which was serving elsewhere on this same station.

They ate, heartily. The Garudas might have been taken for granted but the fresh variety of food they brought with them was not. Sunraysia mainly consisted of grain, grape and citrus farms. They were frequently nicknamed the 'breakfast colony', since all they really produced was the ingredients for bread, cereal and orange juice. There were a few mills and factories on the surface that made the colony self-sustaining in the event of isolation. Otherwise, many of the colonists had little hydroponic gardens in their living quarters, and there were small patches of non-produce fruits and vegetables on the surface but there was never enough to keep up with demand. Right now, they were enjoying spaghetti in a fresh marinara sauce, not that preserved stuff they normally had to rely on. There was the fish, as promised, the real prize of the meal since there was absolutely no way they could harvest fish on this floating rock.

It must be uncomfortable for Alan in these situations, Jamal thought to himself. Ma was one of the station's cooks so Alan normally did the cooking at home to give her a break from it. The only time Ma cooked at home was when they had guests over, primarily because Alan's curries were too hot for the uninitiated, but also because the living quarters were so cramped that the only time anyone had guests for dinner was to celebrate something.

'What's the occasion?' Jamal asked before spooning the last few mouthfuls of fruit salad into his mouth.

Pots and pans clattered in the kitchen as Ma apparently dropped them in her rush to answer him. Her eyes were wide. 'You have not heard?' she asked.

Tim laughed and said, 'He was too busy watching the Garudas again, Ma.'

Ma looked to Tim, then back to Jamal. 'The orbital farms worked. We have solved world hunger! No one ever needs to be hungry again!' she said, so excited she was shaking.

'What happens when the world gets tired of eating cereal?' Tim joked.

Ma flicked him with a tea-towel.

'Wow,' was all Jamal managed to say. He looked at the clock on the wall, memorising the date. The clocks here didn't sync perfectly with earth but the colonists still found it useful to track Earth time. July 20th, 2029. It seemed so fast. The first orbital station had only been built six years ago; Sunraysia itself was only three years old.

'This calls for celebration!' Ma insisted, and bustled back into the kitchen where she retrieved a bottle of Earthen Vino. Wine was one of the few things the colony produced that it didn't get tired of consuming, even if the lack of maturity meant the wine had to be mixed to be drinkable. Truly, one could only drink so much recycled water.

The next few months passed much like the ones that came before them. The colonists celebrated; Earth assisted by sending an extra Garuda full of food and supplies to the colonies, its contents including wine that was old enough to drink itself. But in the end, there was only so much fresh food the colonists could eat and the bulk of it was simply frozen for future use. Although the eradication of world hunger was no doubt life-altering on Earth, the reality was that it had almost no impact on the colonists. Every day they still got up to work, driving harvesters or fixing machinery, and every night they drank terrible wine and went to bed early because there was nothing else to do. By the time the additional food had dwindled, Sunraysia had all but forgotten the achievement. In fact, they found out later that world hunger had actually been eradicated in June, not July. The interplanetary communication system had broken down yet again and it wasn't until one of the Garuda pilots mentioned it over the radio as a by-the-by that the colonists heard the news.

In this crazy time where global milestones seemed almost regular, it was difficult to acknowledge the importance of the first human settlement on Mars, for example, when a Jovian expedition was announced in the same year – the eradication of world hunger barely made a mark on the calendar. Lebensraum day was the second biggest day on the calendar after Christmas. Lebensraum was an old German word that meant 'living space'. The name was selected particularly because the

Germans had used the word in World War Two to justify their invasion. The significance was that with a whole universe to settle and mine, there would theoretically be no reason for future wars on Earth. The reality was very different of course; space was dominated by mega-corporations that were frequently wealthier than nations, and sometimes their disputes would be settled on Earth. The worst part was that the colonists didn't even get a day off to celebrate properly.

The very next morning, Jamal and Tim went to work alongside thousands of other hung-over colonists.

'No, the electricians will be down that tunnel today,' Jamal explained. 'They found a fault in one of the grav-drive backup generators yesterday.'

'They claimed to find a fault in the generator so they would be left alone today and you know it,' Tim scoffed in response.

'Yeah alright but the fact that we know that means they'll get caught one day. So we need to be smarter about it,' Jamal said patiently.

'Smart like leaving your tools in the vent shaft?' Tim said bitingly. Tim was not normally much of a drinker, and Jamal was used to him acting like an angry bear the morning after a big night so he tactfully ignored him.

'There's an extraction fan up here that's not making pressure. I had a listen yesterday and couldn't hear anything but I think the belt has slipped,' Jamal told Tim.

Tim wasn't happy at the prospect of working but bit his tongue.

'We'll lock it out,' Jamal continued, 'then head back down the shaft to the electrical store. We know no one will be there since the electricians will all be sleeping in the generator room.'

'That's diabolical,' Tim said, grinning up at his dark-skinned friend.

'I thought you would like it,' Jamal said with a laugh. 'We'll sleep it off in there and then go and get dirty fixing that extraction fan just before knock-off.'

There wasn't much risk of getting caught. There was an unspoken agreement that anyone who could afford to shirk work for the day was going to do so. The trick was just to hide, so that if anyone who couldn't get out of work caught you, they wouldn't get jealous and report you.

They slept the morning away, waiting for lunch time before crawling out of their hidey-hole. None of the workers were expected to lunch in the small crib room that was provided for the underground servicemen, and the room was small and uncomfortable as well as usually being a long walk from their workplace, so on any other day the servicemen would have just taken packed lunches with them and eaten wherever they happened to be when they got hungry. The day after Lebensraum day, however, saw the workers crawl out of the proverbial woodwork to sit around sheepishly in the crib room as if they all felt the need to prove they were awake and had been working hard all morning. The image was completed by the laughing workmen taking digs at the workers who were absent, half-jokingly accusing them of being off asleep somewhere and sitting around looking self-righteously at each other. Meanwhile, the workers who weren't there to defend themselves were probably the only ones who were actually out on jobs.

It was this strange gathering that brought Jamal and his brother back together. Jamal's brother worked and lived in one of the other underground 'cities', elsewhere along the ring. Communication was an ongoing issue on the colonies and although it would only be a few hours of walking to reach the other's underground city, it was rare for them to contact each other unless they needed something. So what was he doing here?

Jamal eyed his brother across the room. They looked similar enough that they could be confused. His brother was slightly taller. Jamal was slightly darker, due to his weekly solar exposure when the Garudas arrived. His brother's expression was hard. Something was wrong.

'How are you, Ez?' Jamal asked. They were alone in the tunnel outside the crib room.

'Mum's on her way out. Dad reckons weeks,' Ez answered soberly.

Jamal leaned against the wall, taking it in. She had been sick for a long time, so long it seemed to Jamal that she had always been sick. Jamal looked at his brother, who had cast his eyes toward the ground. It was hard to read him. They got on well enough but it was a long time since the brothers had been close. They had simply led different lives; it was only coincidence that had put them on the same colony at the same time.

'Why didn't Dad call me?' Jamal asked.

Ez said nothing, gesturing vaguely around them in response. It was enough. The inter-colony communications were bad enough but the inter-planetary communications seemed like they were down more often than they were up these days.

'Thank you for coming to tell me,' Jamal said sincerely.

Ez nodded.

'Are you staying?' Jamal asked.

'For a couple of nights,' Ez answered. 'One of the backup generators is spiking, they needed someone to carry the parts over from Estuary.' That was Ez's city; Jamal's was Solar. Ez was one of the colony's senior technicians, in a different role but sharing seniority with the maintenance supervisors. It was slightly concerning that the backup generator really was faulting.

'Boys have been having some grief with one of the harvester docks lately, I thought I'd take a look while I'm here. They've put me up in Holloway's,' Ez continued. Holloway was one of the farmers - or had been. A couple of weeks ago, there had been some sort of mechanical failure with his harvester. One of the oil hoses had flared and Holloway had been burnt alive. He had managed to escape his cabin but hadn't been able to put the fire out. A whole section of crop burnt to the ground around him before the emergency crews got the blaze under control. That was how they found the body. Another operator was being transferred up to take over his room and job but not many of the Garudas were currently equipped for human transport and they were tasked elsewhere.

The door opened. Lunch was over and the workers came shambling back out. Tim looked from Jamal to Ez and back again. He faced Jamal and said, 'Hi, Ez,' then turned back to Ez. 'Come on, we've still got that extraction fan to fix.'

The brothers laughed. Tim, who knew both brothers very well, must have sensed the dark mood.

'Come on, Tim. We've got work to do,' Jamal said, and headed off down the tunnel toward the extraction fan.

Jamal swore as his shifter slipped, forcing his hand down abruptly and causing him to cut his knuckles on the bolt beneath. His mind was elsewhere.

'I'll get it,' Tim said, pushing into Jamal's position without waiting for an answer.

'And you know better than to use those things,' Tim scolded, raiding Jamal's tool bag for spanners. He held one up to check the measurement in the dim light of his headlamp and went to work. The nuts were already in place, they just needed tightening.

'So when's the grieving?' Tim asked.

'Ez reckons he'll be stuck here for another few days fixing that harvester controller but he's too exhausted after work so he wants to wait until the night before he heads back to Estuary,' Jamal said, moving out of the way to let his apprentice work. Tim was practically a tradesman himself now anyway, so while Jamal normally supervised on the less common or more difficult tasks, they had reverted to taking turns with the mundane.

'That's fair enough. That sun really takes it out of you,' Tim said.

Jamal nodded his agreement, although Tim had his back turned and couldn't see it.

It was their last job for the day and they separated shortly after, Tim returning to his family quarters and Jamal continuing on down the tunnel past the family quarters to the single men's quarters, stopping at 'The Vineyard' where he bought a cask of the local wine and two bottles of the decent stuff.

He had to put his tool bag and box of alcohol down to let himself in his doorway, then pushed the tool bag into the doorway with his foot to hold it open. He frowned at the doorway like he had every day for the last month. It needed fixing, the pneumatic on the door needed re-gassing. Every afternoon he came home to it, frustrated, and vowed to take it in to the workshop and fix it the next morning. And every morning he went to work, the door slamming behind him, forgotten about.

He walked up his narrow hallway and dumped both the tool bag and box of booze on the kitchen bench. His quarters had a storeroom, which was mostly full of tools, and a bedroom, which he rarely used. It was just big enough for a single bed and a locker, so he used it as a second storeroom and slept on the couch in his living/dining/kitchen room instead. The single quarters were much smaller than the family quarters, and the family quarters weren't big. Not for the first time, he wished he'd applied for a job on one of the other orbital colonies. Some of them were run by wealthy families who built huge estates on the surface with wings connected for the employees. Of course, you typically had to already be family for them to employ you.

There was a knock on the door. Jamal opened it and let Ez in without a word. Ez followed Jamal down the hallway to the couch, where he took a seat. Jamal pulled the retractable table out, placed two of his cleanest glasses on it and filled them both with one of the Earthen wines. He sat on the couch next to Ez and they took a drink in silence. Ez let out a long sigh and placed his glass back on the table.

'How much longer are you planning on staying up here?' Ez asked Jamal.

Jamal shrugged. He honestly hadn't considered it.

'I was thinking about getting a trip back for the funeral, and then staying on the dirt for a while,' Ez continued without waiting for an answer.

'Why don't you?' Jamal asked.

Ez was silent for a while. Perhaps that was exactly what he was going to do.

'Someone's got to look after my little brother,' Ez answered after a while. That was an excuse, and Jamal knew it.

'You've found someone,' Jamal accused.

Ez shot him an amused look, then fingered the rim of his glass thoughtfully. 'You know me too well,' he said.

Jamal finished his glass, poured himself another and topped up Ez's. 'You are my brother,' he pointed out.

'Put the TV on, will you?' Ez requested, making himself comfortable and sinking further into the couch. 'And get rid of this damn thing,' he said, kicking the table leg.

Obediently placing the bottle of wine on the floor next to Ez's foot, Jamal retracted the table and switched the TV on. The screen was blue – no signal. 'So who is he?' Jamal asked as he sat back down.

'She, and no one you will know,' Ez replied tersely.

'So she's ugly,' Jamal ventured.

'She's not ugly,' Ez snapped, and snatched the remote out of Jamal's hand and changed the channel. Blue again.

'Fat, then?' Jamal offered. 'Old?'

Ez struck Jamal in the knee with the remote. 'Eliza Winters.'

'Winters.' Jamal repeated, rolling the name around on his tongue. It sounded familiar. 'Wait, Ezekiel's daughter?' Ezekiel part-owned Agrifirm, Sunraysia's parent company. The boss.

'Niece,' Ez corrected.

'Well that explains why your comm system was working when mine wasn't,' Jamal said. 'How long has this been going on?'

'It hasn't,' Ez answered, frowning.

'Wait, one of us is confused,' Jamal said.

'Yeah, me. Or her. I don't know. I had to go up to Pinnacle last week, to try and sort out whatever's causing the electro-magnetic interference that keeps screwing with the comm systems.' He emphasised this last point by gesturing to the TV, which he had been flicking through channels on but which obstinately refused to display anything other than a blue no signal screen. 'I met her up there, she's one of the communication technicians.'

Jamal went into the kitchen, where he started preparing a meal. 'I can still hear you,' he called out.

'Anyway we hit it off, started having lunch together. I asked her if she was seeing anyone. "Not yet", she said,' Ez continued.

Jamal was about to interrupt with another joke at Ez's expense, but thought better of it. 'So did you ask her?' he said instead.

'Yes, of course. She said yes.'

'Well, congratulations then?' Jamal asked, curious why Ez didn't seem happy about this outcome.

Ez waved the congratulations away and continued. 'But then I got the call about Mum. So I jumped straight on the dinger' – that was the buggy that carried workers and equipment over the dirt road that circled the ring – 'and came here. Except the damn comm system still doesn't work so I haven't been able to contact her since,' Ez finished angrily, throwing the remote at the other end of the couch.

Jamal couldn't tell if Ez was upset about Mum dying or angry that he couldn't tell his new girlfriend what was happening. He saw what Ez meant now though: The abrupt departure could certainly be taken the wrong way, and it would obviously be unwise to anger the boss's niece. And now that they knew their mum's life was going to be measured in weeks, if Ez really had been thinking about leaving then now would be the time to do it. Jamal had no solution to offer, so instead he handed Ez some dinner and refilled his glass again.

The following morning, things went from bad to worse. Instead of his usual alarm, Jamal was torn from sleep by the sound of an announcement buzzer. Quickly he fumbled around for the remote, which was jammed in the corner of the couch where Ez had thrown it. The TV blinked into life and displayed Ezekiel's wizened face. The man was visibly shaken. Whatever he had to announce, it wasn't good. Perhaps one of the life support systems had failed. Or worse, a gravity drive. Either would have left thousands of colonists dead within minutes. Ezekiel was talking but there was no sound coming out. The TV was muted. Jamal turned the volume up.

'-overnight. At least one hundred million dead so far, but there is too much radiation to do a count. The toll could be as high as five hundred million. Miami, New York, London, Madrid, Moscow, Beijing, Tokyo, Cairo, Hong Kong, Tel-Aviv, Tehran, Ankara, Istanbul-' the list of cities went on. Jamal stared at the screen in horror. The names passed in one ear and out the other; he couldn't absorb them all. 'Chemical and biological weapons have been used as well as nuclear weapons. It is unclear who fired the first missile. We don't yet know which countries are responsible but many countries have already retaliated. The reason for this attack is unclear; so far it appears to be religious rather than political in nature. A conference is taking place as I speak. More news will be released as it becomes available. Until then, stay calm and return to work. None of the colonies has been affected yet but as we are on orbital stations, your work is crucial to maintaining the safety of all colonists. I say again, stay calm and return to work.' The screen flickered and the announcement looped back to the start. 'The Earth has been involved in a multi-national attack overnight-'. Jamal had heard enough. He turned the TV off and sat back down on the couch, too shocked to move.

A series of horrifying scenarios ran through his head. He tried flicking the TV to other stations, but to no avail. The interplanetary communications must still be out; obviously Sunraysia was receiving radio waves still but no television broadcasts. Either that or things were even worse on Earth than Ezekiel had let on. Broadcasting towers frequently made good strategic targets for bombing if one wanted to prevent news from spreading.

Jamal tried to remember where his family was, scattered as they were. One of his sisters was piloting a ship on the Jovian mission. That left three brothers and a sister somewhere in Australia. They might be far enough to be safe. His parents, however, were in America last he had heard; somewhere in Nevada, working on one of the space programs. And his youngest sister was probably still with them. None of the cities listed in the broadcast were in Nevada but there was nothing to say the list was exhaustive and no way of telling how extensive the radiation was.

He had to find Ez.

There was a knock at his door. It was Tim, dressed and ready for work. Jamal checked the time. Where had it gone? He had been so distracted by the news, he must have zoned out. He was supposed to have started work an hour ago. Tim looked him up and down, still dressed in his clothes from the night before.

'Did you miss the announcement?' Jamal asked.

Tim shook his head soberly. 'No,' he said. 'But the announcement said to return to work as usual and I couldn't think of anything else to do, so-' he finished with a gesture toward his uniform.

'What do you think happened?' Jamal asked. 'Sorry, come in,' Jamal said, realising that in his distraction he still had Tim cornered in his hallway.

Tim frowned and bit his lip at that. 'Ma and Pa were fighting about this morning. Both of them blame America,' he said thoughtfully.

'You don't sound like you agree,' Jamal noted.

Tim shrugged, walking past Jamal to sit on the couch. 'I honestly have no idea,' Tim admitted. 'Ma seemed to think it was the Muslims again but Pa says it's a conspiracy.'

Jamal's brows furrowed in confusion. 'I thought you said they both blamed America?'

'Yeah,' Tim said, 'Ma thinks either America's attacks on Islam pushed them to another attack like that one in 2001. Pa thinks the Americans launched the missile and are blaming Islam for it.'

Jamal had heard all this before. The twin towers attack of 2001 was still taught in school, including the twin theories of whether it had been a terrorist attack or an American conspiracy to start the so-called 'war on terror'.

'The announcement said the attack was religious, not political,' Jamal said.

'Yeah, which kind of supports the theory, I guess,' Tim said. When Jamal said nothing, Tim continued. 'I don't know, it just sounds to me like the twin towers all over again. Attack out of nowhere, and it looks like a setup for America to blame Islam and carry out their war all over again.'

'That makes no sense,' Jamal said. 'Even if the war on terror was over oil, who cares about oil anymore? We have fusion power now. And the attacks weren't limited to America. Even if America wanted war with Islam again, I doubt they would have the balls to directly attack their allies to start it.'

'The attacks were mostly on America and her allies,' Tim pointed out. 'And any of the others could be explained as either retaliation or collateral. Islam is the only religion volatile enough to oppose the globalisation of America's secularism, so they could be responsible for the attack. But on the same hand if America wanted to get rid of Islam for good, the attacks on their allies could be seen as very good incentive for them to join the fight. I don't know that I believe that though. It seems awfully risky.'

Jamal nodded his agreement with the latter. 'So you think it was Islam then?' he asked.

Tim bit his lip again. 'That seems exactly as unlikely. I honestly just can't believe it happened. It's been so long since anything like this has happened and with so much Lebensraum now, what's the point of squabbling over anything anymore? The trouble is, the religious mobs are getting all uppity about it. They're worried they're going to take the blame for the attacks and they'll be persecuted by the Secularists again.'

'What?' Jamal said incredulously. 'That makes even less sense. It's been a long time since any religion – other than Islam – has been persecuted. And they're only persecuted because they refuse to assimilate.'

'Can you blame them?' Tim asked.

'No, I guess not. I mean if that's what they believe then that's what they believe. To them it must look like us refusing to assimilate with Islam. But what about the other religions? Your parents are Catholic and Hindu, what do they think?' Jamal asked.

'The Muslims called a meeting at the chaplaincy about it this morning, straight after the announcement,' Tim said by way of answering.

'It's that serious?' Jamal asked, shocked. 'But it has nothing to do with us, all the way up here. Shouldn't we banding together, worrying about family down there and doing what we can to help them?'

'We've never been persecuted, so I guess we can't understand?' Tim said, throwing his arms out in an exaggerated shrug. That was one of the standard lines that the religious mobs liked to bandy around when they weren't getting their way. 'I think the Muslims expect to be the scapegoats again, so they called the meeting pre-emptively, to try and head off some of the persecution that might be coming their way,' he continued more seriously. 'The Christians and Muslims had some success working together in the 2010s, so I guess they thought they would try it here.'

Jamal shook his head. 'So now the rest of the faiths have allied with Islam and the Secularists are the scapegoats instead?' he said, more to himself than anyone else. He just couldn't wrap his head around the whole thing. He was just worried about his family down there. How were people confusing this catastrophe with a religious persecution?

There was a loud banging on the door.

Jamal looked to Tim, who returned his confused expression. He opened the door and was surprised to see the maintenance supervisor standing in the doorway looking furious.

'What are you two doing!' he demanded.

Jamal opened his mouth to answer and started – his eyes were drawn to the cross hanging around his supervisor's neck. Working with machinery being what it was, it was unusual for someone in maintenance to have dangling jewellery on their person.

'Sorry sir, but the news-' Jamal began.

The supervisor, however, had caught his gaze. He fingered the cross, staring Jamal in the eyes. 'Is there a problem, Jamal?' His voice had softened, but was somehow more menacing for it.

'No sir,' Jamal answered. He was tense. The supervisor turned his stare toward Tim.

'No sir,' Tim echoed.

'Then get to work. You're two hours late and you aren't even dressed,' the supervisor said, dropping the cross. He spun on his heels and stormed back out the door, not even bothering to close it.

'What do you think that was all about?' Tim asked as Jamal hurried to get dressed. He hadn't even had breakfast yet; he would have to take something with him.

Jamal didn't answer, he just dressed as quickly as he could, grabbed his tools and went to work.

The work day, after starting so late, went very quickly. Just as Jamal returned to his room, the PA system clicked into life and the well-known voice of Elizabeth 'Lizzy' Steinbach, Solar's popular city manager, announced that there would be a mass grieving that night.

Each city had an above-ground building called a chaplaincy, which was a large building with a single entrance but normally the internal area was divided into sections where each of the faiths separated for their own private rituals. However the building was also designed to be used as a community hall, and was able to be converted into an emergency shelter if something were ever to happen to the underground systems. For the mass grieving, the dividers had been removed, leaving the room looking like an oversized version of the Harshavardans' living room with the bizarre assortment of religious ornaments and shrines littering the walls. All of Solar's population as well as the nearby farmers were there, with the exception of a few detractors and the skeleton crew required to monitor the control rooms.

Where Jamal expected the colonists to band together in this time of strife, he couldn't help but notice that most of the colonists had filed in to where there faiths normally gathered. They were easy to tell apart now, all dressed in their funeral attire as according to their faiths. There was Ma and the Catholics on the right-hand side with the other Christian denominations, dressed traditionally in black suits and dresses. The Hindus were dressed casually in white; and Muslims, some covered, some not, all dressed in various subdued colours, were on the left-hand side. Jews, Pagans, Buddhists, Confucians and a myriad of other religions filled the middle. The cities had gathered for other occasions in the past, mostly for Christmas and other holidays, but this sort of division had never happened before. The majority of the Secularists were left at the back, dressed smartly but in all manner of clothing, squeezing in wherever they could find room. Some of the Secularists who had arrived earlier found themselves in the middle of tightly knit crowds. They could feel the eyes on their backs and they felt vulnerable. They kept their children close by and clenched their loved ones tighter than normal.

Jamal, Tim and Ez looked around nervously. There would be a short speech and a minute's silence for the general crowd, followed by the re-division of the chaplaincy so that the faiths could mourn in their own ways. There was an unspoken agreement between them that they would leave as soon as the ceremony was over. Although they couldn't understand why, and had personally done nothing wrong, it was clear they weren't welcome here.

Lizzy, Solar's city manager, came out of a back room and stepped onto the little stage that had been constructed at the far end of the room. She stood all of five foot tall and had an unassuming face, but her actions in the early days of the colony had earned her the colonists' respect. The moment her foot touched the stage, the murmuring of the crowd ceased.

'Colonists of Sunraysia,' she began formally, 'unfortunately, we have not yet received further word from Earth, and so I can offer you neither an explanation for the catastrophe that has taken place, nor the extent of the damage. Regardless of the reasons why, everyone here has been affected in some way, we have all suffered great loss and we are together in our grief. I hand you over now to the chief chaplain. Dante?'

Lizzy stepped back from the microphone. Dante adjusted the microphone up to his height and spoke into it softly. 'Ladies and gentlemen, we are gathered here this evening to grieve for our lost friends and comrades that we left back home. I now ask for the heads of each denomination to offer a brief prayer or speech.'

The Christian leader spoke out first, saying the Lord's Prayer. He was followed by the spokesmen for the other faiths, taking turns clockwise around the room, each offering brief funerary prayers. Where prayers from other faiths would contradict or offend, those who would be offended simply bowed their heads and politely covered their ears with their hands. The Secularist spoke last, simply stating the collective sorrow at the loss and offering his condolences to those affected.

'Thank you all,' Dante said simply, and stepped off the stage.

Lizzy pulled the microphone back down and washed her gaze over the crowd before speaking again. 'We will now observe a minute's silence,' she said. She bowed her head and the crowd did likewise. Stock images of Earth and its people were projected onto the walls of the chaplaincy. The members of those faiths who found it offensive to view images of the deceased simply bowed deeper and directed their gazes toward the ground in front of them.

When the minute was over, Lizzy spoke again. 'My fellow colonists, I appreciate that there is some tension amongst the community at present. I urge you all to set that aside. We must remember that we are alone up here and that we need each other to survive.' She paused to let her message sink in, then finished, 'there will be an interlude of thirty minutes as the dividers are replaced and the rooms refurbished, and then individual services will continue as planned by your denominations.'

Ordinarily, Secularists were allowed to utilise the various meditation rooms within the chaplaincy, or even the prayer rooms between services. There would be none of that now, so the Secularists had nowhere to go. Jamal, Ez, and Tim went back to Jamal's room for a drink and some quiet contemplation before splitting ways and returning to their own quarters.

The next few days passed by in a strange kind of haze. There had been no further communications from Earth, so the colonists were beginning to get anxious. Paranoia took hold of the colony.

There was no more shirking work; previously, the supervisor would spend the bulk of his time in the maintenance control room and the only times Jamal and Tim ever saw him was for a meeting at the start and completion of their shifts, which was roughly twice a week. Unless the supervisor got bored, in which case he might drop in on them for a chat. Other than that, they would receive task sheets electronically and issues or procurements were sent back the same way. There was no need for anything more than that since if Jamal and Tim didn't do their job it would become quite clear when sections of the ventilation started failing.

Since the attack however, the supervisor had started checking on them regularly, at least twice a day. At first they had taken it personally, thinking it was either an attack on their diligence or due to their both being Secularists, which was currently enough reason for them to be treated with suspicion at all times. It wasn't, though. Ez confirmed that there had been a meeting and all the supervisors had received the same instructions, to ensure that work continued regardless of social tensions on the station.

The high-ups had wanted to keep it quiet, but apparently one of the other colonies had already experienced rioting. The only thing that had stopped the riots was the failure of one of the gravity drives. Luckily, a backup drive had kicked in almost immediately so no one died but it could have been catastrophic. The colony engaged a kind of martial law after that, arming the few police they had and deputising others. They had tried to lock up large groups of the rioters but it didn't work since the rioters were necessary to maintain the gravity, power and other life support systems on the station. It was chaos.

Obviously, Ezekiel was worried about the same thing happening on Sunraysia. The supervisors' intervention kept everyone honest to some extent but it was also causing more problems as people related it to the 'big brother' tactics of the previous decade. And it didn't stop people from talking outside work hours, when the religious mobs cloistered themselves in the chaplaincy for all-night meetings. They were doing it for their own safety, they said, as they feared Secularist retribution. The trouble was, that very action was making the Secularists suspicious. Where previously they may have trusted the people they had been working beside for the last three years, now they had to wonder exactly what it was they were planning at those meetings. Perhaps the religious mobs were planning on overthrowing the Secularists, to ensure that they would not be persecuted. In turn, the suspicion the Secularists displayed only served to justify the faithful's concerns of persecution.

It was a self-fulfilling prophecy.

Jamal hardly saw Tim anymore. Tim had started meeting Jamal at the jobsite instead of his house, and began going straight home instead of stopping at Jamal's for a couple of drinks after work. Jamal didn't ask, but he got the idea with Tim having two religious parents, he was under pressure to hide his secularism, and that meant at least appearing to cut ties with Jamal.

Eventually, the communication link was restored, and the news came through. It wasn't delivered by Ezekiel or the other station staff however, since the TV signal came back at the same time. And it was all over the news, on every channel that was still operating. Apparently, a radical Islamic group called Ikrama Sabri was taking the credit – or the blame, depending on which way you looked at it – for the attack. The newscast showed a photo of the man, a Muslim who had to be at least in his late fifties and was so remarkably expressionless that he actually looked bored. A taped radio sermon from 1997 by a one-time Sheikh and Grand Mufti, the group's namesake, played in the background. 'Oh Allah, destroy America, her agents, and her allies! Cast them into their own traps, and cover the White House with black!'

'Well, their inspiration is clear,' Ez said. With all the paranoia, Ez had moved out of Holloway's and into Jamal's.

'This isn't good,' Jamal said, stating the obvious.

'I don't think I'll be going to work today,' Ez said.

Jamal chewed his lip thoughtfully. 'I've probably got enough food here to see us through the week.'

'Let's hope it doesn't come to that.'

'It might pay to start finding containers for water though,' Jamal said. 'If things get too crazy, the services might go down.'

'If the services go down, water will be the least of our problems,' Ez pointed out. If the gravity drives or life support systems failed, they would die long before they would die of thirst.

They stayed in Jamal's quarters for the next five days, watching the news and talking quietly.

On the first day, the corridor outside was silent, like the rest of the colonists had come to the same conclusion. Around lunchtime, an announcement came over the PA system. 'Please be aware that Sunraysia's police service has been activated to maintain control,' the announcement said. 'Please remain calm, this is only a precautionary measure. Additional deputies are required. To ensure fairness, police membership will be equal numbers faithful and Secularist. If you are interested, please apply through your supervisor.'

Jamal and Ez just looked at each other. The police activation was more likely to escalate the situation than control it. And it was unclear whether or not this was a trap. As a senior technician, Ez effectively was one of the supervisors, and he had no information on this turn of events.

The second day was even more alarming. There was noise and movement in the corridor all day, sounds of running feet, raised voices, and something being dragged. They heard knocking, starting up the corridor and coming closer until the knocking was on Jamal's door. They didn't know if it was supervisors rounding up workers, or groups of people rounding up Islamists – or Secularists, or someone in trouble, looking for somewhere to hide. They didn't open the door to find out.

On the third day, the newscast was interrupted for a colony announcement. The Sunraysia banner flashed on the screen, followed by Ezekiel's face. He looked angry. 'Colonists of Sunraysia,' he began, his voice quivering as he visibly tried to remain calm. 'Following the detention of violent protesters yesterday, rioters have seized control of the police station and are now armed. The rioters are urged to relinquish control of the weapons and police station peacefully in return for a full pardon. We're living on an orbital space station, you morons. If the colonists cannot safely return to work, everyone on Sunraysia dies including you!' Ezekiel lost his composure and raised his voice toward the end. He snarled at the camera and spun on his heels. The announcement blinked off and the newscast continued, unaware of what had just transpired.

Jamal and Ez remained locked in Jamal's quarters for another two days, hoping the rioters would relinquish the police station – or at least the weapons – but no further announcements were forthcoming. However, they couldn't wait any longer. Even if they were to continue to hide out, they needed to resupply. Jamal cautiously opened his front door and poked his head out. The corridors were clear. He stepped out, Ez following. He turned to close the door behind them and stopped. Ez caught his stare.

'What is it?' Ez asked quietly.

'Look,' Jamal told him. Ez did, turning to look where Jamal was staring. There was a red 'S' spray painted on the front of the door.

Ez shot a look back at Jamal, who was still staring at the S, frozen with disbelief. 'Come on,' Ez urged.

Jamal nodded, and they silently started walking up the corridor. 'You hear that?' They heard the hiss of someone whispering farther up the hall. The brothers froze in place. There was no way of telling whether it was friend or foe.

'Go back,' Jamal said. 'I've got an idea.'

They retreated back to Jamal's quarters and closed the doors. 'Listen,' Jamal instructed.

Ez stopped and listened carefully, but shrugged. What was

he supposed to be hearing?

'I noticed it yesterday. The ventilation fan in this section has stalled,' Jamal told him.

'But there's still good airflow here?'

'Of course,' Jamal said matter-of-factly. 'There's still three other fans in the area. Only two are needed, the rest are precautionary.'

'I'll take your word for it,' Ez said. 'What about it?'

Jamal ignored him and went into his bedroom. It was an absolute mess as he had had to clear enough space for the bed since Ez had moved onto his couch. Jamal stopped rummaging for a moment and popped his head out of the room. 'This might take me a while. Grab a couple of bags, fill them with water and food,' Jamal instructed.

Ez obliged without question. Whatever his brother was up to, he trusted him.

'Here,' Jamal said five minutes later. He was holding two masks. Ez took one. 'Are the bags ready?' Jamal asked.

Ez handed him one of the bags, but Jamal pushed it back into his hand. 'Hold it for a moment, you'll need to pass them up to me. We're going to crawl out the ventilation shaft.' 'Where?' Ez asked.

'The surface,' Jamal answered, already donning his mask. Ez rushed to pull his on. Jamal climbed up on the table and reached for the vent cover. His practiced hands had the cover and filter removed in moments. He reached up to the sides of the opening and pulled himself up. Ez handed him up the bags and Jamal grabbed his arm and pulled him up.

The shaft was very tight. It was lucky that both brothers were slim and although Ez had never been in one of the shafts before, as a maintenance technician he was used to working in tight spaces and didn't get claustrophobic.

'What are we going to do once we get to the surface?' Ez asked.

'I have no idea,' Jamal answered honestly, pulling himself

along the shaft like a caterpillar, pushing the bags in front. Ez followed as best he could.

'You have a better idea?' Jamal called back.

'No,' Ez admitted.

There was a technique to crawling in such a tight space, it seemed. You couldn't simply wriggle your way along, there wasn't enough room to position your elbows. You had to lift and slide your body.

'Are you sure the fan is off?' Ez asked.

'Yes,' Jamal said. Between the exertion and the mask, his voice was barely more than a pant. Sweat was pouring down his face and he could barely see through his fogged-up mask. Jamal didn't have the heart to tell Ez, but he was sure the fan had stalled. In fact, now that he was up inside the shaft, he could tell it wasn't just the one fan. The air flow was minimal and warm. There was probably only one fan in this area still working. It was lucky they were escaping now: never mind the rioters, if they had stayed in Jamal's quarters much longer, they would probably have succumbed to an oxygen-deficient sleep and simply never woken up again.

At last they reached the point Jamal was working toward. He rolled over onto his back and sat up into the vertical shaft, then wriggled his way to his feet. He tied the bags to his belt and climbed his way up the ladder. There was a hatch in the side of the shaft, which he opened. This was the surface; it was a stack rising above them, like a big chimney. He climbed out and pulled the bags up. One snagged, but Ez pushed it up from beneath and climbed out after it.

They were free for now, but still very much in danger. They had food and water with them, but no home to go to, nowhere to hide, and unless sanity prevailed the critical services would fail and the entire colony would either run out of oxygen or simply float off into the vacuum of space.

They were on the surface. It was dusk but with no hills or other high features, the sun still beat down on them. They could see the unmistakeable orange glow of fire in the distance. They couldn't tell from here whether it was the crops or one of the surface buildings.

After the brothers took in their surroundings they turned to each other.

'What do we do now?

THE QUEEN OF MARS
By Marc Murkin

Author's note: I'm 29 years old, and my day job is in logistics. My story is loosely inspired by a lot tensions we are experiencing right now in the world. Many people believe it best to simply leave and start again somewhere else, away from the world's problems. But ultimately if things don't change here first, these problems will follow you, and take root at the very foundations of a new society. That is the inspiration for my story.
I chose to go this way because I feel the themes are relevant, despite the Sci Fi genre. I also chose to write a female main character. It occurred to me that I have not many female characters, and I wanted to challenge myself personally to broaden my own viewpoint.

Chapter One - May 2049

As she floated, Erin dreamed of a time before the accident. She was in her Uncle James's home in Queensland, lounging in her favourite chair overlooking the backyard. It was the only spot where she couldn't see the skyscrapers that rose out of the rural landscape. Progress, the Terran Union told the public, with perfectly choreographed pride and joy. The thought gave Erin an idea for another blog piece, but she shelved the idea for another day with a click of a few keys. She wanted to maintain her good mood, opting instead for a more lighthearted piece. The scent of mozzie coils and freshly brewed coffee permeated the air, leaving her in a bubble of comfort. Erin needed all the comfort she could get before deployment. She heard a noise coming from the yard below. James shouted as the gas plates finally burst on, close to his face. Her parents laughed as they watched him fall onto his arse.

No. No that's not what happened, thought Erin. They've been gone a long time.

Submerged in the machine, Immortalis, Erin stirred involuntarily. Her limbs, those real and ghostlike, twitched, bringing her out of the dream. She did not sink, the liquid held her in place like a baby in the womb, pulsing with warmth, and life. She felt her long hair brush against her nose, though she didn't feel the irritation she would normally feel. It seemed like she had been there for days, within Immortalis. Her mind had relaxed, melding with the underwater feeling. But it never lasted, not when she thought of life before.

Erin could hear the whirring of the machine. Scans were scouring every part of her body. It started with her missing toes. Pain, at first only minute, slowly spread up her legs, through to her knee and thighs. The pain grew as it spread throughout her body. Her ruined hand clenched and unclenched as the liquid that held her grew warmer.

Pain like she had never felt before burned behind her eyes. She was back at zone 23. The chaos of the moment, when all order had been lost, and she had lost a part of herself. For a moment she regretted accepting the proposal. No job was worth this agony. But in the end, it did relent. And it *was* worth it. Erin had to repeat it in her mind, over and over as she adjusted to the pain that was now a constant behind her eyes. This was a gift she could never repay.

A voice reached out to her from the dark. "Undergoing muscle memory re-creation."

Despite herself, Erin fought against the warmth, fought against the drugs that kept her still, those same drugs that were meant to keep her in a dreamlike state, a place where she wouldn't be feeling the process. Submerged as she was, Erin could not cry out. Would anyone hear, and even if they did, would they stop? She lost control, and it took her back to a point of complete darkness in her life. Erin's mind repeated the words she spoke - not to doctors or psychiatrists, but to herself.

Am I such a ruin? What purpose is left for me?

"You must relax," said the voice. "Breathe."

Was this the true price, Erin wondered? The liquid that held her now crushed her under immense weight. It forced its way in, into every pore of her body. The pain was intense.

Ages passed Erin by, until the liquid receded from her touch. Had it really drained, or had she absorbed it into her body? She only knew the sensation had passed. It was no longer pressed against her body. The full procedure of Immortalis had never been fully disclosed to her. Even if it had been, she would not have cared. The only details she'd heard were that it would heal her, make her like she was before.

Erin could finally move, but she had a terrible feeling, one she felt every time she fell asleep. Erin felt herself falling.

"Operation complete," said the voice, which was clear to Erin now the water had drained. "It's over Erin, we'll have you out of there very soon. Please refrain from opening your eyes until I say."

Immortalis whirred and hummed all about her, lifting her up in metallic arms until she stood on her own feet. The sensation shocked her. She could actually feel her feet. Erin looked down and 10 wriggling toes of flesh and blood stared back at her. Immortalis opened up wide with a sharp release of pressure, and a searing light that blinded her.

"Help me get her out," said the doctor.

"I can't see," said Erin, not recognising her own voice, so raw with emotion. Blind, Erin fell away from the machine and was caught up in many arms. She hugged her chest, conscious of her naked body. Her breath left her at the realisation of what she had accomplished. She could walk, even though it had only been a few steps. Memory of the time before flooded her.

Tears welled in her green eyes that now saw the bright room with perfect clarity.

"I did try to warn you," said Doctor Martin, the voice from inside Immortalis. "The sensitivity in your eyes will pass. How do you feel?"

Erin could not answer as she lost what little remained of her voice and her head bobbed with unashamed cries.

Erin completed the final eye examination. Even before the accident, she could never read the lowest line on any eye chart. At the best of times she needed glasses while reading. Everything seemed easy now. For days she had run through rigorous testing, ensuring her body worked exactly as it was meant to. A smile slowly spread across Erin's face.

"Very good," said Doctor Martin. With a flick of his hand he dismissed the eye chart, bringing the background displays forward. Erin looked at her digital form on the display screen. She thought digital Erin stood proudly, her chin held high. She remembered standing tall like that once. It was like she was looking at a stranger. At five foot six, her feet dangled in the overly large leather seat, making her feel very small. She felt digital Erin needed a haircut, her brown hair well past her shoulders. The screen was dismissed before Erin could finish her judgement. She watched the doctor, who murmured quietly to himself as he continued to flick away file after file into some unseen folder in the virtual space between them.

"Am I okay doctor?" said Erin, after what seemed like a long enough pause between speaking. The doctor turned to Erin with a comforting smile. He brought his hands together, dismissing the display. "Erin, please call me Martin. Your body is perfect. You accepted the regenerated tissue very well. Thanks to the muscle re-creation program you should feel like you did before the accident."

"I feel even better," replied Erin, kicking her feet back and forth underneath her chair. "I've never felt better in my life. I feel like a teenager."

Martin chuckled quietly, his blue eyes shone above dark rimmed glasses. "All of our clients say that, but I would hardly call 24 old. You're in the prime of your life. Immortalis not only fixed all damage from the accident, it removed your genetic history of cancer. Your immunity to disease has strengthened. Your body can take care of itself like never before. But, I have concerns with some of your tests."

Erin felt the deep foreboding return, sitting heavily by her stomach.

"You awoke during the deep sleep phase. Given your background, steps were taken to ensure you an appropriate level of comfort. I've been running Immortalis since its inception, and I have never seen anyone fight against process as much as you did."

A dozen responses came to mind, and after a quick evaluation, none of them seemed fit for polite conversation.

"I've always had a strong rejection to medications," Erin said lamely.

Martin's smile dimmed, his forehead creased. "Immortalis heals the body, not the mind. I've recommended further time planet-side before your deployment."

"I've been through enough therapy. I know what my issues are. Unresolved trauma from my childhood. I left a large piece of my heart in Sydney when the nerve gas hit. Grief doesn't have a time limit, but I've learnt to not let it cripple me. That was half a lifetime ago. I've found new purpose. I'm due to leave soon. Are you stopping me from going?"

Martin sighed. "No. I also understand time is needed for the mind to heal. A new start will be therapeutic, therefore the decision has been made to give you clearance. But I do wish you would reconsider about your implants. There is still time for another session to complete the Immortalis treatment?"

Erin tapped her left hand against the armrest, her long fingers counted a rhythm on the leather. It was the only thing she had not let Immortalis change. She had flatly refused, despite extreme pressure from her Uncle James. "I need this," Erin said, more to herself than to Martin, "to remember. I can never go back into that darkness."

„Well, I can see there is going to be no convincing you. You may find some of the modifications I've added to be of great use to you. As a last gesture from us, I'd like to offer you the latest in skin grafting. We've been able to engineer skin grafts that won't reject your bionic implants."

"I didn't know that was possible? That's kind of creepy." The thought of robots in human skin frightened Erin. She'd begun to grow used to the sight of her mechanical hand.

"It's a new advancement, a revolution for victims of severe burns, along with cosmetic applications for people conscious of their implants. Consider it on the house. After all, nothing's too good for our colonists. Once your therapy is complete, you will be given your briefing. Auscon thanks you for your service, future citizen of Mars.

Chapter Two - January 2050

Erin hated long flights, and this by far was the longest she had ever been on. Disgusting food and cramped quarters, her hands touched the walls in the only place she could stand. The bunk itself was selected specifically to fit Erin's exact height, and little more. The periods in and out of stasis were more than she could bear. The constant thrumming of the bulkhead only compounded her fears of a breach that would shoot her and the several thousand other passengers into space. Sure, space flight was the safest way to travel, so all her online followers and friends had assured her on her blog before boarding at Woomera Spaceport.

She rummaged through her bag, removing a small pillbox and her phone. Everyone had told her it was so 2030s, but Erin couldn't help but love the classics. Besides, hardly anyone even carried phones anymore, preferring mobile glasses or retina implants. But after her experience with Immortalis, Erin wasn't willing to risk messing with any more implants. At least, not yet.

She decided to take a Mars re-entry selfie. She stared at her image in the inverted camera. Green eyes and light freckles, and a smile she hardly recognised stared back at her. Her brown hair had been so long and wavy, if a bit ratty, Erin could admit. She had shortened it to her neck, a more manageable cut, plus it made for a better fit in the helmets she had to get used to wearing. Her entire life was changing, one haircut wouldn't hurt.

She hadn't washed properly since leaving Woomera Spaceport. Her eyes were puffy, cheeks haggard. The typical picture after a long flight on an old decrepit jumbo, the kind she remembered taking as a child. Click. Approved and sent. Perfect, Erin thought, as she reviewed her photos. She pondered how long it would take to connect to her website once she arrived. It was unusual for Erin not to post for more than a few days. It got to the point where she answered to her online tag, Queen of the North, more than her own name. She hoped Mars had better signal strength than Townsville. Cynic that she was, Erin suspected it was almost deliberately bad so nobody could use it. She had made it the highlight of one of her recent blogs.

Erin flicked back through old photos of some friends from Townsville. She had never been happier, surrounded by friends. There were older pictures of Uncle James and his girlfriend Roz. He cut a pretty good figure in his day, in full fatigues. The pictures were years old from his last campaign, before retiring. She reached a particular date and stopped browsing, placing the phone back in its case, back into a pocket, taking comfort in the weight on her leg.

The light above Erin's bunk flickered. A pleasant voice advised of the descent into Mars's atmosphere. She braced herself.

Nothing in the spaceliner pre-training or online guides could prepare her for the descent. It did not help that she had read too many horror stories and watched far too many low-budget airline crash vids. Why they have those available for free during flights, Erin would never know. *Futuristic spaceflight my arse.* She smiled as she touched her left hand, taking comfort in the smooth skin. Erin opened the pillbox with a practised twist. *Valium always will be the greatest invention of mankind,* in her opinion. She closed her eyes and waited for the rumbling of the descent to end.

Erin squinted behind her raised hand as she stepped out onto the tarmac. She looked about groggily, not knowing what time it was. She could not determine where the sun stood, but the sky seemed to glow almost like earth daylight. The line of dazed and fatigued passengers seemed like the worst conga ever as they proceeded wearily through a sealed tube towards the spaceport lounge.

It had taken a few more valiums to get herself into the stifling suit. Despite the closed in feeling, she was happy enough to wear it. Aside from the obvious lifesaving qualities, it was a snug, form-fitting suit. It was when she had to activate the helmet to close around her face that things started to feel wrong. Despite all efforts, enough accidents had happened in the recent past that all passengers were required to have active life support whilst departing a spacefaring vessel. It was a standard safety procedure, but one that made Erin feel utterly helpless.

The entire colony was situated in the Hellas impact basin, a broad crater in the southern hemisphere. According to the logs, the spaceport was situated apart from the other complexes, at the very edge of the basin by a large mountain that put Everest to shame. Erin could see at a distance the long transport tube connecting the spaceport with the rest of the colony, an enormous mess of skyscrapers and silver domes that filled the basin.

Erin watched the rhythmic patterns of the designated skylines for air and gravity bound transport ships, both trade and long range passenger liners. One particular transport had flashing lights. Erin pondered at the need for a police force in a relatively new colony. Larger transports hummed all around them, refueling and preparing for take-off, to the outer colonies, Erin guessed, or even Tau Ceti. It was only then she realised how far away everything was. Some of the vessels were barely in orbit. Erin marveled at her newly repaired vision, but also felt a twinge of fear. How could anyone see that far? Should they?

The spaceport loomed before her. The baggage cars looked the same as the ones on Earth, along with the crew carelessly collecting what few precious personal effects the Union allowed for transport. Erin's possessions were few apart from some small family keepsakes, and she had kept them on her person at all times. Her only large item was her personal computer and workstation for her new position. As the line passed by the baggage handlers, Erin craned her head to search for the large steel case with the yellow tulips embossed on the side. She didn't trust the handlers to be gentle with it, but she had little say in the matter.

Erin didn't expect heavily armed soldiers. She had read about the latest in the aptly named power armour, but had never seen it up close. They certainly weren't the same military-grade issue back home. Even the SAS didn't have access to this kind of hardware. They excelled more in stealth technology than brute force.

Everyone was intimidated as they walked between the lines of soldiers. Erin doubted she could even lift the needler rifles they carried, though she eyed the sidearms at their waists. She had enough training to use the latest gyrojet pistol, though she hoped her skills would not be required. The suits were bulky, but they moved about with complete ease.

The cynic in Erin pondered the reason for the soldiers' presence. She was surprised to hear her thoughts voiced by a passenger behind her.

"Are they supposed to be here for our protection?" grumbled an old man, catching up to her long-legged stride. Erin pretended to adjust her bag so she could study him. He was perhaps in his late fifties with grey curly hair. He appeared weighed down by more than his two bags. His blue eyes stared back at her above small glasses that seemed to rest a little too far down his nose. Erin tried hard not to notice the tremors in his hands. It pained her to see his failing health, she knew him too well.

"Doctor Martin! You didn't tell me you were coming to Mars."

"Hello Erin, it's good to see you," said the doctor.

"Is it always like this? Security seems a bit excessive."

The same polite voice began again at the entrance to the spaceport. "Welcome to Mars," said the voice with delight. "Enjoy your new stay, your new life. You are the forerunners of the Terran Union's glorious advance into intergalactic civilisation. Work hard, and your names will be remembered in honour. Welcome, first citizens of Mars."

"Mars," said Martin, clamping his shaking hands together, "a paradise of innovation and new beginnings. A strictly controlled beginning at that."

"We already passed all their tests for Mars citizenship," replied Erin. "What do they have to fear from us when we've already arrived?"

Martin only smiled and nodded in agreement as they passed a cluster of watchful soldiers. It seemed to Erin that most of the passengers were equally as disturbed at the show of force. She could hear muttering all around her towards the heavily armed escort.

"Mars has never been the same since the so-called accident. What a sham. You think these are police? No. All security forces are courtesy of Ortega Industries to ensure the *safety* of the port's clientele."

The Typhon Expanse

The polite voice over the intercom repeated its greeting over and over again until all passengers had entered. Inside, a new voice instructed on the layout of the port, pointing out directions to the baggage retrieval and exits. The new voice was a bit gruff compared to the one outside. The difference was jarring, the welcome mat swiftly rolled up out from under them.

The line of people began to spread out as the tunnel ended. Erin stood back with Martin as they watched the people proceed. "They have little more than the clothes on their backs," Erin said to the old man.

"Corporations provide everything," said Martin. "These people will be given everything they will ever need. Jobs on the colonies are advertised quite attractively."

"They need to be in such a desolate place," replied Erin.

"And that's why you're here?" probed Martin. "A lucrative career move? For Auscon and glory?"

"It's a little more to it than that."

The old doctor merely smiled and shook his head. "This is my third flight to Mars, I believe this will be my last."

"You plan on dying here?" said Erin with a smirk.

"I hope not. I have plans beyond Mars, there are too many secrets here. Maybe to Tau Ceti. I hope it isn't the same there, at least not yet. I will go beyond, if more planets are found. Mars no longer feels like the outskirts of civilisation that gave me my drive in life. Look at it out there. The colony is almost full, the Big Four petition weekly to branch out beyond the basin. What little space that remains in our bubble is being filled with looming towers of steel. Yes, I hope for something beyond even Tau Ceti."

"That's a wonderful dream," said Erin. "I hope you make it there. I might just join you someday."

"Erin Rowland?" said a strange voice.

Erin turned around at the sound of her name and immediately regretted it. She looked upon a line of intrusive virtual advertisements. They began to heckle all the passengers.

"Miss Rowland," repeated the virtual face. It smiled, excitement digitally pasted on its bland face once eye contact was initiated. "Welcome to Mars! When was the last time you checked your insurance premiums? Did you know you could save eight point seven five per cent on your appointed income as an employee to Ortega?"

Erin broke eye contact and walked towards baggage claim, but the virtual presence followed her. It was not bound by the usual constraints.

"Miss Rowland, based on your recent personal pictures and statuses, your appearance has dramatically changed beyond your last recorded scan. Prosthetics? Scanning now. We have a wide range of safety footwear that applies to your workplace health and safety regulations. Feeling tired from your flight? Ortega has a wide variety of chemical solvents that are guaranteed to make you feel refreshed. Excuse me, Misss Rowland, it is considered rude to ignore a dedicated salesperson of Ortega Industrial. Scans take longer if you move. You are required to be still."

"You are not real," said Erin in clipped tones, "and it's not an offence to ignore someone trying to sell me shit I don't need, human or no."

"Not yet," replied the virtual presence, appearing in front of her, "at least not until proposition 2369-T is approved for mandatory advertisement quotas. I'm afraid your salary would not cover the fines based on current Mars living expenses. You should reconsider your words. Ortega Industrial currently employs over 30 per cent of the workforce in the Hellas Basin and rising. It would be a shame for you to miss out on future opportunities due to such a minor slight on your record. All you need to do is provide your digital signature, here, and this violation can be forgotten. Erased."

Erin shuddered, took a breath, and continued on straight through the virtual presence, her left hand outstretched. The presence jolted, pained as Erin's hand punctured its body. It grew distorted, erratic. The presence roared at Erin before blinking out. She sighed, harassed by a volatile AI advertisement booth after being on Mars for less than an hour. It did not bode well for the state of the colony.

"One moment, Miss."

Erin froze at the voice. It was certainly not a virtual presence. Rough, distant, digitally projected through the mouthpiece of an enclosed helmet. The soldier's accelerator rifle rested comfortably on his shoulder. It was inactive, though his free hand rested comfortably on his live sidearm.

Erin stammered; knots grew in her stomach. "I'm sorry. I'm just not used to the AIs. I've got a headache-"

The guard interrupted. "Come this way. Now!" The soldier's tone brooked no further argument.

Erin felt the eyes of everyone in the security line.

"One moment," said Martin. "I think there's been some mistake here. Return to your post. This woman is my head of security. We don't have time for this rubbish."

The guard stood a full foot over the doctor, who waited quietly. Erin held her breath, caught in the middle of a standoff.

"Apologies Director Terrance," said the guard, before nodding a salute and returning to his post.

Erin watched the old man as though she were seeing him for the first time. The pleasant old doctor was gone. In his place was a stern man with a gaze like steel. A man who was fully unaccustomed to having his orders questioned.

"Miss Rowland, apologies for not being forthcoming from the beginning. My name is Martin Terrance. Auscon is my company."

Erin did not enjoy being caught off guard. "Hello boss."

Chapter Three - 2051

I've been escorted off the floor," said Erin into the subdermal radio. "You sure about this?"

"He's the one," replied Martin, his voice heard only in Erin's ear. "Plant the seed, show him the truth and he will find you again. My source is certain the information we need is on the 48th floor."

"You trust a source from Auscon? We aren't technically part of them anymore."

"ImagiCorp and Auscon are still connected as long as I own Immortalis. Keep him busy, I need to get things ready. Take care of yourself Erin."

"Roger that."

"Did you just say 'roger that'? I'm 53, even I think that's lame. Be careful, little bird."

Hours passed as Erin waited in the room a soldier had left her in. She fidgeted nervously in her seat. Less than a year on a new planet and already in trouble, she thought grimly. The room only had one light directly above her. Erin snorted. All that was missing was the good-cop bad-cop routine. She flexed the fingers of her left hand. Now was not the time to test the gifts she had been given.

The door opened opposite the one she came in. A dark-skinned man stepped through, dressed in a neatly pressed blue security uniform.

"So you like vandalising AI's huh? I watched the footage from the lobby; I've never seen an AI crash like that before." He moved across the room, touching a panel Erin would never have distinguished from the rest of the wall. He pulled out a large canister and two cups.

"Coffee?"

Erin smiled. "Yes that would be great. Thank you."

The man nodded and spoke without looking at her. "Australian accent, from Queensland?"

"That's right."

"I'm from Alice Springs myself, but I spent time in the

tropical north. Connor Frances of Terran Security Corp, Mars Division." He handed Erin a cup, the steam wafting between them. "First of my family to go off-world. You look familiar. Did you serve?"

Erin nodded. "Four years. In zone 23."

Frances remained standing, taking a big gulp from his cup. He eyed the remaining brown contents with suspicion. "Zone 23, that used to be Tokyo? Now I remember you. I used to read your blog. Well, before I came here anyway. You can't get that kind of stuff working for Ortega. I hear the other corporations are banning it too to support the new laws."

A spark lit in Erin's brain and her face paled, not responding for a while. "Half my life is online. It wasn't like this when I first got here."

Frances tried to ignore the use of present tense, internet being highly illegal. He shrugged his shoulders and took the seat opposite her. "I'm sure the Union are working on a fix to, well you know, make it more regulated."

"Am I in trouble?" asked Erin, as Frances sat across the table from her.

He browsed through a tablet, his brown eyes flicking up every few seconds. "You have a bit of a history since coming to Mars. Not your first time killing AI salesmen, no wonder security pulled you off the floor so quickly."

"Trouble's followed me since I got here. I know I shouldn't have been rude to the AI, they're just so annoying. I've had a file ever since."

Frances waved his hand. "Honestly, don't worry about it. Those things are awful. According to your file, that particular salesman from the spaceport was decommissioned one week after speaking with you, after it went nuts on other passengers."

Erin took a sip of hot coffee before breaking the silence. "So, why am I here?"

"Well that AI's in the lobby flicked out of action when you went near it. Care to share how you did that, along with why you were in the lobby of Ortega Industrial in the first place?"

"ImagiCorp engineers have a meeting with Auscon today," said Erin, "I'm on escort duty, but I have a few hours to kill. I was scouting out the perimeter while they, you know, meet. The sales guy started bugging me."

"Sure sure. So innocent like." Frances's eyes flicked up to Erin briefly, and back down to the screen. "Sorry for being forward, but you had been seriously injured. Today's scans do not match with ones pre-Mars."

Erin glared at Frances. "You've already scanned me? I haven't even been through a checkpoint! Don't you need permission for that kind of thing?"

Erin watched the heat rise on France's cheeks. "New legislation, just came through last week. Terran Union requires all citizens to be regularly scanned at checkpoints, the spaceport especially, but there is a larger network being developed throughout the basin. Every corporate lobby now has scanners installed. I'm sorry, I didn't mean to be rude. Surely ImagiCorp have them too?"

Erin sighed. "I usually go through a side entrance. Part of the job I guess." Erin already knew about the scans, she was just annoyed that she had not found a way to tamper with it. "If you must know, I spent some time at Immortalis before leaving Earth."

Officer Frances's eyes bugged out. "My god, I'm sorry. I mean, not sorry that you had it. It's just, well, expensive. That's a one-percenter kind of medical treatment. You look great, is all I'm getting at. Probably should have just stopped talking, from the beginning. Okay, stopping from this point on."

"It's okay. Really, thanks. Everybody asks, I just don't always like to talk about it."

"It's just unreal," continued Frances, looking through his tablet. "I've never heard of anyone, much less seen a person without a 10 figure salary who has ever undergone Immortalis. I'm definitely working for the wrong company if Immortalis sessions are part of the package. That's strange. Miss Rowland your file has been black flagged. I cannot access any further."

"He doesn't need to read any more of that," said Martin through Erin's subdermal implant, "I'm ending this conversation. Operation is a go."

Erin tried not to brace herself.

The walls shook, and an explosion rocked the building. The room turned black, until orange emergency lights came alive in place of the solitary light above Erin's head. Officer Frances leapt from his chair, receiving instructions through a wall intercom.

"We have to leave. Now."

"What about my engineers?" shouted Erin.

"You'll have to meet up with them later. They have a different emergency point from us. Ortega security will lead them out with the rest of the staff."

The emergency stairwell had wall-to-wall windows. The view from this height momentarily staggered Erin in a moment of vertigo. She could see most of the Hellas Basin. Erin and Francis leapt two steps at a time down the staircase.

"Only 47 floors to go," said Frances between short breaths.

"No look. We can't go on," replied Erin, her breathing smooth and even. Below them the staircase glowed in flames, the heat could be felt from the many floors above, the stairwell filled with smoke. Erin and Frances raised their arms to their faces to block out the haze.

"Damn it," swore Frances, coughing. "Cut across through that door. We can make our way to the other stairwells. Hopefully that whole floor isn't burning."

The side door opened for Erin, leading back into the lobby of the 48th floor of Ortega's science division.

"It's empty. They must have evacuated already. This way."

Light in the main lobby was limited to dim red panels situated at regular intervals. The only sound was the echo of their quickening footsteps. They reached the centre of the room. The exit was lit up in a red glowing aura. Frances quickly stepped forward, banging his head against the door.

"Shit," he spat, rubbing his head. He swiped his card on the panel beside the door. Fail. Even a fifth time his card failed. "My card should have clearance for this floor, why won't you work? Damn it, comms are down too."

"Are we trapped here?"

Before Frances could answer, the full glass windows of the lobby shattered, sending pieces throughout the floor. Erin pulled Frances down behind the empty receptionist counter to shield themselves from the blast.

"What the hell?" shouted officer Frances. He peeked around the side of the counter. He ducked back his head when multiple shots blasted their cover. They both fell prone as the reception's counter was riddled with holes.

"Stay down Miss Rowland."

"Friends of yours?" said Erin.

Frances glared at her. He pulled out his sidearm as his envirosuit extended over his head, protecting him from the harsh, high-altitude atmosphere outside. Erin did the same, activating the suit all citizens wore, though she was not armed.

The soldiers all wore sleek black power suits. They took places throughout the lobby and one held up Frances before he could even stand.

"Drop your weapon officer," said the soldier. He nudged his needler rifle closer to Frances's head for emphasis. France's gun clattered onto the tiled floor.

"Remove them," said another soldier. "We're moving on to secure the objective." With that the rest of the team moved on to another area.

The needler rifle rose again.

"No, don't do it!" shouted Erin, her left hand outstretched.

The rifle did not fire. The soldier checked his weapon for faults. Erin dived forward, grabbed the fallen pistol and fired.

The soldier fell to the floor. Frances stared at Erin, relieved but fearful. Erin realised she may have gone too far. She stared back at him. Her green eyes were afraid, but her breathing was normal. Her hand didn't shake as she offered the gun back to him.

He waved it away taking up the rifle of the fallen soldier. "Keep it, we need to move."

"Who are they?" said Erin, nudging the dead soldier with her foot.

"Not ours," whispered Frances, "They must be from another corporation. Nobody else could afford those kind of suits. Decals removed, this is a black ops corporate hit."

They moved away from reception and into the dynamics department.

"Espionage?" said Erin. "What's here that's worth stealing?"

"I don't know," replied Frances, "truth is I've never set foot on this floor. There's never been a need to come down here, and there are other security officers who work the rounds."

"Poor fool," said Martin through the subdermal, "he doesn't realise it's his own people. Erin, leave no witnesses, he will discover the truth soon enough."

Dynamics department was empty. They walked by tidy cubicles, all recently emptied. Workstations were left open, coffee cups half full and cooling.

"Seems odd," Erin said, "for head of security to not have access to a particular floor. What are they working on here?"

"Alternative fertilizer, life support, the important stuff. There's a joint operation on the continued research of planetary terraforming between the major four corporations. Terraforming is taking way too long on Venus. With the population exploding, there's only so much space left here in the basin. Things have never been the same here since the big accident. Funding for agriculture was cut after the explosion at the spaceport. I tell you, it's bad news for the colony."

They moved into a long hallway. The entire western wall

was a view of Hellas Basin. Skyscrapers dotted the landscape, covered with glowing advertisements in multiple languages. Erin and Frances's shadows stood out boldly along the wall as they moved through the hallway.

"Is there another way off this floor?" said Erin.

"Yes. There's another stairwell on the opposite end. Don't worry, I'm sure they've managed to seal the fire. Well, I hope they have. Seeing these guys here, I don't imagine it was a waste paper basket fire."

"So what's up this way?" said Erin.

"I don't know."

"You don't know? Head of security doesn't know-"

"Alright then," hissed Frances. "No, I don't know what's back here. Are you happy now? This is clearly some super-secret floor conducting some super-secret enterprise that security doesn't know about. Are you frigging happy now?"

"Yes," said Erin eventually. She picked up her pace without making any noise, moving lightly on the balls of her feet. She took point in front of Frances. Martin had told her it wouldn't be difficult. Things would come back to her with time. The fluid movement of her muscles. She remembered the feel of the pistol in her hand, the surprising weight of it, her fingers wrapped tightly around the grip. The sights up at eye level, Erin felt she didn't even need them. Even the muscles of her arm didn't waver. Her bionic arm supported the weight.

The corridor ended in a larger office wing with no name. The door was already open. The card access panel was a mess of static.

"This has been hacked open," whispered Frances.

Erin raised her hand for silence. She stopped and listened. Footsteps, almost imperceptible on the smooth office carpet. But Erin heard them. She theorised that if she heard, then they must surely have heard Frances's whispers and his booted feet.

She pivoted around the corner of the doorway, firing successive rounds into the room. Without a pause, Erin rolled forward, taking cover in the front reception's desk.

"Did you get anything?" said Frances, but he had to take cover in the corridor as bullets thundered around their position. "Shit."

"Get in here!" shouted Erin. She moved to the right of the room.

Three offices were separated by glass walls. She fired off more rounds into the room, ducking her head before the return fire began. Frances took the opportunity to enter the room, but he was slow. He dove forward to avoid the incoming fire, though it was concentrated in Erin's direction. She was covered in shattered glass.

He charged the rifle, brought it up over the counter and fired. Ducking back down, he knew at least two were down from his shots. He watched in disbelief as Erin vaulted up over the glass-strewn desk and into the first office. Frances laid covering fire, allowing Erin to move into the next office, but not before being forced to hide under more concentrated fire.

Erin came face to face with a black ops soldier. He couldn't bring his rifle in close quarters. Throwing it to the ground, the soldier took a baton from his belt. It extended out as he lunged towards Erin. She raised her left arm, taking the brunt of the swing against her forearm. The soldier stopped, a digital gasp emitting from his helmet. "Shit, Cyborg!"

Erin was also shocked. She had never tested the limits of her arm. It never occurred to her just what kind of limitations she possessed before Erin swung a vicious backhand, breaking his mask and knocking him senseless to the ground.

"Are you alright?" called Frances from cover.

"I'm fine. I think that's all of them."

Frances crept through the room, counting the fallen bodies of the SF until he reached Erin. "You're bleeding. Let me help."

"I'm okay," replied Erin with a weak smile. She had multiple cuts from the broken glass. Her breath had finally come short. Her green eyes darted about the room. "I'll be fine really. At least until the adrenaline slows me. Let's find out what they were looking for."

Frances didn't reply. He walked slowly toward a large display of a ship. It looked similar to your typical personnel carrier, but there were some clear and disturbing differences. The kind that neither of them had ever seen, except in basically every science fiction movie and TV show ever.

The floating display ship was covered in weapons.

"What the fuck," breathed Frances. "Why would we even need these? Ortega have found a way to build them onto a working ship."

"So it would seem," said Erin. "Look here, is that the ship's name? Xerxes."

"This is bad. Alternative agriculture my arse."

Erin remained silent. Before entering the room, she had activated the recording device imbedded in her arm. Erin connected to the Net, and began uploading to her blog. Her followers on Earth would see what was really happening on Mars.

Chapter Four - 2052

The streets were thick with people. Erin tightened her long jacket against the chill. Even after a few years, she had never become used to the life support on Mars. At the very least her jacket helped with extreme heat during the day, and the bitter cold at night. She refocused her optical lenses as the sun finally dropped beyond the Hellas Basin. The altered light frames allowed her to see better in the dark. Lighting was poor in Athens District, what little power available often spiking, causing brown outs. Not that much street lighting was necessary. Mecca District produced enough light to simulate the sun, even at night.

Erin's optics automatically adjusted as she crossed a busy

street, otherwise the distant skyscrapers would have seemed too bright, blurring her vision. As her eyes adjusted back to normal, she bumped into a man. She made an apology and moved on. The man barely acknowledged her, his head lowered. How absolutely dejected have people become, thought Erin, when pedestrians no longer have the strength to argue over nothing? She felt homesick.

At this time of day, the streets were filled with people. They trudged along in columns, leaving from dayshift, going to nightshift, it didn't matter. Few people adjusted well to Mars Time. Erin skipped ahead to avoid the incoming tram. She watched it go by. It was filled to the brim with people.

Rollo's Cafe was just ahead. It was busy. There was a mixture of clientele who remained simply because their suits were built from an older design. They did not protect so well against the cold, but Rollo's Cafe helped with that. The interior was dimly lit, but the smell of various soups brought the life of the room up.

"He's been asking for you," said Jordan, behind the counter. She passed a bowl to Erin as she walked by. Jordan wore a wool knit beanie over her short cut blond hair. A beanie wasn't exactly practical headwear on Mars, but few things about Jordan seemed practical. Her purple lipstick added matched her contact lenses. She brought a smile to Erin's face.

"I know, I'm late," said Erin. She took a deep breath of the vapours hovering up from her bowl. It didn't taste like real pumpkin, but the smell was just right. It made her think of home, wherever that was now. Jordan had even snuck a few extra croutons into the mix.

Erin took her soup down a twisting hallway, into a back room. It was empty except for a single chair and a desk with an ancient laptop. After placing the soup on the desk, she returned to the door and locked it. She sipped at the soup greedily while the laptop hummed to life. It was slow going because the operating system was at least 20 years old. It took quite a bit of time getting this from the marketplace. Luckily Erin was well funded in her operations.

After a few minutes the brown walls turned clear, revealing the mass of servers, their blinking lights a rainbow of activity. Everything was running at optimal settings. Over the years she had managed to upgrade her hardware. Erin looked proudly at her primary computer with the yellow tulips embossed on the sides. Her network had grown. Her followers had grown. She gave them something nobody else could.

Erin checked her phone. Her lifeline from another world. Literally. There were at least 30 messages from Frances. She knew what they would say.

Finally, the system was ready for use. It was loaded with old junk, outdated software and dinosaur virus protection. Erin knew what she was looking for. Hidden in the waste was a single application. She clicked okay to proceed.

A screen appeared out of thin air beside the desk, an image displaying somewhere else. Erin frowned at the level of distortion, which had gotten worse since she last checked in. The clever blend of old and new technology could only go so far.

The screen revealed a crisp, clean office. A man in the far background was closing the full-wall window overlooking the Hellas Basin cityscape. Martin Terrance brought his plush chair closer to the screen and sat down.

"Erin," he said.

"Martin."

"You're late. You were supposed to meet me a week ago. Things have escalated here. Where the hell have you been?"

You haven't changed, thought Erin. Martin maybe had a few more greys, and his shaking had worsened to the muscles on his face. It disturbed Erin when she realised how long she had been out in the cold. Too many ops. She had been gone for months.

"I know," said Erin after another gulp of soup, not wanting it to go cold. "It was too risky to come in person."

Martin scoffed, leaning back in his chair. "My own chief of security can't meet with me in my own building. But I must insist. I need you back here. Something's happened, or is about to happen that could ruin everything."

"I know. That's why I called you. I did some digging with Frances. The Big Four are planning something big. Xerxes is not solely funded by Ortega Industries. Auscon, Noxxe Corp and Amero are in on it too. At face value they seem like your typical warring corporations. But Frances found something big. There's a secret facility 50 kilometres underground right here on Mars. They are planning to build a shipyard in orbit. What they plan to do is far worse than anything the Terran Union have done on Earth. Mars is the new staging ground to travel even further. They will control everything if we don't wake everybody up to it. Xerxes is just the beginning."

"What can be done that we aren't doing already?" said Martin. "The Union's primary weapon is apathy, misdirection. The citizens of the Union are more slaves now than they ever were at the turn of the twenty-first century."

"We have to give them a new hope," said Erin fiercely. Her soup had cooled to a thick paste.

"Very dramatic," replied Martin with a slow clap. "I'm sorry, that was rude. I'm, just so tired. You are of course right. You have all but confirmed my worst fears. It's coming closer and closer for us to leave, but we are at least 15 years too early. I didn't finish what I was saying before you interrupted me. We have been noticed. The Big Four have eyes on me."

"I've been careful! I've covered all my tracks."

"I know, it wasn't you," said Martin," you're like a ghost. The stories about you out there. Do you know what they are calling you? Look, not important." Martin looked away from the screen, his face distorted in the display. "It was me."

"You? How?"

"I over extended my reach. ImagiCorp has grown too large, too quickly. We've become a threat. I've defended myself against two separate takeovers. All suits and boardroom kind of events. I regret ever selling Immortalis to Auscon. Any hopes of turning it into mainstream medicine is now a distant memory. But now, some of my backers have gone missing. The situation has grown too quiet. I'm concerned about a different kind of assault. You are to report back here ASAP. Where it's safe. We must hold our ground against whatever comes, and I cannot do it without you."

Erin sighed. She knew this would happen eventually. Erin had singlehandedly made the Net available to those with the balls to look for it. Her blog had grown into something much more for the people in Hellas Basin. It had become a manifesto against everything that was wrong with the Terran Union. She had always hoped for more time. She had one more post to send to the people. There was still time.

"Please come, as soon as you can," said Martin before cutting the connection. The room darkened once again and the only light shone from the old laptop screen, illuminating Erin's paled face. That light was snuffed out as she punched the screen, then the keyboard. With her left hand, Erin tore open the laptop, smashing the interior to tiny pieces. The servers disappeared, replaced with plain walls. She could never return to Rollo's Cafe. Erin hugged her chest at the sudden chill, and left the room behind her.

Erin knew something was wrong immediately upon re-entering the common room. When she had first arrived, her optics had marked every single person. Everyone was different, except for Jordan behind the counter. She hadn't been in the room long enough to warrant the change. Men and women sat by themselves or huddled in small groups talking softly. Head held high, Erin approached the counter, trying to ignore the bowls of soup gone cold, in front of people who didn't buy them.

"I might not be back for a while," she said to Jordan. "Can I have a soup to go please?"

"Of course," said Jordan with a smile before turning to fill a takeaway cup.

Erin was grateful for the optic shutters concealing the tears in her eyes. If Jordan was at all genuine, she should be nervous. Not alarmed in any way by the tension in the room. A man entered the cafe. He looked proud and confident. Nothing at all portraying the mood of Athens District. He headed straight for the counter.

"Here you go," said Jordan, "no, no. On the house, you can pay it back when you come by again."

Damn her.

Erin took a sip. Traitor or not, Jordan at least gave her another weapon.

The man behind Erin screamed as scalding hot soup burned his unprotected face. He received a brutal kick to the stomach before the cup hit the ground.

The room erupted with the sound of mismatched chairs and benches scraping hard against the floor. Before the confident man doubled over, Erin made use of his imbalance and pushed him towards the closest group of patrons descending upon her. Erin ducked down at the sound of guns charging. She couldn't help but flinch seeing Jordan take a clumsy hit in her place, but the shot was not lethal. At least, Erin hoped it wasn't.

She pulled a small device from her jacket pocket, flicking it out until it unfolded into a small pistol. Erin stunned two women before they could grab her arms.

"Bring her alive," said someone in the back. The confusion of tables and chairs and bodies slowed movement in the small cafe. Erin deepened her breath as she felt the onset of claustrophobia. She raised her hand towards the lights, turning them off along with all other power in the room. She punched another man square in the jaw, dropping him. Erin lamented the need, feeling his bones crunch under her attack. She leapt over a table and fired a few more shots into the darkness before slamming open the front door.

Nobody followed her out, but Erin wasn't about to pause long enough to make sure. The street was clear. This was all an ambush, she realised. Erin wondered how big the net was to catch her. She raced into a narrow street and stopped, slumping her shoulders against the cold wall. Night had fallen and the exterior heating was inefficient as she watched her own breath float up in front of her eyes.

"Pull yourself together Erin," she murmured between sobs. She hugged her arms against her chest, slumping down the wall onto the ground. She touched her hands, her legs and feet, reassuring herself of their presence. "You don't have time for this."

"Erin," said a voice in her subdermals.

"Boss?" she murmured, taking in big gulps of poor quality air. "This line isn't safe. They could be tracing it."

"From your vital readings I think we are past that. Besides, we are under attack here too. Where are you?"

"I'm about a block away from Rollo's. A whole district away. I'll never make it."

"You must," said Martin sternly. "You're here because of me. We both came here to change things. Mars can never become another Earth, that's what we said. The Union destroy everything they touch. The people here are slaves to these brutal conglomerates. Over the years I've done what I could. Selling off Immortalis to them was the hardest thing I've ever had to do. My biggest achievement to mankind. But it's gone now, only the wealthy can access it. My dream of curing the world of sickness, even of age itself! Now they control everything. Erin, listen to me. It's time. Time to be remembered for something. Now get up!"

Slowly, Erin pushed herself up. "I'm ready."

"Use everything you can. Make them see."

Erin removed her gloves and pulled up her left jacket sleeve.

Her skin was porcelain smooth, unaffected by the cold. Despite breaking a man's jaw a few moments ago, her knuckles were clean, untouched.

With gritted teeth, Erin pulled at the skin below her wrist. She couldn't bring herself to watch as she tore her own skin down her arm. She shuddered, tears filling her optics. In her mind, Erin was back at zone 23. The deafening fire-fights. The screams of people caught in the crossfire. What a failure the mission had been. The EOD team had swept through the area prior, but they missed something. And it cost Erin more than she was ever willing to give.

Erin forced her gaze back to her opened arm. The smooth synthetic skin was gone, in its place gleaming metal. She pressed the thumb of her right hand onto a panel. Her hand lit up and a thin beam of light pushed out in front of her. Erin had learned to type well with one hand, and her delicate fingers flicked over the holographic keyboard.

She was connected. It felt good to be online again. Like re-connecting with a long lost friend. Erin thought of her uncle, and everyone she had left behind. But she no longer went by the tag Queen of the North. She changed her tag when she arrived on Mars. Everyone would be watching. She wondered how long before it would reach Earth through the correct channels. Would they be able to block it? No, Erin couldn't think like that. They would all be watching the Queen of Mars.

A light moving past the alley diverted her concentration. Her fingers were a flurry on the keyboard. She only had one more protocol to activate. Erin closed her eyes as she felt her cybernetic hand release a series of chemicals directly into her bloodstream. The adrenaline that had faded and robbed her of energy returned with a deafening howl in her ears. Her pulse quickened to dangerous levels, but finally receded to a more controlled pace.

The hologram faded as Erin folded her jacket back down and put her gloves back on. With a press of a button by her collarbone, her suit constructed a helmet over her head, sealing it along with the rest of her body.

The toxins coursing through Erin's body gave her more energy than an artificial pumpkin and crouton soup ever could. She avoided the ground patrols by scaling the building in front of her with unnatural ease. She listened as a team closed on her former position below. Without her suit, Erin would have frozen from the cold. She looked out into the night. The horizon was teeming with skyscrapers and lights, the shipping lanes high above coiled like an ever-moving serpent.

In her mind, she heard the playbacks of the last year. Her arrival on Mars, the discovery of Xerxes, the months spent uncovering the truth, Rollo's Cafe, it all played back to her. Everyone online saw her run along the rooftop of a building in Athens District. They watched as she was momentarily blinded by the spotlight of a patrol ship looming above her. Teams of soldiers burst through the roof access door, a voice called for her to surrender.

Erin ran. Without a pause she leapt up and over the edge of the building. She barely made it to the other side. Erin rolled through the landing, getting back to her feet. Another patrol ship joined the first. They took chase as she jumped from building to building, their engines roaring in the night.

Erin took a wrong turn. She could go no farther without another building close enough to jump to. On the ground they would surely catch her. A third patrol ship joined the chase. They formed around her, their spotlights pointed at her. Erin's jacket whipped about as the ships grew closer together. She had never used her cybernetic hand against anything so large. But with the chemicals running through her, she felt no fear and the thought of failure ended as she raised her clenched fist towards the patrol ships.

She released the pulse through her hand, more than she had ever released before. The ships faltered. Their spotlights flickered, calls for her surrender ceased through the failing speakers. The ship to her right went into a spin, spiraling out of view to the street below.

"Get away Erin," said Martin inside her head. "We cannot hold them."

"I'm not leaving you there," shouted Erin. The growl in her voice frightened her.

Erin leapt towards the second faltering ship as it lined up with the rooftop. Her cybernetic hand dug into the ship's hull, anchoring her to the top of the cockpit. Her keyboard lit up, taking control of the ship from the outside. She veered it into the remaining patrol ship, hoping to god she wouldn't go down with it. But the ship clipped against its starboard engine, sending it into a spiral like the first one. Erin's body was drenched with sweat at the exertion her hand had forced from her. She raised the patrol ship up higher, above the city. She marked out the ImagiCorp building easily and set course.

With little room remaining in the domed area, Hellas Basin had grown up instead of outward. Mecca was an overcrowded mess of skyscrapers, each fighting to become the largest.

She was almost there. She panted, control over the ship's systems beginning to slip from her grasp. The ImagiCorp building was before her, a small spire amongst behemoths. She scanned the building for survivors, but all that remained was the penthouse floors. She made out a single life sign, Martin. The floor below was teeming with little red blips in her vision. Erin could hear the muffled screams of the pilot below, trying to take back control. She pulled out her pistol, firing as she crashed into the building.

Erin lived. She didn't know how it was possible, but she lived. She knew from the aching all over her body that her leg was broken. Erin was alarmed by the dead weight of her left arm. Its power had been completely drained. But she was still connected. Her online followers would see everything!

Her aim had been true. She guided the ship into the area of

highly concentrated soldiers, but not before disconnecting and breaking her way into the penthouse floor above. Even still, the floor was on an angle. The patrol ship must have driven through two more floors before stopping.

She gazed out at Hellas Basin. Explosions rocked the skyline. Remnants of ImagiCorp's security patrols battled furiously in custom made ships, designs courtesy of the stolen Xerxes plans. At least they had the technology to fight back.

"You certainly know how to make an entrance." Martin sat behind his desk in a daze. His hand rested on a series of gyrojet sidearms, and what appeared to be grenades. "You could have brought down this entire building with your recklessness. It may still fall."

"It won't," said Erin as she got to her feet. "You know, I don't think I've been in this room before."

"Few come in here and live," said Martin ominously, a whiskey glass shaking in his loose grip. Erin thought it was a joke, but couldn't be certain.

The walls were covered with replica swords and posters.

"You like those?" said Martin. "My favourite, the one in the middle. Excalibur. Ah the days of chivalry and magic."

Erin walked up to the poster next to Excalibur. It depicted a very frail man in a wheelchair with a quote underneath him.

"However difficult life may seem, there is always something you can do and succeed at."

"Stephen Hawking said that. Brilliant man. If any man deserved Immortalis, it was him. Would that he was still around today, I always thought I could have saved him. We could have used his intelligence, amongst such blind stupidity."

Erin could hear movement outside the door, only then realising she had lost her own weapon. She tried to drag herself closer to Martin to take a weapon, but the look Martin gave her held her back. "Stay unarmed," he said. "It's your only chance." It was the same steely gaze she remembered him giving the soldier at the spaceport. The stern features of a man not to be questioned or trifled with. Martin looked into her eyes, but Erin knew deep down, he was looking at *them,* those watching. He was no longer talking to her.

"It's time to come out of the dark, little birds. Time to fight for a new home. Freedom. I regret I cannot follow you. But you will know who to turn to when the time comes. I can't tell you what you should do, use your imagination."

Erin's ears rang from the blast of the office door shattering. Soldiers in nondescript power armour poured into the room. They had no decals on their suits, no insignias. This was a black op. A hostile corporate take-over.

Erin couldn't hear her own scream over the ringing in her ears as Martin's body was hit repeatedly by rifle fire. She collapsed. The room was filled with soldiers. Erin didn't have the strength to move her head to see who spoke. She was exhausted.

"Martin's down. So is the woman."

"Clear. We're done here. Not our department to clean this place up."

"Looks like the Big Four are going to be fighting over who's going to get this place. Hey, the woman is alive, she hasn't been hit. Pretty one, aren't you? Oh shit. Shit, get over here. She's online, connected. She's recording, someone jam her fucking signal."

Erin took a hit to the side of her head, then nothing more.

Chapter Five - March 2064 (Fourteen Years Later)

"Sir, that's the last of the convoy," said Emir, a young and vibrant second officer. His suit was pressed sharply, as though he would be on parade at a moment's notice.

"Finally, it's about bloody time. Which one is this from?"

"Gulag seventeen, orbiting Mars. Sir, didn't you serve on Mars for a time?"

The dark skinned man looked at his young protégé with a wistful look. "A very long time. Long before the war started. I was a low level officer overseeing Ortega security. Terran Security Corp was only a new conception then, compared to now. And to think I thought Mars would be the farthest I would ever go. Yet here we are, a stinking hot new colony. Orbiting yet another star, getting ready to rocket off even farther."

"It's really quite amazing, how far we have come as a people. It's such a shame such an enormous portion of our population is a waste. I hope they don't ruin the new colony."

You have no idea, thought the senior officer. He wiped sweat from his brow. Despite the interior insulation of the base, the intense heat of outside could still be felt. Much of the base's power had been redistributed towards preparation for the mothership convoy. He made a mental note to call maintenance, requesting a slight decrease for comfort's sake.

"Here they come sir," said Emir. All available Security Corp personnel had turned out to get a chance to look at the latest batch of convicts. The senior officer allowed it, since he himself had leaked that a living legend was among the prisoners.

"Do you think she's hot?" wondered a soldier, one rank behind.

"I doubt it," said another. "I hear life's pretty rough in the Gulags, Mars ones especially. Besides, she must be nearly 40 by now."

"I hear they call her First Lady on Gulag Seventeen. She was Queen of Mars!"

"You idiot, she killed hundreds of Terran Security before she got brought down."

"Shut up, the doors opening."

Hundreds of prisoners filed out into the departure lounge. They all wore the same bland, mustard coloured space suits, the barest no frills technology. Even if their helmets raised in case of emergency, it was doubtful whether the suits would protect the wearer for more than a few minutes.

"There she is."

"She is cute."

"Shut up!"

Half of her face was covered by wavy brown hair. She wore the same mustard suit, but markings made her stand out. It was almost like an order of rank. The highest rank, thought the senior officer.

She was completely surrounded by other convicts, forming a protective barrier between them and the security corp. They loved her, he realised. Their adoration for her was plain to see. They would die if anyone made a move against her.

He raised his hand, the cue to halt their procession.

"Miss Rowland."

She lifted her head to the speaker. Almost indifferently, she noted the ranking on his uniform. The crowd began to murmur. They prepared for the worst.

Boldly the senior officer strode forward, his retinue rushing forward to push through the convicts. Not that it mattered; they parted to let them through.

"We need to come to some understanding of the rules here," began the senior officer. "Since you clearly speak for everyone, I think it would be easier if we had a little chat."

She didn't reply. Not a word. Just a nod of the head. She tried to look downcast, but he saw through it. Chin held high as she allowed herself to be escorted away.

They didn't have to go far. A room had already been arranged.

"Sir," said a voice behind him. It was Emir. "I respect your decision to not have an escort, but please be careful. She's the first radical."

His only reply was a pat on Emir's shoulder.

The door locked behind them.

"We need to get a few things straight convict," barked the senior officer. He motioned her to be seated at the table. "I control things on this rock. We are on a strict timetable here. Since you are the so-called queen of these people, I think we need to talk."

He marched over to the wall and pressed his hand over the panel. The wall hissed aside. From the small alcove he took out a case with yellow tulips adorned on the sides. He placed it on the table between them.

"We've been picking up some pretty disturbing chatter between the Gulags. Care to explain this?" said the officer, as he opened the case.

It was her old cybernetic hand. The lights flickered, and eventually evened out.

"Camera's disabled now," he said softly. "You have no idea how good it is to see you."

"It's good to see you too, Frances."

Nearing 39, Erin showed her age. Life was hard on the Gulags, and she had resided there the longest. The first woman to do so. But Frances still saw the old Erin. Her hair was much longer than he remembered. When she moved to give him a hug, her hair fell back from her face. Those same green eyes had not lost their spark after years imprisoned.

"I assume by your lack of surprise you've been receiving my messages?" said Frances as he crossed the room. He pressed on another panel in the wall. He brought out a canister and two cups. "Coffee?"

She nodded. "God, thanks."

She took a light sip, but her eyes bulged. She took a bigger gulp.

"Yes, it's real," he said, bringing the cup to his mouth. "I made sure we don't get that same Mars crap here."

"I love it," replied Erin, taking her seat back. She couldn't help but glance at her left hand in the case. "I'd gotten used to not having it. It's been so long."

"Take it, it's yours. It took me a number of years to get this. A few mutual friends helped me locate it. A few ImagiCorp staff managed to go underground."

Erin raised the left arm out of the box, but placed it down as she looked at the remaining contents of the case. Her phone stared back at her. She couldn't grab at it fast enough. To her astonishment, it still turned on. It was the photos she wanted to see. She needed to see them. She flicked through days, months, years. Erin choked up as she reached pre-Mars. Her Uncle James smiled back at her in his backyard. She went back further, back to memories she couldn't bear to see again. Her parents, holding her in their arms. The family home in Sydney, before the nerve gas destroyed Erin's life, the driving force that brought her to this moment. But she didn't blame it anymore. She looked at the photos until tears blurred her vision. Her cybernetic hand was forgotten. Frances gave her all the time she needed before she finally spoke.

"Fourteen years, Frances," she said. "Fourteen. Fucking. Years. I hope it's been worth it. Tell me."

Frances smiled, taking another gulp of coffee. "You have no idea. The old man hid his funds well. Upon his death his files transferred to me. Shell companies dating back to when he sold Immortalis. He made some pretty clever stock purchases to the same companies who took him down. There's a big mothership out there, courtesy of Martin, with your name on it."

"Martin," said Erin wistfully. "I wish he was here."

"Me too."

Erin was silent for a moment out of respect. "How many?" she said.

"What?"

"Your men."

"Not all of them, unfortunately. Those will be left behind. The colony here is ready, we aren't leaving them to die. Although I cannot speak for what the Terran Union Hierarchy will do with them when they lose over twenty million convicts under their watch. No, there are far too many young idealists who would only cause trouble. I've watched them, tried to bring them round to a different way of thinking. But they are all straight out of Earth. They haven't experienced the atrocities on the other colonies. Mars, Triton, Galatea. They were the last bastions of freedom, and they were all murdered, or imprisoned. The Officer Academies are practically city-states, and they are quite thorough in their indoctrination. Ten years ago I went back to Earth. They gave me a medal, I only wear it during the ceremonies. I was acknowledged for my service to the Corp. My career off-world was a shining example to everyone back on home soil. They offered me a teaching job, recruitment. I was to help recruits through the Academy. Would've been a great chance to be close to my family."

"You refused?" said Erin, tapping the back of her cup above her mouth.

"You wouldn't like Earth now. I mean, that was 10 years ago. I don't even read the news these days. It's all Terran News crap. They talk a big game, how they are eradicating the last remnants of rebel ships. Everyone is imprisoned. At least, that's what they tell you anyway."

"Are we well defended here?"

"Space is empty. Xerxes should be up there, but I got some pretty solid intel. Very reliable. Xerxes is out cleaning up the remaining ImagiNation activists on the outer fringes. That's what they call it now, out of respect for the old man."

Erin's smile was genuine.

"That's not even the best part," said Frances. He brought up a holographic display between them. Erin squinted at the image. It was a terrible shot. A blurred picture of what appeared to be people standing around a large very inhuman creature.

"What is that? Looks like a dinosaur?"

"I'm not quite sure what they call themselves. Communication is sketchy at the moment, since we are losing. In other words, first contact. We are not alone Scully."

Erin had nothing to say, despite the utterly lame reference.

What could she possibly say to fully appreciate the magnitude of the news.

"It gets better," said Frances.

How on earth could it be better, thought Erin.

"That there," pointed Frances, "is their homeworld. The Terran Union has no idea it's there yet, courtesy of ImagiNation hackers. Hopefully it will be decades before they find it. Relations with the natives are going well, maybe a little too well if you talk to a few Buddhists. They gave us a gift."

Frances minimised the image of the alien species. He brought up a star chart. Erin could see Earth, it seemed so far away now. It never occurred to her until now that she would never go back. Not once had she thought of going back. She had become so enamoured with Martin's dream.

"That there, is confirmation of Martin's plan. The Typhon Expanse. It's time for our freedom, Erin. The start of a new kingdom."

Frances zoomed the star chart out further. The distance was great, greater than what Tau Ceti was to Earth. Nobody had ever travelled so far.

"Home."

THE DAWN OF CHANGE
By Joelle Cronin

Author's note: This short story is the beginning of an epic adventure involving science, revolution, genetics and courage. Set on an overcrowded and derelict mining planet, it is the tale of one of the few societies still struggling under the brutal regime of The Corporation. Science Fiction is a genre I rarely dabble in but I was grateful for the opportunity to participate in such a fantastic group anthology project. As a 24 year old health professional, my five-year plan involves finishing both my first novel and a post-graduate degree in clinical pharmacy.

Chapter One

Lanie was grateful for the screams. The screams meant her sister was alive. Each howl of pain echoed off the steel walls and throughout the tiny bunker. It pierced through Lanie's throbbing head, intensifying her nausea and guilt. She was to blame for her sister's suffering so every cry hit her like a rogue train.

Lanie's mother, Mari, rushed from the back of the bunker towards the kitchen. She ripped open the pantry doors and began searching through the deep cupboard. Lanie watched her fearfully, still frozen to her spot in the middle of the sitting room, her sister's cloak clutched in her fist.

"Mother." Lanie's voice wavered uncertainly.

Mari did not reply. She reappeared from behind the pantry door with a large glass storage jar filled with a white grain tucked under her arm. Her fingers, wet from water and blood, fumbled with the lid before desperation took over and she lifted the jar above her head and threw it at the fortified wall.

The jar shattered, sending glass and grain scattering across the tiny kitchen and into the sitting room. Lanie flinched, surprised by the action more than the sound. She barely had a moment to process what had happened when she saw why. She watched wordlessly as her mother stepped through the mess to pick up a small glass vial that was lying against the far wall. The vial was roughly the size of a shotgun shell, stoppered with a piece of cork.

Lanie's mother hurried back towards the back of the bunker. She did not make eye contact with Lanie as she passed her. Lanie tried to speak, to beg for an answer, but her voice was stolen away by fear and intimidation. This tiny woman marching around their home wasn't her mother. She had become a soldier, activated by the task at hand. She had seen the blistered state of her daughter, burnt by the star's radiation, and had leapt into action.

The minutes passed and the purple-tinged potion in the vial began to work because Elda's cries were subsiding. Lanie remained motionless, her black eyes darting anxiously around the room. She was vividly aware of every sound now – her sister's muffled whimpering, the low comforting murmur of her mother's voice, the deep creaking of the metal roof as it expanded in response to the temperature change brought about by the brutal early morning rays. She could also hear her own raspy breathing, her lungs still aching from the exertion of having to carry her sister.

It wasn't until her mother reappeared to clean the mess that Lanie dared to move again. She took a step towards the kitchen, a piece of wayward glass crunching under her tattered boot.

"Mother."

She still clutched the yellow cloak in her hand but didn't have the strength to raise it off the ground. Fatigue had set in, causing every muscle in her body to protest against performing even the simplest tasks. She let it hang limply at her side and dragged it with her.

"Stay over there," Mari commanded and brandished a hand dismissively. She turned her back on Lanie and crouched down. "Not safe," she murmured. Her weathered hands were trembling as she began to sweep the shattered glass and grain into a pile using a small brush. She didn't dare turn around. She could hear her daughter approaching, the mess on the floor grinding together between the leather sole of her shoes and the steel floor. She could hear Lanie dragging the cloak behind her, the metal buttons scratching against the floor.

"Mother." Lanie was standing over her.

"Lanie, go to your room." Mari brushed more grain and glass together in a pile, pained at the sight of a week's worth of food wasted on the floor. She felt guilty at the stray thought; it was the least of her worries at the moment. How could she care about food when her daughter was dying in the next room?

"What is wrong with me?" Lanie's voice wavered in desperation and panic.

Mari hurried to her feet, disturbing a pile of grain in her haste. "Nothing is wrong with you," she said dismissively, her eyes still downcast. She smoothed her white dress absent-mindedly.

"Then what am I?" Lanie stood before her mother in a sea of white grain and glass, a stark contrast between the deep, dark grey of the floor. Her mother made an attempt at a reply but faltered and buried her face in her hands, overtaken with emotion. Lanie let out a frustrated cry and clasped her mother's wrists, wrenching her hands away from her face.

"Look at me! I'm a freak!"

Mari finally relented and let her eyes wander over her daughter's unblemished skin in amazement. Her heart fluttered anxiously as she replayed the events from earlier. She had seen both her daughters come in the door at the same time. Lanie had stumbled in, 70 minutes after curfew, her sister clutched in her arms, crying for help.

Curfew was enforced one hour before star-rise and was continued one hour after star-down to ensure the citizens' safety. When neither girl came home that morning Mari had thought them both to be dead. The radiation incapacitated in minutes.

But then Lanie came in the door, unhurt, her skin undamaged despite being exposed to the same level of radiation as Elda. It was wrong. It was unnatural. Lanie should've been burnt. Lanie should've been gravely injured like Elda.

Mari had lived on Tiria her entire life and no one had ever gone out into the radiation and survived. There were no old wives' tales or fantasy stories about heroes who had gone into the starlight and lived because there was nothing to base the story on. The *only* reason Elda was still alive was because Lanie had been there to carry her home. Without Lanie, Elda would have remained in the street where she would have continued to burn until she was identifiable only by her shoes and her dental records. It had happened before and it would continue to happen as long as the government had totalitarian control over its people.

Lanie was a miracle and now no one could know about her.

"Do not use that word." Mari shook her head, pulling herself together. She manoeuvred her hands so she was grasping Lanie's wrists. "Hush!" she said as Lanie began to object. "No, you're not a freak. Just…" She sighed and looked around the sparsely decorated room. "Keep your voice down. Please, Lanie. Be sensible." She swept her eyes down her daughter's frame. She was tall, a trait that was extremely unusual on the planet. Most of the individuals on Tiria were short, their growth retarded during childhood due to the residual radiation.

"Mother, no one has ever survived being outside before."

"We don't know that." It was a lie. Mari knew that Lanie was right. The day The Corporation became aware that an individual could tolerate the star's radiation was the day that individual became a human test subject. The Corporation would take her and use whatever means necessary to replicate whatever mutation Lanie had in her DNA.

Mari bustled over to the cupboard and found a tatty old broom. Much like everything in the bunker, it was well worn, a clear reflection of the poverty the family was facing.

She shook the cloak, agitated. "Then why didn't I burn?"

"Because you didn't go outside." Mari's answer had an air of finality about it.

Lanie frowned. "Yes I did. Mother, you saw me save Elda."

Her youthful innocence was painful for her mother to witness. All Mari wanted to do was protect her family, save them from the mines and slavery. She grabbed Lanie's shoulders and shook her fearfully. "No, Lanie. You didn't go outside. That's what you will tell the guards or anyone who asks. You will tell them it was only Elda who missed curfew and you stayed home to study. Elda made her way home by herself. You must tell no one of this. You must not ever tell your father. Promise me, Lanie?"

Lanie shook herself free of her mother's grasp, her mouth agape. She nodded once, a terse promise, and stormed away, dragging the cloak after her, scattering more grain across the tiny dwelling. Inside her room she threw herself against the threadbare rug on the floor. She clenched her eyes shut as hard as she could before opening them and gazing at her outstretched arms. She studied them closely, searching for any sign of a scorch mark but her brown skin was flawless. Giving into the exhaustion and emptiness, Lanie climbed into her cot and tucked the cloak over her body. Here she would wait to see if her sister made it through the day.

Chapter Two

One by one, Lanie watched people file into the Corporation building ahead of her. She was near the back of the queue that snaked and wound throughout the city. The rich and highborn had priority, then the free citizens, then the debtors and their children.

It was Exposure Day. The first day of every month saw every citizen of Tiria forced to leave their homes to report to their closest Radiation Monitoring Centre and surrender their *Hexie* to the Corporation for evaluation. *Hexie* was the nickname Lanie and the other debtors gave to their radiation monitoring devices. The *Hexie* was a hexagon crassly emblazoned with the Corporation's logo. It was small, deceitfully heavy and fit neatly into the palm of Lanie's hand.

Lanie clenched her fist around the small gadget and peered anxiously over the heads of the mass of people ahead of her, quickly evaluating and calculating how long she had left until she would reach the doors of the centre. The queue was moving forward at a steady pace. Lanie would be inside within the hour and she knew she would not be leaving.

The frustrated barks of the Corporation guards about forming an orderly line seemed distant and muffled as Lanie shuffled forward with the crowd. People she attended school with smiled and waved to her but she couldn't muster anything in return. Instead she looked away guiltily and clutched the *Hexie* tighter in her hand, cursing it to Hell.

Lanie took another step forward as the line surged toward the Corporation building again and as she moved under the stark fluorescent light, it suddenly began to flicker ominously. Lanie shot a look up at the sputtering bulb over her head and as she did a cold shiver whipped down her spine. It was almost as if the light knew what she had done and was signalling to someone. Signalling to the Corporation guards to warn them she was a flight risk. Or it could be a sign of her impending doom.

Look here. Look at this girl. Watch her. Just look at her. She's a freak.

As the word freak shot through Lanie's mind the light

suddenly died, sending the surrounding area into darkness. The people around Lanie murmured in annoyance and Lanie caught several discontented remarks about the state of disrepair of the city. But that was not what she was concerned about.

She could run. This could be her chance to slip away from the crowd and head towards the mines and the desert. It was nearly midnight. Star rise would come within the next six hours and the city would be deserted again. Normally she would have to seek refuge inside, behind reinforced steel walls, like she had done every day of her life for the past 15 years, but there was no refuge in the desert. She would have to stay exposed. She would have to hope she survived, like she did the first time.

"Move!"

The Corporation guard shone a bright torch in Lanie's face and shoved her forward. Lanie gasped at the dazzling light and stumbled forward into the poor man standing a few feet in front of her, all thoughts of a daring escape dashed from her mind. The guard laughed obnoxiously and switched off his torch, sending the area into darkness again. Lanie and the man she had stumbled into steadied themselves and watched the tyrant guard saunter away, swinging his flashlight haughtily.

"I'm sorry," Lanie murmured and tried to focus on the man's form, blinking rapidly to readjust her vision. She towered over him, as she did with most people in the town. Her height was another reason she knew she was a freak. She was taller than most of the full-grown men in the town.

"Yeah, yeah," the man grumbled and resumed his place in the line, turning his back on Lanie.

The crowd moved forward again. Everyone had resumed their regularly programmed roles after the mishap with the Corporation guard. It was the same everywhere Lanie went.

Work hard. Speak not. Pay your debt.

It was the unspoken slogan of the Corporation. If you followed those three principles you would survive. Everyone around Lanie was following the second principle. Speak not.

No one dared speak up about the way the guard had acted towards Lanie. Lanie stared bitterly at the Corporation guard who had intimidated her. He didn't have to act so vulgar when he was just doing what every single other person this end of the line was doing – paying his debt.

Lanie's anxiety intensified again as she was suddenly able to see the Corporation logo on the panelling above the door, which was flanked by two more heavily armed Corporation guards. The guards had their visors raised so they could survey the crowd and make eye contact with people as they were marshalled through the doors into the dark room beyond. The process seemed stricter and more sinister this year, as though the Corporation knew people had misbehaved and they were predicting runners.

It wasn't exactly a false inference. Elda had misbehaved. Lanie had misbehaved. They had been out trying to acquire unauthorised extra rations. Now, Lanie was at risk of running. The Corporation had invested too much money in her to lose her to the desert or to have her out of action due to radiation poisoning. Lanie's heart began to beat wildly in her chest as she inadvertently made eye contact with the blonde guard by the door. Every vigorous beat resonated throughout her body, pounding in her ears, throat and left temple. She instinctively reached up to rub her head, wiping away several beads of sweat that had trickled down from her hairline. She was close now. They herded people inside in groups of 12 and she would be included in the next cut.

Lanie opened her clammy palm and stared down at her *Hexie*. It was covered in a gleaming layer of sweat. The marshal came out and began to beckon people forward, counting under his breath. Lanie wrapped her fingers back over the *Hexie* and allowed herself to be herded inside as number nine.

Lanie held the number nine card tentatively in her spare hand and stood with the other 11 debtors, waiting for their next orders. She tried to slip subtly towards the back of the group, towards the wall and away from the guards. The nausea had set in now, an unsettling ache in the pit of her stomach that was slowly creeping up her throat. Lanie swallowed twice in quick succession in the hopes nothing she'd eaten would make a reappearance.

The marshal materialised and directed them to their stations. Lanie made her way falteringly over to the table, her pace nothing more than an amble. The #9 station worker watched her expectantly, a black look growing over their face as she dawdled. To the right about four metres was an emergency exit – unguarded – Lanie noted. She could make it to the exit in a few seconds and be out the door and into the night before anyone knew what was happening. Yes, it would be star rise in a matter of hours and she would barely make it a third of the way into the desert by the time the brutal rays were unleashed. But she'd survived them once, she might as well try them again. Either the star killed her or the Corporation killed her and at least the star would be quicker.

Lanie was mustering up the adrenaline to make a run for the door when someone seized her upper arm and dragged her towards the station. Lanie staggered towards the ground, her *Hexie* flying from her grasp as she instinctively threw her hands out to cushion her fall. But Lanie's unknown assailant did not let her fall, wrenching her into an upright position. Lanie quickly found her footing and spun around to meet the furious face of the marshal.

"Hurry up, you pathetic debtor. I'm on a schedule," the marshal growled, his moustache twitching in rage at Lanie's insolence. Lanie stared at him in shock, her arm throbbing from his iron grip.

Lanie nodded dolefully and dropped her eyes, trying to appear meek. The marshal relinquished his grip and pushed her to face the worker at the station. Lanie dropped to her knees and retrieved her *Hexie*, which was resting at the base of the booth.

She stood again and held out her trembling hand, surrendering her *Hexie* to the worker. The worker gave her a sympathetic look, all previous frustration and distaste gone from her face. She accepted the *Hexie* with one hand and readjusted her glasses with the other. Lanie suspected she was being sympathetic because of the way the marshal had treated her and that it wouldn't last. Not once the results from the *Hexie* returned.

The worker girl inserted the *Hexie* into the computer and set it to run. It was not a quick process. The technology was still rudimentary. All funding the Corporation provided to the planet was immediately channelled towards the mining sector. Health care, non-mining technology and education were severely neglected. The only chance you had of receiving an education from the Corporation was if you were being groomed as a future miner. Lanie was one of those lucky children. From a young age the Corporation had paid for her to attend school, rather than send her away to work in one of the more menial jobs.

The computer whirred as it sluggishly drew the past few weeks' worth of incriminating data from Lanie's *Hexie*. Lanie could see the yellow lights on the monitor flickering out of the corner of her eye. She could see a faint reflection of the computer screen in the worker girl's glasses. The Corporation's logo sat in the middle of the screen, rotating slowly.

It took almost a full minute for the *Hexie* to be processed. The Corporation logo vanished from the screen and the worker's eyes widened in shock. Her entire demeanour changed. She sat back, her hands gripping the edge of the desk as she tried to comprehend the information on the screen.

Lanie's mouth went dry. It was exactly as she had feared. All her doubts that had been intensifying and festering over the past few days culminated into this one moment. The moment where the worker tore her eyes away from the screen, gazed fearfully up at Lanie and slowly set her finger down on an orange button on her desk.

Chapter Three

The light above the desk flickered on and red and yellow beams of light started flashing obscenely, attracting the attention of every person in the room. The red and yellow meant only one thing on Tiria – radiation. Lanie felt the eyes of everyone on her and her heart began to race again. She glanced around before focusing on the emergency exit.

She had no choice now. She had to run. Lanie inhaled sharply and held her breath. She tensed the muscles in her thighs, priming them for the flight. Her hands clenched into fists so tight her knuckles went white. She tossed her head, flicking her hair out of her vision, exhaled, and focused on the door.

Lanie launched off the spot and took two long, powerful strides before she was flung backwards onto the ground. The marshal had appeared seemingly from nowhere and seized the collar of her jacket. Lanie landed heavily. The marshal leered over her and grasped Lanie's forearm, pulling her to her feet. Lanie fought back and tried to pull away but his grip only tightened. He dragged her over to the computer, took a cursory look at the screen and marched her over to a set of red doors opposite the entrance.

Nobody moved to help Lanie. They all stared mutely at the proceedings, afraid. Two security guards rushed over to Lanie and the marshal but they were immediately dismissed. The marshal exchanged words with the guards but Lanie couldn't comprehend them. Her panic levels were critical and her body was struggling to cope with the overwhelming amount of adrenaline surging through it. Her vision kept going black, as if she might faint, but every time the marshal jerked her arm, the pain centred her, clearing her vision.

The marshal adjusted his grip up Lanie's arm so his leather-clad hands were closer to her shoulder. Now with more control, he steered Lanie through the red doors and down the corridor. It was deserted. Lanie began to speculate wildly about her fate. Was he bringing her here to kill her? He guided her down a set of stairs. Was she under arrest? They moved swiftly along a starkly lit corridor. Surely he had figured out about her immunity by now. Lanie saw the computer screen herself. She saw the level of radiation she had exposed herself to by going outside during the day. They were making their way towards a single door at the end of the corridor.

They stopped.

"Please," Lanie began to beg.

The marshal let go of Lanie's arm and she recoiled. Her shoulder hit the corridor wall and she clung to it, her eyes narrowing as she faced the marshal.

"Don't –" Lanie was about to beg him not to kill her when he shushed her. He swiftly entered his pin into the number pad by the door and Lanie heard the door unlock. Was this where they put prisoners?

Lanie turned back to look at the corridor they'd come down. It was long and narrow. There was nowhere to hide or run. She spun back towards the marshal and gasped. He had drawn his weapon; it was hanging loosely by his side. Lanie was instantly on guard. What was beyond that door that he had to threaten her with his gun to make her comply?

All Lanie could do was stare at the blue air pistol as the marshal slowly raised it, deliberating on his next move. His hand was shaking as he spun the pistol in his hand and offered it to Lanie.

It was a trick. Surely it was a trick. But suddenly instead of staring into the blackness of the pistol's barrel, she was being offered it. How many more years of imprisonment was he trying to trick her into serving? Taking a marshal's weapon – that was surely worth at least 10 years. But perhaps she could use it to her advantage. Lanie raised her arm, hesitant.

"Take it and shoot me."

Lanie withdrew her arm, clutching it tightly. "What?" she whispered. She was suddenly afraid of who was listening to this treasonous conversation.

"I can't just *give* you my weapon. We need to pretend we fought and you overpowered me. So, shoot me." He brandished the butt of the gun towards her.

Lanie slid sideways along the wall, away from the marshal. She didn't understand what the marshal was asking her to do.

"Lanie," the marshal thrust the gun towards her. "We don't have a lot of time. The guards will have reported your results by now. It's not safe here anymore. You need to leave the city or –"

"Why are you doing this?"

"Do you know where the deserts are?"

Lanie wrapped her arms around her abdomen, clutching herself tightly.

"Lanie! Do you know where the deserts are?"

Lanie nodded. She remained silent. Of course she knew where the deserts were. The deserts were forbidden territory, so naturally every child had been there. The Corporation said it was too dangerous to go near – that the sand retained radiation so even during the night it was still possible to die of exposure.

There were other rumours, rumours of people living in the deserts – the rebels – people who wanted to bring down the Corporation. Rumours were rife that they were the reason why the Corporation forbade access to the deserts – to prevent further recruitment.

"Run *towards* the deserts – they won't follow you out there."

"Why are you doing this?" Lanie repeated her question.

The marshal dropped his arm, retracting his offer to Lanie. "If they have you, they'll do tests on you. They'll try to figure out what gene the mutation is on, so they are able to test for it. And they'll figure it out sooner or later. Then they'll be looking for others. And then they'll find my Kadie and who knows what they'll do to her. Who knows what they'll do to you, Lanie."

Lanie darted forward. "There are others like me?"

The marshal's reply was interrupted by the sounds of heavy feet traipsing down the stairs. In one swift movement, the marshal turned the gun on himself, aiming it at his uniform-clad leg.

Lanie stifled a scream as the gun went off, sending a pellet into the soft flesh above the marshal's right knee. The marshal collapsed to the ground with a grunt, the gun falling from his hands. With a determined look, the marshal batted the gun towards Lanie's feet. Lanie ripped her gaze away from the dark, sticky pool of blood that was forming on the floor and bent to pick up the pistol. She held the heavy weapon loosely in her hand and stared helplessly at the marshal who was trying to stem the bleeding from his leg.

The footsteps were growing closer. It would be another few seconds before reinforcements would arrive and Lanie had to start moving. She lunged forward, grasped the door handle and wrenched the steel door open. She stepped through the doorway and slammed the door shut behind her, muffling the cries of the approaching guards.

Lanie realised with a gasp she was standing outside. She waited a few moments for her eyes to adjust to the blackness before taking a tentative step forward. She had never been down this alleyway before and had no idea which way to head. There was no time to deliberate; she could hear a large group of people gathering on the other side of the door. She took a deep breath, tightened her grip on the pistol and set off.

She had barely reached the end of the alley when the guards burst through the door, calling for her to stop and surrender. Lanie glanced both ways, recognising what street she ran into. The deserts weren't far. She could make it. She sprinted off towards Town Hall, the guards barely 50 metres behind her. They were calling out but had not yet fired upon her. Either they had realised the probability of hitting a moving target was low or they wanted her alive.

The entrance to the desert was only a few minutes from the Town Hall and Lanie reached it effortlessly. She tore past the warning signs and ducked under the barrier. She kept running until the grass became sparser and the coarse sand underfoot slowed her footsteps to a heavy trudge. She glanced over her shoulder at the guards. Two had begun to follow her out into the desert but the remaining dozen hovered anxiously at the edge of the grass, raising and lowering their guns in frustration.

Lanie quickened her pace and walked deeper into the unknown territory. She tread carefully, worried about falling down a sandbank and breaking an ankle or stepping on a sand scorpion and angering it. The star had not yet begun to rise and the whole land was in blackness. The only light came from the two guards who were tailing her.

The blissful quiet of the darkness was cut suddenly by the wailing of the star rise siren. It echoed across the land, sending a shiver down Lanie's back. There was exactly one hour until the star began to rise. If she wanted to seek shelter, she needed to turn back now. The guards obviously had the same thought. They stopped at the sound of the siren and Lanie could faintly hear them arguing in the distance.

Then, mercifully, the light of their torches began to grow fainter until it disappeared altogether as they began the long journey back to town. Lanie kept walking until she heard the second siren. She stiffened. Star rise was merely minutes away. She had survived exposure to the star once but it was only for a minute. She realised that she may be about to be burnt alive. Suppressing her terror, she turned to the horizon and waited.

Chapter Four

The Typhon Expanse

The star rose, as it did every morning, sending piercing rays of light and radiation flooding onto the planet's surface. Lanie had never seen a star rise before. She had spent her entire life locked inside a steel bunker during the day. She couldn't comprehend the astonishing array of colours smeared across the sky. She had never seen anything other than darkness.

She could feel the heat on her skin but she felt no agonising pain. It was a comforting feeling after a lifetime of bitter coldness. She peeled off her coat and set off walking again. Now the desert was brilliantly lit by the rays and Lanie could see clearly in every direction. In the distance was the indistinct outline of a building. She hastened her pace as she realised she was approaching the outskirts of an old, abandoned mining community. The community was a dark part of Tiria's history. It was one of the first settlements to be established on the planet, enclosed by one of the Corporation's protective shields. The shield was intended to be a barrier between the radiation and the people, allowing them to venture outside after the star rise. Productivity and mining returns from the community were unparalleled. However, less than six months after it began to prosper, the shield inexplicably failed. Every soul in the community perished under the brutal rays of the star.

The Corporation tried to pretend it never happened and let the town fall into ruin, punishing anyone who spoke of the tragedy. Rumours were rife that the shields had been faulty for months and the Corporation had neglected to do anything about it.

A few weeks after the first shield failed, the strength of the other shields began to waver. But rather than evacuate the planet they ordered the people into the cities and built bunkers, confining them to the steel prisons during the star rise. Eventually, one after another, the shields began to fail and the *Hexie* was introduced to monitor exposure levels. Mining of plutonium never wavered for an hour during the ordeal. The Corporation and its iron grip over the planet remained strong.

Lanie approached the mining community cautiously. A cold shiver ran down her back as she stepped off the red sand and onto one of the roads at the outskirts of the town. The star's rays were beating down relentlessly on Lanie's bare skin. A thin layer of sweat covered her body and several beads of perspiration trickled down her neck. She scanned her surroundings for shelter. She may not have died immediately from the star but it was dehydrating her and she could feel her skin stinging as it began to burn.

There was a building ahead of her, an old guard outpost for the town. She thought of the soldiers who would have manned it. They were there to watch the town and keep the people inside the border. Their job had been to keep everyone a prisoner. Lanie approached the door, a wave of grief washing over her as her keen eyes spotted a pair of brown shoes in the street. It was all that was left of the person. Their body and clothes had perished many years ago but their shoes were untouched. The shoes had become a tombstone.

She entered the guard tower and climbed to the top to survey the town. Shoes littered the streets, from large steel-capped boots to tiny white slippers. The star's vengeance on the planet's first inhabitants had been vicious. Lanie gazed out the window, feeling better already now she was sheltered from the full force of the star. Suddenly, her eye caught something in the distance. She clutched at the side of the window and leant out, squinting at the building. Then, she saw it again – movement. There was something moving around in one of the dilapidated stores along the main street.

She ran back down the stairs to the street and cautiously hurried towards the store. It was a clothes store; an impressive display of mannequins posed elegantly in the shop window. Peering closely between the models she saw the blur of movement again from the depths of the store. She inhaled sharply and stepped back. The blur resembled the shape of a human. How could there be anyone living out here? Her mind began to race at the thought. She could only think of two possible explanations – ghosts or the rebels. Both possibilities frightened her.

She was warring internally about whether or not to enter the store when the shadow she'd seen came into focus. An older woman came to the window, standing between the mannequins and gawking at her. Her face was worn and lined, a sign of radiation exposure. Most of her body was covered by a thick, hand-woven black shawl. After a long minute had passed, the woman regained her composure and beckoned Lanie inside.

Despite every survival instinct telling her to turn and run, Lanie had nowhere else to go. The Corporation would be coming after her eventually. Lanie entered the clothes shop and came face to face with the woman.

"Are you wearing a shield?" The woman was abrupt and accusatory.

Lanie shook her head and glanced down at her body. "No. I'm –" Lanie's response was cut off as the woman raised a withered finger.

"Where did you get a shield from?" the woman demanded and lunged forward to clutch at the air around Lanie's shoulders.

"There is no shield," Lanie insisted and took a step back to escape the woman's crazed swiping.

"Did the Corps send you?" the woman questioned. "Did they send you with their magical shield to kill us?"

Lanie's eyes widened at the accusation. She and the woman were circling each other now. "No! I'm not here to kill anyone. *They* want to kill *me*. And, *there is no shield*!"

The woman laughed and stopped in her place. "So you ran away from the Corps?"

"Yes."

"Did they follow you?" The crazed woman turned and began to walk away. She beckoned for Lanie to follow.

"Only part of the way. They turned back at the first siren."

Lanie began to trail after the woman as she made her way towards the back of the shop. She wondered if this woman was one of the rebels she'd heard rumours about.

"Why are you here?"

Lanie shrugged. "It was an accident." She watched the woman disappear into a small dark tunnel. "I figured I would keep walking until I was out of their range."

"Wise choice," the woman said shrewdly.

Lanie frowned but continued to shadow the woman along the tunnel. They walked in silence and in darkness until eventually the suffocating blackness ended and Lanie could see a light ahead. As Lanie exited the tunnel she realised with a jolt that she was inside one of the deserted mines. Except, it was no longer deserted. She could see people everywhere: men, women and children.

"Rebels," Lanie breathed.

"Is that what they call us?" the woman asked curiously. She half-smiled. "I suppose we are. Come with me. There's someone you need to meet." She ushered Lanie into an office and shut the door silently, trapping Lanie inside.

The leader of the rebels was an old man. Lanie considered him apprehensively. She was standing a few metres from him when the woman spoke from behind her. "Grey, look what I found. She was wandering around. *Outside.*"

The leader, Grey, raised his head slowly, a tiny smile on his lips. He glanced at his wristwatch, confirming the time. He looked at Lanie and then to the woman. "Claire, you've done well." He dismissed the woman and invited Lanie to sit with him at a stone table.

Lanie remained standing, wary.

"What's your name?"

"Lanie."

"How did you get here, Lanie?"

"I walked."

Grey's smile grew even wider. "You walked during the day?"

Lanie nodded, studying Grey closely. He looked excited, as though something amazing had happened.

"May I take your hand?" he asked and slowly extended his hand towards Lanie.

Lanie was immediately suspicious. "Why?"

"I want to show you. He nodded down at his own hand and Lanie looked. His hand was covered with silver streaks and blotches. "Have you seen this before?"

Lanie quickly held up her own palms and studied them closely. "It's a sign of radiation toxicity," she mused. "I don't have any yet because I'm young."

Grey shook his head. "No, you don't have any because you're different. My body retains the radiation like it's a precious resource. It's ingrained in my cells now. They've mutated to ensure I cannot survive without it."

Lanie's eyes flicked from her palms to Grey's face, waiting for further clarification.

"No one can leave the planet, Lanie. The star, its radiation, we now need it to survive. The one thing that can kill us has become the one thing that sustains us. We tried to evacuate the planet once before. We sourced a ship and supplies but as soon as we were out of the planet's atmosphere people fell ill and began to die, one by one."

Grey gestured out to the bustling crowd. "We realised too late that it was the *lack* of radiation that was causing people to die so we were forced to return. We can't leave this planet. We never made it to the rendezvous point. We couldn't raise the alarm and call for help."

Lanie did not react to Grey's stirring words. She was already beginning to realise what point he was trying to make.

"Lanie, I think your body is different. I believe your cells do not retain the toxic waste matter like mine do. Your cells will not die once you are out of the atmosphere. *You* will not die. You can leave the planet and bring us help. We have allies outside of union space that will come. We just need to get a message to them."

"How can you be so sure?"

"I'm not sure of anything except that the Corporation is afraid of you for a reason. And I think that reason is your potential to bring on their demise." Grey spoke passionately, decades of bitterness lacing his words.

"But, my family…. My sister, Elda, is hurt."

Grey nodded. "I can have them extracted from the colony by the next star rise. That's no problem."

"Good. But, if I do this – I'm going to start a war, aren't I?"

Grey looked genuinely happy for the first time. "Yes."

Lanie nodded. "Okay."

THE ALIEN INTEGRATION ACT
By Ash Rutherford

Author's note: I am 20 years old and when I am not writing, I am either Insurance Broking, studying, dancing or eating peanut butter Tim-tams.

'The Alien Integration Act' is a story about betrayal and self-awareness. I chose this section of the timeline as I have an interest in how humans might interact with alien races in the future. I found it very challenging to put myself in the shoes of an alien race who would have absolutely no knowledge of life outside their own planet and community. The story is very character driven, and I hope that readers will be able to empathise with and even relate to, River's plight.

I have loved every minute of working with the Townsville Speculative Fiction Group, who are a family of talented, patient and caring people. I have learnt a lot about myself, writing and the publishing process and I am so thankful to be involved in this project.

Happy Reading!

Year 2072

I let out a small sigh of relief as a cool breeze ruffled the hair that lay slick to the back of my neck. My relief was short-lived however, as the next strong gust whipped the bedraggled black strands across my face and into my eyes. Catching a rather large chunk in my mouth, I choked and sputtered, breaking the thick silence that had hung over our congregation like a cloak. I winced. It was a mark of our colony's discipline that not a single person turned to glare at me disapprovingly, although I could almost sense Elder Frost's third eyelid twitching irritably, even from my position at the back of the group. I sat straighter, ignoring the side-ways glares I received from my pride-mates. I'd long been considered the 'odd one' in the T'Ca community. According to my tutors, I lacked the 'natural grace and patience' of the females of our race. Personally I liked to think my vivacious personality was simply a source of jealousy. That aside, even I couldn't deny that too often I found myself in uncomfortable situations I'd unwittingly brought on myself.

A dribble of moisture slid down my back, joining the other droplets of sweat that were forming a formidable lake at the base of my tail. I shifted in the heat, willing my legs to uncramp themselves. The small movement caused me to brush against the girl crouched respectfully on my left. Her posture stiffened, the set of her mouth radiating disapproval. I let out another sigh, this time in frustration.

Our congregation had gathered in the Sacred Valley, beneath the shrine of the Sun Gods, to pray for a safe and prosperous Mid-Cycle. Group prayer and extended fasting ensured our continued grace in the eyes of the Gods. At this time, when both Suns scorched the land and our already limited water supplies grew even scarcer, survival became a top priority. Unfortunately, prayer was all the colony could fall back on in harsh times. Me? Well, I was somewhat of a cynic. I wasn't sure that any amount of prayer was going to push us through this Mid-Cycle, which already appeared bleaker than usual. That said, I wasn't able to offer up any life-changing alternatives to our predicament either.

Don't get me wrong, I firmly believe in the existence of the Gods. Whether or not they have a hand, or even an interest in our measly existence? Well, I couldn't help but speculate. I wasn't the only one either. Many of the youth felt it was time for a change in leadership, time to discuss new ideas, approach the growth and survival of our race from a new direction. The

Elders were steadfast in their traditions though; the structure of our leadership allowed for no argument from the general population.

So here we knelt, the heat beating down on us from both the East and the West, the sand beneath our knees growing hotter and hotter, my stomach practically about to grow legs and go in search of food itself, and the stench of sweaty bodies quickly becoming a fainting hazard.

Unfortunately, it would only get worse as the Suns neared their peak.

The wind had picked up in earnest now. I raised my face to the sky, closing my eyes and allowing myself to enjoy the small respite. Abruptly, a shadow fell across my lids. I frowned. The wind was abnormal, but clouds? Rain at this time of the rotation was unheard of.

As the wind grew stronger, I became aware of an unusual whining sound.

I cocked my head to the side, ears flicking back and forth in confusion. Around me, the T'Ca colony grew restless, many even daring to stir from their prayers to squint into the sky. Just visible against the glare of sunlight, a small blot of darkness appeared to be growing larger. At first the faces around me registered only mild interest and confusion. Excited whispers travelled around the group. Somewhere at the head, Elder Frost squawked at us to remain silent. His words were quickly lost as the whirring sound built to a deafening roar. In panic, people struggled to their feet, robes flapping about them wildly, their braided hair becoming whips in the wind. Strong gusts threatened to bowl people over, forcing them to the ground as if they were nothing more than leaves underfoot.

Someone screamed. The raw, discordant sound signaled a mass stampede towards the mouth of the valley.

I stood slowly, my heart leaping into my throat with each beat, bodies surging around me in pandemonium and my eyes focused upward as the creature descended. A strong feeling, excitement to the point of nausea, running to the point of flying, the sharp sting of fear, flooded my system in alluring waves. Poised on the edge of my feet, I stood transfixed as I identified strange grey wings, loud spinning contraptions that appeared to be the source of the noise, and an eclectic jumble of feet, pointed objects and smooth panes.

A shoulder slammed into my side and I was knocked to the ground. A heel ground into my shoulder, another foot kicked sand into my eyes and mouth. Blind and spluttering, panic suddenly a huge, insatiable weight in my chest, I fought desperately to stand amid the chaos. A knee to the face drove me straight back into the dirt. For a few minutes I struggled to crawl in harmony with the madly dashing feet, my head spinning as the colony trampled me in their efforts to escape the new threat. Finally a hand clutched the back of my robe and pulled me roughly to my feet. I stumbled along with the last of the crowd, dizziness threatening to overwhelm me. At last we entered the relative safety of the tree line. A canvas of greens and purples and browns whirled around me, their shapes blurred and blending into each other like a dream. I stumbled, my arms extending a moment too late as I fell into the welcoming folds of shrubbery on the forest floor. I felt the leaves brushing my face. And then I didn't feel anything at all.

I jolted awake as if I'd been splashed with icy water, my heart still hammering against my ribs. My first eyelid blinked rapidly, the blurriness of sleep giving way to a thick, dark canopy and dense woodland where hundred year old buttress roots and hardy shrubs twisted together like a maze. A layer of wilting brown ferns carpeted the forest floor, the first victims of drought.

Buffeting winds, giant grey wings, panic.

I shuddered in a deep breath and prepared to sit up. Propping myself against a nearby tree trunk, I took stock of the damage my body had incurred during our mad dash into the woods.

The Typhon Expanse

Apart from a throbbing headache, a large, foot-shaped bruise decorating the back of my right shoulder and a few scratches here and there, everything appeared to be in functioning order. I grimaced at the dirt and sand matted in the ridges of beige fur that protected the topsides of my arms and the backs of my hands. Unfortunately for my pride-mates, I was too achy to scale the cliff and take a dip in our ever-dwindling river. Hopefully the threat of being eaten by a giant grey bird would take precedence over any disfavour my bad body odour might invite from the Gods. I grinned. Elder Frost's third eyelid would certainly be getting a workout today. Cleanliness was more important than breathing to our Dear Elder.

I sighed and rested my head against the rough bark. The adrenaline from the day's events was fading from my system, leaving weak, twitchy muscles behind. I mourned its loss with a fervour that surprised me. So much of our lives were taken up by prayer and meditation, it was difficult to remember the last time I'd run as fast as I could, the last time I'd felt shock, or fear or excitement. It was thrilling. Even now, the threat of becoming bird food was the only thing keeping me from rushing back to the valley to humour the insatiable curiosity that circled my thoughts like a persistant fly.

I often wondered whether the colony's coveted 'Peace' was really worth the sacrifices we made, emotionally and physically, on a daily basis. I understood the theory behind it, living a modest life, dependent on each other and separate from material greed simply because we had nothing to begin with, was indeed peaceful. But it was also unforgiving. Not a single T'Ca, young or old, was untouched by death or suffering. When I thought about the giant bird descending from the sky, when I wondered where the herds went during the Mid-Cycle and how the desert toads could survive the harshest of sand storms, I became painfully aware of just how little we knew and understood about the world and what it had to offer. Even at the risk of becoming greedy, or starting wars such as those

118

we had long ago, shouldn't we be utilizing the gifts the gods gave us, our minds, to harness those resources and better our lot in life? Perhaps if we'd known more, my littermates, my family, would have survived the disease that took their lives so many years ago.

I squeezed my eyes shut, conjuring up memories of the giant bird instead.

A warm, salty wind penetrated the forest, lifting the hair from my face and cooling the beads of sweat that had gathered on my forehead. I raised my head and sniffed, detecting a heady, unfamiliar scent on the breeze.

The wind died down and the forest became eerily still. The scent trailed behind, lingering on my skin and gathering in the fine hairs of my nose. I wrinkled my nose up in distaste. It was sweet smelling, and very much *alien*. Thoughts tumbled in my head, gathering more and more excitement as I leapt from idea to idea. I welcomed it. Could it be the bird? Was it still in the valley?

Another gust of wind rustled the leaves on the forest floor, this time bringing with it the jumbled sounds of voices. Voices? I was halfway to my feet before the guilty little voice in the back of my head spoke up.

I *should* get back to the colony. I *should* clean myself up. I *should* finish my prayers. The words sounded empty even to me. A familiar, nervous energy was already bubbling in the pit of my stomach. A healthy dose of fear mingled with the excitement, which only made the idea of rule breaking, of chasing the source of the odour, still more compelling. The wind was undoubtedly coming from the valley. Even thoughts of meeting my end at the beak of a giant bird only gave me pause for a moment.

I wove through the trees at a crouch, the tips of my fingers braced against the ground and my tail held aloft for balance. Less than a minute passed and I was nearing the edge of the forest. A wash of sunlight broke through the tree line, highlighting where the cracked earth became yellow sand. Even beneath the cover of the canopy, the heat from the valley was stifling.

The smell was much stronger now, overpowering the natural, earthy smells I associated with the forest and leaving a bitter taste on my tongue. The thickness of the aroma rendered my sense of smell completely useless, and as such, I didn't realise who I'd accidentally stumbled upon until their voices suddenly became more than unintelligible murmurs. That was, because they were yelling.

"How dare you!" Elder Frost's voice crackled like lightning. I felt myself instinctively shrinking away. Had his anger been directed at me, I would have been running in the opposite direction before a single word had left his mouth. Evidently, whoever was bearing the brunt of his wrath was made of much stronger stuff.

"You have knowingly entered and tarnished a very sacred site and interrupted our prayers, possibly bringing cycles' worth of misery and suffering upon our people!" Elder Frost's rant continued, uninterrupted. I strained my ears, picking up on the nervous shuffling of more than one set of feet. Ducking around a broad tree trunk on my left, I took cover behind an overly enthusiastic growth of succulent. Hesitantly, I leaned out and peered into the valley. My heart leapt into my throat at the strange scene that confronted me.

The bird was perched, no *crouched*, about 200 steps from the tree line. Its nose was rounded, jutting forward from the main section of the body in a long, smooth prism. Its wingspan was at least 100 steps, the tips turned upwards to the sun. The bird's body seemed to widen at the back. Much like the wing tips, a long thin tail (or was that a fin?) was held erect towards the sky. A second tail, slightly larger than the first, was aligned behind it. Whilst the bird appeared to be a splash of different whites and greys, a strange marking, almost like a brand, stood out in bright colour at the base of its second tail. The image was oval in shape and slightly off kilter, with a deep blue centre interspersed with greens and browns. It reminded me of lakes and islands.

Not 20 steps from my position in the forest, a standoff was in full swing. Elder Frost's wizened chest was rising and falling in quick succession, his slanted eyes flashing with an anger that made my palms sweat. Behind him, their light brown apprentice robes billowing in the wind, stood two other Elders. Their heart-shaped faces were calm, but even from here I could detect fear in the twitching of their noses and the tips of their tails.

Directly across from them, gathered in an eclectic group, stood some of the strangest creatures I'd ever seen. Hairless and pale, their limbs and body were protected by sections of fitted material, the colours of which were previously unimaginable to me. Deep blues, bright yellows and angry reds. Each of them had a tuft of fur protruding from their round skulls. The one closest to my hiding spot surveyed the forest warily, his eyes hovering a little too long over my position. I suppressed a gasp. They were a piercing blue, like the sky on a clear day. Too bright, unnatural. The smell too, originated here. It rose off their skin in waves, but with none of the natural odours I would normally identify with an animal. I couldn't detect the flavour of fear, excitement or happiness. It was a big, bitter cloud of nothing.

The creatures seemed at a loss as to what to do. They muttered together quietly, their gestures and language completely lost on me. Finally, the one closest to me stepped forward. In perfect T'Ca, it said, "With all due respect Sir, we had no choice but to make ground. Our ship," it pointed to the bird, "is damaged. No choice."

This one was bigger than the others, its jawline strong and its chest smooth and flat. I wondered if it was male.

"You need to leave. Now." Elder Frost's words were non-negotiable.

The creature's mouth stretched into a disturbing grin that flashed two rows of white teeth. "Or what?" he said, stepping forward.

Elder Frost and the creature were similar in size, but violence was not our way. His tone was much less threatening when he said, "You may not believe in our Gods, Human, but I can assure you they will seek retribution for the pain you have caused here." Elder Frost and his contingency turned to leave.

"You're a fool," the creature, Human, yelled to Elder Frost's retreating back. "We have the ability to save your people from suffering. You could have everything at your fingertips. Yet you turn us down again and again." Human shook his head. "*You* are the reason your people die each cycle!"

Elder Frost didn't look back as he entered the woods just to my left.

My heart in my throat, I held perfectly still. But the Elders passed by without incident. I breathed a sigh of relief. In the valley, Human and his companions were making their way back to the bird, wrapping strips of material about their faces and donning strange, brimmed headdresses. Perhaps they were leaving after all. I stood, wrapping my arms about the trunk of a tree and leaning my cheek against its cool surface. Disappointment coloured the emotions that swirled in my gut. They could save our people from suffering, he had said. I wondered if it was true. How could the Elders have turned down such an offer? Surely they don't hold the favour of the Gods, who had not yet given physical evidence of their tampering, over saving the lives of hundreds? Or, what if it was the Gods who had brought us this opportunity? After all, we are their sons and daughters. We've proven our devotion cycle after cycle; maybe this is their reward? People who can help us.

As engrossed in my thoughts as I was, I didn't hear the crack of twigs behind me, or the rustle of fabric. I didn't hear the sharp intake of breath or sense the nervous excitement on the air. The creature rose from behind and wrapped warm, calloused hands around my mouth and nose. I had a fleeting moment of wide-eyed panic, in which my vision turned red and I struggled against the creature's crushing grip, before darkness engulfed me a second time.

Something hard and rough nudged my side, bringing my mind halfway to the surface.

Voices. But they were jumbled and stilted, as if I was hearing them through an inch of water. The 'something' dug into my side again, this time a little harder. Sudden, sharp pain lanced through my head. My lungs opened, filling with air. I remembered I had eyes.

Light flooded in, blindingly bright. I peered around blearily. My thoughts seemed to travel at a snail's pace, sluggish and distorted. My head had been replaced with a giant boulder, my neck was barely capable of holding it up. It took me a moment to remember how to move my hands and then another moment to rub my eyes, clearing them of the sleep that had gathered in the corners.

When some of the fogginess had faded, I took stock of my surroundings. I should have been afraid, I should have been panicking. The emotions were there, but they were stunted, trapped behind a wall. Instead, I felt oddly carefree. Curiosity bubbled warmly in my stomach.

The room was long and narrow, with plain grey walls and a smooth floor that was hard and cool to the touch. A narrow, unadorned bench with a row of seats on either side was situated in the centre. The walls were uneven, crisscrossed with thin tubes and dull, protruding objects that appeared to hold the plating together. In the ceiling, tiny little suns flooded the room with white light.

Two seats were currently occupied. Closest to me was Human, his strange blue eyes observing me with mild curiosity. On the opposite side, another creature leant casually against the table, his long legs crossed and a hand scrubbing the underside of his chin. From my position on the floor, I had to tilt my head to look up at them. I waited for the adrenaline to kick in, for fear to take hold. But again, I felt nothing.

Human leant across the table and muttered something to his counterpart. They shared a look. From beneath a swath of material around his neck, Human's counterpart pulled a thin, rounded object with two dainty, black attachments on the right side. He fitted it easily over the curve of his skull, the first attachment sliding smoothly into his ear cavity and the second resting on the side of his mouth.

"My name is Matthew," he said. My head throbbed. He spoke into the device in his own tongue, but it was being translated and emitted in T'Ca. The jumble of voices was a little too much for my pounding head. He smiled, guessing my thoughts. "I'm sorry, you'll get used to it." His eyes were warm.

"Where am I?" I asked. "And who are you? What are you doing here? Why were you arguing with the Elders?"

The creature cocked his head, a shock of black fur falling into his eyes. He ran his fingers through it while he absorbed the translation of my questions. "That's a lot of questions." He laughed.

I looked down, abashed. I was often chastised for asking too many questions. I put a hand to my head as the throbbing increased. "I don't feel very well," I murmured.

"It's the drug leaving your system."

"The drug?" I said, rolling the foreign word over my tongue.

"It's something we gave you to make you sleep. We didn't want to scare you. But we thought you might be able to help us." I frowned. The feeling of weightlessness had all but disappeared, finally allowing the trapped emotions to rise to the surface. Logic was starting to weave its way into my thoughts. I knew I shouldn't be here, but curiosity kept me rooted to the spot. I wanted to know more about how they could help us.

The creature shifted in his seat. "If you will allow me, I'll explain. From the beginning."

I met his eyes and the thundering of my heart quieted. His features might have been alien to me, but the look of concern in his eyes was universal. I wet my lips. "You want me to help you?" I said, clasping my sweaty palms together to hide their shaking.

The two creatures nodded. Matthew leant forward, his face growing animated. "We want to save your race. But we can't do it without help from the inside."

There was that little voice again, telling me to get the hell out of there.

I stared up into the creature's passionate eyes. Whatever I was getting myself into this time, it was no longer child's play.

It was outright rebellion.

The ship shuddered as the engine roared to life beneath our feet. I gasped, my grip on Matthew's arm becoming a stranglehold.

"Uh, River, a little looser if you don't mind," he said, his brown eyes watering. I yelped and let go immediately.

"I'm so sorry," I said, backing away. Matthew and his company had explained to me that whilst my race, the T'Ca, appeared to have genetic links to mankind, evolution had gifted the T'Ca with incredible strength.

"It's what allows your people to scale cliffs and mountains so easily," Matthew had explained, brown eyes twinkling with laughter as I'd expressed my awe at their knowledge. The Humans had been studying our race for nearly a whole cycle, developing cures for some of our most high-fatality diseases and strategies for improving our way of life. They could build shelters that could withstand the most powerful of dust storms. They could make water from the air and build sustainable greenhouses to grow crops all cycle. I was in a constant state of nervous excitement. All this knowledge was at our fingertips. With one obstacle: the Elders.

Vibrations from the ship's belly travelled up through my feet and into my chest. I pressed a hand against my heart, fearful it would lose its rhythm.

Matthew grinned at me. "Don't worry, you'll be fine. You might want to hold onto something though!" The words had barely left his mouth when the ship leapt into the air, quickly gaining in height and momentum. The sudden jerk saw me nose-diving the deck. My arms went out with only a second to spare, saving my face from a violent end. Somewhere on the ground below, there was a pile of all my internal organs.

I cowered on all fours until the ground had stopped shaking and the noise had dulled to a low growl. With Matthew's encouragement, I wobbled to my feet like a baby testing its legs for the first time.

The view from the cockpit was like nothing I could have imagined. The sky was an endless expanse of blue, the white clouds almost close enough to touch. Down below, the ground was a smear of browns and golds. On the horizon, a ridge of deep blue mountains rose out of the earth like clawed hands reaching for the sky. The dunes, which had always seemed so terrible, were tiny by comparison.

I held onto Matthew's arm for dear life. Despite their assurances, glass was not a concept I had managed to wrap my head around. I was certain that any minute now we would all be sucked out into the abyss to fall to our deaths below.

Matthew took my hand and led me to the back of the cockpit, where two seats could be pulled down in the corner.

"Are you ready?" he asked, his eyes boring into mine with a mixture of concern and excitement.

I broke the gaze, my eyes falling to the floor. "Can't we try to reason with the Elders one more time?"

"We've tried that, River, many times. They won't listen. We need to take action, we need to force them to see reason, otherwise the future of your race is doomed. We've been over that."

I nodded dejectedly. He was right, there was no other way.

"River." I met Matthew's eyes again.

"We are relying on you. If our laws would allow it, we'd intervene ourselves. But we can't. We need your help." He squeezed my hand and I rewarded him with a small smile.

"Maybe you can come with us, you know, after all this is done. We could explore the galaxy together. The Union would consider you a hero."

I gasped, "You would take me with you?"

"Of course. But this has to be done. Each stage, *exactly* the way we planned."

I swallowed. "Once this is done, you'll help the Colony survive the Mid-Cycle?"

Matthew nodded impatiently.

"And no one else will be hurt?"

"River."

I grimaced. "Okay, I'll do it."

Stage One.

A bead of sweat trailed down my forehead and dripped into the cavity between my nose and the corner of my eye. I ignored it as I stretched my body to its maximum capacity, my right arm desperately searching for a sturdy handhold in the wind-battered stone. My legs shook like leaves in the wind, the muscles screaming for a moment's rest. A cry of relief came unbidden to my mouth as my searching hand gripped a small outcrop. With a powerful upward thrust, I pulled my exhausted body onto the jagged ledge. It would be my last break.

Above me, our smallest sun was at its lowest point in the sky, the coolest time during Mid-Cycle. Even still, the heat was enough to bake the cliff-face and melt the skin off my back. It was suffocating. On my right the smooth stone was marred by a huge, shallow groove, worn down by the relentless fall of the great river over thousands of years.

On the other side of the groove, in the valley far below,

was the T'Ca colony. The cliff was riddled with natural caves and it was there that the T'Ca hibernated for the worst of the Mid-Cycle, surviving only on stocks of dried crops, meat and stored water. It was never enough. In the coolest part of the day, runners would make the climb up the cliff-face using a beaten track on the other side of the groove. They would fight tooth and nail with the animals gathered around the puddle that was what remained of the river, hopefully returning with a casket of water. Sometimes, they would have to dig down into the bed of the river to capture the water that lay just below the surface. There were always casualties.

I was about to make things a whole lot worse.

Guilt held my heart at knifepoint. Not for the thousandth time I wondered if I was doing the right thing.

With a strained groan, I twisted my body and began the next section of the climb. I'd chosen this side of the waterfall to avoid undue notice from my pride-mates. I had been missing for days, and no doubt my presence would draw suspicion. But as I inched along the cliff-face at a snail's pace, my fears no longer seemed quite so valid.

Finally, I pushed upwards from the last foothold and wriggled over the edge. Body trembling, I lay in the sand for a moment, my arm still dangling over the ledge and my heartbeat thundering in my chest. I counted to ten, drew in a sharp breath, and scrambled to my feet.

The river was a 100 steps-wide pool of stagnant, muddy water, surrounded by dry, cracked earth and dying plant life. To my right, sand dunes rose and fell as far as the eye could see. In the far distance, the heat rising off the dunes created colourful mirages that stung the eyes. A herd of Gafti, their huge ears flapping at persistent bugs, milled around the lake, picking at tufts of brown grass that still struggled for life at the edge of the water. A set of beady, red eyes watched them hungrily from beneath the surface.

My heart heavy, I reached into my robe and withdrew a small

glass vial filled with yellow liquid. Floating in the liquid was a single algae stem. I struggled to recall what Matthew had told me about the cell.

Matthew held the vile up for everyone to see, the white lights reflecting off the glass.

"This piece of algae is currently fostering live Crandula cells. If left untreated, the bacteria is fatal to the T'Ca. Normally it exists here in land fungi, like mushrooms. However, we have modified it such that it can live off algae in the water. When it breeds, which is often, it produces inactive cysts which can survive in water for an immeasurable period of time, until it makes contact with a new food source."

I swallowed. Once the cysts were ingested by the T'Ca, the disease would begin to breed in the digestive system, killing the host shortly thereafter. Matthew had assured me no other creature would be affected, which brought some measure of comfort. But nothing could free me from the guilt I knew I'd feel once I tipped the contents of the vile into the lake. I alone would be responsible for potentially dozens of deaths. Matthew's voice reasoned with my consciousness.

"We will initiate the third step of the mission six days after the release of the disease. There will only be minor casualties, River. We can cure the remainder of the sick once the mission is complete."

I released a breath I hadn't realised I'd been holding.

"There are always casualties in war, River."

"Is this a war?"

"We're fighting for a better future for your people aren't we?"

"Yes, we are."

Steeling myself, I uncorked the vile.

Stage Two

Okay, so I wasn't as small as I used to be. Breathing heavily, I wriggled and squirmed until I finally managed to squeeze through the narrow crevice in the rock-face. Breathing a sigh of relief, I peered back out into the tunnel. Torches lined the smooth, grey walls, the flickering lights creating false shadows. Thankfully, the tunnel remained quiet and empty. I couldn't imagine how the T'Ca would have reacted to the sight of my overly large butt wedged tightly into the crevice like some grotesque sandwich.

Ahead, the fissure rose into a narrow shaft, just wide enough to crawl through. Somewhere near the top, a narrow sluice of light entered through a crack in the cliff face, cutting through what would otherwise be a very dark hole. On the rare occasions that it rained, the shaft flooded with water and the colony residing in the caves below was gifted with a small waterfall. For the most part though, it was dry and empty.

I screwed up my nose in distaste. It'd been some time since I'd visited this place. I'd forgotten how tight and claustrophobic it was. I'd spent a long time exploring these caves as a cub, spurred on by the thrill of rule breaking. It had been a small victory when I had discovered this place, and more importantly, where it led, even though I was caught and punished more times than I could count.

I crouched, allowing myself a preparatory breath before sliding forwards on my belly and wriggling into the tunnel like your regular earthworm. The abrasive stone walls scraped against my skin as I inched upwards. I would no doubt have battle scars to show for my efforts today.

My arms were about to quit in protest of their abuse when the tunnel widened slightly, allowing me some room to move. Only a few paces away, the wall on my right ended abruptly, the narrow path giving way to an enormous cavern.

I crept forward as quietly as I could, knowing even the smallest noise would bounce off the walls in the cavern below, alerting the round-the-clock guards to my presence. A gust of wind whistled through the crack in the cliff face, flooding the crevice with warm, stale air. Praying that my scent wouldn't carry to the guards, I peered hesitantly over the ledge.

Close to 300 paces wide, the natural cavern was roughly circular in shape. The floor had been worn down over hundreds of years by the feet of thousands of T'Ca, but the edges of the cavern were still home to twisting formations of stalagmites, their counterparts reaching down to them from far above. In autumn, when the river above began to flow in force, the empty cavern echoed with the tinkling of falling water droplets.

During Mid-Cycle, the cavern was a storage place for the food that would sustain the T'Ca through the season. The floor was piled high with woven bags of dried crops and meat. Stacked neatly against the wall directly beneath me, was a mountain of wood and kindling. It was too risky to have open flames in the room, so the only light flowed in from the passage beyond the archway on the far right wall. My twitching ears picked up on the occasional shuffle of tired feet just outside the entrance.

In slow motion, tongue in cheek, I twisted my body into a more comfortable position. Once again sheltered inside the crevice, I pulled out the small, metal contraption Matthew had given me earlier in the day. His face had been stern when he'd placed it delicately in my palm.

"Whatever you do, don't get it wet," Matthew said, and then grinned at the irony. I nodded, turning the small sphere over in my palm and gazing at the reflection of my face in its shiny surface. The metal was cool to the touch.

"It's called a Burner. This is the keypad and this is the screen. When it comes time to use it, you'll need to program it."

"Program it?"

"You'll need to tell it what to do. The Burner is used for routine fires. It's sensitive to different types of kindling and has a heat and flame option depending on the efficiency required for the job. Every few minutes it sends out a kind of pulse, measuring the strength of the fire and the area burned. It's a method of containment. The stats get sent through to me and I can then shut it down remotely if necessary." I watched his mouth move with a cocked head, mesmerised.

I loved listening to Matthew talk; I was addicted to every word that came out of his mouth. He was a born teacher and I an over-eager student, yet he never seemed to grow tired of my questions. I was learning more and more every day. It was liberating, it was exciting. I couldn't get enough. And soon, everyone would get to feel the way I felt. I would no longer be an outcast and the possibilities for our race would be endless.

I just have to get through this, I thought, my heart pounding as I punched in the code and selected the correct setting.

I held the Burner over the ledge, my fingers trembling. The device flashed, signaling its activity. Neon blue letters traipsed across the screen.

Device Active. Fire Setting: High Intensity. Containment Level: Difficult. Warning: Please check area before setting your device. Do not activate device in suburban areas. Keep out of reach of children. Countdown will begin now.

Heart in my throat, I tipped my hand and watched the sphere fall until the neon letters were out of sight.

Stage Three.

Under the cover of the trees, Matthew and I watched in silence as the T'Ca colony poured out of the caves amid a billowing cloud of thick, dark smoke. Some were limping, others crawling, some carrying the sick on makeshift gurneys. The valley was filled with a cacophony of cries and splutters. Each hopeless wail another punch to the gut. Along the cliff-face, ribbons of smoke curled from the cracks and fissures and wound up into the sky.

I stared at the scene in horror. I'd done this.

Matthew's hand clapped down hard on my shoulder. I jerked, turning my wide, horrified eyes to him. He was grinning.

"You did it, River. This is it." His eyes flashed, with excitement or something else, I wasn't sure. I couldn't bring myself to feel happy, even with the endless opportunities that lay ahead of me now.

"We're going to initiate Stage Three in a few minutes. When it's safe, come out and join us. You did well." He clapped me on the back again, and then he was off, speaking animatedly into his earpiece. Not 10 steps from me, a T'Ca cub sprawled over a boulder, his frail body convulsing as he dry wretched into the dirt. There were bruises around his eyes and a trickle of blood trailing from his nose. A victim of the disease I'd released into the river. I took a step back as his blood-shot eyes stared into the forest.

For the first time, I prayed to the Gods, desperately needing assurance that I'd made the right decision.

Minutes later, the Human contingency entered the fray. At first, the T'Ca were afraid and standoffish, but the Humans quickly made their intentions clear. A group of six entered the caves, their faces shielded by air-filter masks and their skin protected by fire-retardant mesh. Within minutes, they'd pulled more than a dozen bodies from the cave, all seemingly alive. A small team of nurses administered to the smoke-affected and the wounded, while another group rounded up the surviving victims of Crandula and began dispensing what treatment they could. Unbeknownst to the T'Ca, another contingency of Human soldiers were surrounding the small valley. I watched with relief as the young cub was carried away, hoping it was a sign from the Gods.

Finally, when the smoke had stopped rising from the caves and the T'Ca had grown somewhat accustomed to the Human presence in the valley, Matthew walked to the front of the group. I watched as he adjusted his translator. His back was to me, but his nerves clearly showed in the tense set of his shoulders and the clenching of his fists.

A hush was developing over the crowd as I emerged from the forest. My heart stopped when I caught the eye of Elder Frost, standing slightly apart from the rest of the group. His face was smeared with ash and his ceremonial robe was blackened at the ends, but the only expression I could detect on his face was resignation and pain. I broke the gaze and turned to face Matthew, guilt weighing on my chest like stone.

Matthew's gaze travelled slowly over the group, finally meeting my own. Something cold flashed across his face before he turned away without a wink of acknowledgement.

I wiped my palms against my thighs, leaving a smear of sweat.

"Your attention, if you please." Matthew's voice, made louder by the additional mouthpiece attached to his translator, boomed over the crowded clearing. Frightened by the strength of his voice, many of the T'Ca cowered away, some even throwing themselves to the ground and exposing their bellies in submission. A wave of whispers travelled the group. From the rabble, I heard the phrase 'Is it a God?' repeated a number of times.

"My name is Matthew and I am a human ambassador for the Terran Union on planet Earth. We have been observing your planet and your people for a long time now, with the view of establishing an alliance between our two cultures. However our offer was rejected by your Elders and we made preparations to leave."

I glanced around at the crowd. Many, particularly the young, wore expressions of confusion, but others were sharing nods of understanding. It gave me hope. They would not understand many elements of Matthew's speech, but it was clear that the humans came in peace.

"Given recent, horrific events: the contamination of your only water source, the burning of your home and food stocks," Matthew made an expansive gesture that encompassed the whole valley, "and a new respect for the suffering your people endure during the Mid-Cycle, we have made the decision to put our offer now to you, the people, as we believe you should have a say in your future. We can provide water, we can provide shelters, we can provide food, we can extend your life expectancy, we can cure almost all your diseases and we can provide a strong government that will protect and support you through all future misfortunes. Please, join us, and your people will have a chance at a new life." At the promise of water, food and shelter, conversation suddenly erupted amongst the group. The T'Ca were standing up, shouting, staring at each other in awe and excitement. My heart warmed at the sight. I felt the weight lift slightly from my shoulders.

Smiling, Matthew nodded to his blue-eyed friend on his left. Blue-eyes acknowledged the nod and they shared a meaningful look, before he disappeared into the forest. Moments later, he emerged with a long, thin pole. Flapping at the end of the pole was a sheet of material depicting the same image that was splashed across their ship's tail. With a grunt, he raised the pole above his head and drove it point first into the ground. The hubbub continued unawares, the T'Ca deeming this minor event unimportant. But as I looked around, I could see the expressions of triumph on the Humans' faces. Something significant had just occurred.

"I hereby declare this planet property of the Terran Union. Henceforth, this planet shall be named 'Saati' and all inhabitants will be subject to the laws, traditions and customs as dictated under the newly formed Terran Union Alien Integration Act, effective immediately. As per Terran Law, all public religious or spiritual worship is decreed illegal. All groups are henceforth disbanded. Lawbreakers face severe punishment, not excluding deportation or execution. Saati's Orbital Space will be immediately opened to Terran forces, corporations and potential colonists."

Deathly silence met Matthew's formal announcement. The

speech blurred together in my head, so many new words making it barely comprehensible. One thing that stood out to me though was the outlawing of religion, a practice that was not only a source of comfort for the T'Ca, but a way of life. They couldn't take that from them. The smell of fear rose above the group in a foul wave. The people sensed that something was wrong.

"You cannot do this. I will not allow it." Elder Frost was, ironically, the voice of reason. I watched Matthew's face, expecting a spark of sympathy or a warm smile. Instead, his eyes narrowed, flashing with what could only be described as malice.

"I'm afraid it is too late, Elder. This planet belongs to the Union now."

"You will never take our Gods away from us." Elder Frost's face glowed with pride and defiance, but deep down, my heart contracted with fear. Matthew did not look affronted, he looked gleeful.

"Arrest him."

The scent of human thickened in the valley. My ears flickered and I heard the sounds of shuffling feet and clinking metal closing in on all sides. Two burly humans, dressed in crisp uniforms depicting the Terran Union emblem, emerged from the tree line behind Matthew and surged forward. Wizened and frail as he was, Elder Frost could do nothing as his arms and legs were clapped in restraints and he was hauled to the front of the group. There, he was forced to his knees in sub-mission. The T'Ca cowered, but no one spoke in his defence.

Matthew stared down at Elder Frost's submissive form with disgust.

"Let this be an example to you all. Public religious displays will no longer be tolerated. This T'Ca is considered a threat to the Union." He nodded to the guards. The human on the left of Elder Frost stepped back, drawing a small metal object from the case at his hip. He held it against Elder Frost's head. The sun reflected off the metal surface, temporarily blinding me. The crowd drew in a collective breath as the tension mounted.

Bang.

I stumbled as the booming sound penetrated my eardrums and reverberated through my body like a physical shock. The world spiralled out of control as terrified wails erupted around me. I lurched forward, my fingers brushing the dirt.

I wasn't aware I had been moving until I was kneeling in Elder Frost's blood, my hands shaking his lifeless body of their own accord.

"River." I looked up into Matthew's dispassionate gaze, my vision blurred with tears.

"You told me… you said…" My body shook with the force of my guilt.

"I said and did nothing. You did it all on your own."

"But the plan…"

Matthew raised an eyebrow. "What plan?" My vision went red as panic set in, the meaning behind his words slowly becoming apparent. Matthew knelt so his mouth was level with my ear, seemingly oblivious to the blood that pooled around his boots.

"You were just a pawn in the game, River. You see, this planet is huge and rich in resources beyond your wildest dreams. We tried diplomacy for the sake of image. Taking over a planet without consent from the people would look pretty bad in the press. That said, the only thing the Union hates more than bad press is returning home empty handed." His grin stretched wide. "So, we had to turn to alternative methods. And, lo and behold, poor little River, the dreamer, stumbles into our midst. A few fancy words and empty promises, and you were off to do our dirty work for us."

I leant over my knees as his words sunk in. Too enthralled by the fantasy they'd painted, I'd never wondered what had originally brought them here. My mouth opened and closed, my lungs gasped for air, but I couldn't seem to get enough.

"You know what the press will say now, River?" He leant

closer to my ear. "Terran Forces save intelligent race on newly discovered planet from terror plot within." He laughed and drew back so he could watch my reaction. "Terran Union liberates race from dangerous democratic government and provides life-saving assistance to struggling society." The words were delivered with a dramatic flourish. He clapped me on the back and stood, not quite able to wipe the grin from his face.

"Corporal Williams, this creature has confessed to crimes of a terrorist nature and will suffer the maximum penalty."

"Yes, Sir." Someone gripped my arms and hauled me to my feet. The world spun and I slumped in his grip, unable to bear the weight of guilt and pain on my shoulders.

"Do it discreetly, we don't want to cause any more panic."

"Yes, Sir."

"I'm truly sorry, River. But we can't have you blabbing, now can we?"

I was dragged away from the chaos like a puppet, my head lolling awkwardly on my neck and stars flashing in my vision. The T'Ca had no understanding of violence, they were completely at the mercy of the humans. It was all my fault. I'd walked into their trap, I'd hurt my own people. I'd killed Elder Frost, the one person who had understood what the humans' intentions were the whole time. I'd taken him for a fool. *My fault, all my fault.*

Under the cover of the trees, I was shoved to the ground, my face mashing the dirt.

There was a click.

I turned my face upwards, registering the glint of metal.

Adrenaline kicked in.

Bang.

THE ECHO OF NOTHING
By Michael Huddlestone

Author's note: I guess you would call me a hybrid. A cross between a logical thinker and a creative dreamer, with a dark streak rippling just below the surface. By day I swim neck deep in an ocean of numbers, data and code; by night I write. I am a horror writer who recently re-discovered his lost passion for writing. Normally I firmly reside within the horror genre with this being my first sci-fi piece. The moment I discovered the legend of UAV Discovery i knew that it was the perfect place to hurtle the genres together and write something to make you check your vessels doors at night. And what better way than a good old fashioned ghost story.

Daddy, when we go through the sky to space, will we go through heaven?" The voice was tender, possessing innocence that was reserved only for the young. Bruce watched her crystal blue eyes eagerly anticipating his response; sun reflected off her blond hair as she sat on the tartan picnic rug.

"No Chelsea, heaven isn't in the sky my sweet," Bruce responded.

"Where is it then?" The wonder of her questioning tone made him consider how he would answer it. Bruce took her tiny hands in his. They were soft. Small enough to fit in the palm of his hand.

"I think heaven is all around us." Chelsea's eyes went wide in wonderment. "We just can't see it yet. If you look closely, you might just get a glimpse of heaven and the ones we love who wait for us on the other side." Through his closed eyes Bruce watched the vision play out.

Immersed in memories of days long past, Captain Bruce Sampson sat in his quarters, propped up against the wall of his bed. The memories were always the same, always of his daughter. The first of the shockwaves rippled through the ship. Objects falling on steel echoed like thunder through the halls. Grabbing at his bottle of scotch and steel cup, he saved his only method of escape from shattering to the floor. Gulping down a mouthful of the amber liquid, Bruce tucked the half-drunk bottle into the safety of his bed sheets before grabbing his Capitan jacket and rushing out of the room.

He stood in the hallway surveying the damage before turning his attention towards the flight deck to his left. The soft mechanical hiss diverted his attention across the hall. Lieutenant Sonya Bretts emerged from her quarters. Sonya's stature filled more than three-quarters of the height of the doorway and only half its width. The dark gray and black flight suit clung tightly to her slender athletic build, with her sidearm strapped to her thigh. Sonya never ventured outside her room without the weapon. The last traces of her white undershirt disappeared from view as she did the last of her zips up. Sonya's cognac-colored eyes met his, looking to him for answers he didn't have. "Summon the crew to their stations then meet me on the flight deck."

"Yes sir," she responded, Bruce walked towards the flight deck to her right. Sonya allowed the door to close before reaching for the intercom on the nearby wall. It would be more affective in getting the attention of the crew rather than her collar communicator. A faint noise coming from her left caused her to hold her breath, delaying the order. Stepping out from her doorway she gazed down the empty hall; it led past the remaining crew's quarters and opened out on the upper level of the cargo hold. She knew the crew's quarters were empty as she had left them to their game of cards just before the shockwave hit. They were playing in the gallery on the upper level. Sonya turned, looking to the stairs that led to the gallery. Nothing. She heard it again; it was quicker this time, yet still faint and distant. She could have sworn it was the sound of footsteps. The investigation would have to wait; Captain Bruce's orders were the priority. "All crew to your stations, code blue, I repeat, code blue." The sound of scurrying footsteps came from above. With no further noise from the hallway and the notion that she'd just heard things, Sonya made her way to join the captain on the flight deck.

Bruce was already in his control seat on the right side of the flight deck; Sonya assumed her pilot seat to the left. She felt caged. The steel observation shield was still down, as was protocol while on autopilot. They had been drifting on autopilot for the last three days, since leaving the main colonisation ship Discovery. It was her third mission with Captain Bruce Sampson and the crew of the Careus, a reconnaissance vessel, part of the UAV Discovery's fleet. UAV Discovery was an explorer class vessel currently on a voyage from the Hermes System to the Zeus System. Their mission always had the same undertone: to search for new colony planets, although this mission was slightly different. The brief was to investigate a smaller planet on the far outer edge of the Hermes System. It was identified late in the journey and marked as uninhabitable, but corporate still wanted it checked out briefly before Discovery journeyed too much farther.

"Crew have been summoned Sir." He didn't turn to respond, his gaze focused on the illuminated screen in front of him.

"Thank you Sonya." He had dropped the formalities.

This is serious. Despite being a civilian contractor, Bruce was once in the service of the Aero-Space Union, keeping true to the regiment and formalities of the service long after he left.

"What is it, Bruce?" Sonya asked; he finally raised his eyes to meet hers. He was in his late thirties, but the job had aged him, making him look mid-forties. Burrowed lines creased his forehead.

"I honestly don't know." His gray eyes gave the same answer as his words, sending a shiver down Sonya's spine. He turned his head back to the front. "Careus… Shields Down." The ship's computers obeyed the command, and the Observation Shields split in the middle and retracted to the left and right. The blackness of space and the distant glimmer of millions of stars came into view. An eerie green glow rippled across them, disappearing briefly before shimmering again, like the static of a broken video feed. The sight was enchanting; neither of them had seen its like before.

"Captain to the engine room, Darius do you read me?" Static sounded over the com before the deep voice of the ship's mechanic Corporal Darius Legate echoed through the flight deck.

"Here Captain."

"Damage Report."

"The engines are dead sir. Life support operational. Hull integrity at a hundred per cent. Whatever that shockwave was, it's only affected the engines."

"Is it repairable?"

"I'm currently running a full diagnostic on the engines to pinpoint the issue. Will have an update for you in half an hour."

"Thanks, Corporal. Captain Out." He ran his fingers through his short dark hair. Silvering strands added to the appearance of a man 10 years his senior.

"Captain to Engineering, Dee are you there?"

"Yes, Captain," the young voice of Engineer Dymphna Muer replied. Despite being one of the youngest of the crew at 25, Dymphna could hold her own and put anyone on the floor who called her by her first name. Dymphna was Gaelic for the Little Poet, but it was a name she hated, so everyone called her 'Dee.' Anyone who called her 'Little Poet' was soon on the floor. There was some irony though; when it came to engineering, she could design and put anything together and make it work superbly. She was a poet, just not in the lyrical sense.

"Damage Report."

"A few crates have moved. One of the heavy terrain suits took one to the helmet, shattering the visor. Nothing that I can't repair sir."

"Good work."

"The engineering bay looks like a kid has left his toys out with tools laying all over the place, but that will teach me for not securing the tool box's second lock earlier."

"Do you need any assistance?"

"No sir, don't want anyone messing up my bay." Bruce smiled briefly, as did Sonya.

"Captain out." He paused before checking the last station, the armoury. "Captain to Armoury."

"Armoury here Captain, Corporal Leeks reporting." Corporal Martin Leeks was a serving member of the Aero-Space Union, as was Sonya. It was his first mission on the Careus. He was regimented, a soldier through and through, but she was still unsure just how to take him. He and Bruce had a past, neither speaking about it since his arrival.

"Damage Report Corporal."

"None sir, all weapons still secured. Medical also sustained no damage."

"Thank you Corporal."

"Sir, what the hell was that?"

"Still trying to figure that out Martin, will let you know when we know. Captain out." He breathed a sigh of relief before turning to Sonya.

"Well Lieutenant, we are dead in the water but still functional with unknown environmental disturbance just outside our front window. What do we do now?" He watched her, awaiting a response. She sensed this was some leadership test but wasn't expecting it and was instantly on the back foot.

Can't let him see I'm unsure.

"Report back to Discovery advising of the current situation with a further update once Darius has more information."

"Correct Lieutenant. Rule number 1, always call home, you never know when you might need them to pick you up." Sonya smiled. "I'll leave you on deck. Call home and see if they can help us work out what is happening to my ship."

"Yes sir." Sonya watched as Bruce left the flight deck.

Always testing me. Her gaze fell on the control seat. Command, it was something that she longed. When they returned to Discovery, she would go before the advancement committee. It was her last chance for promotion to Captain. Her last chance to command her own ship. Her last two attempts suffered the familiar tone of self-doubt. The official rejection statement was still etched in her mind.

Request for advancement denied; Failure to demonstrate leadership in the face of challenging situations.

"Not this time," Sonya whispered under her breath. She turned and faced the void as the shimmer illuminated the flight deck, flooding it with a sea of fluorescent green. "What the hell are you?"

"Daddy… Follow me Daddy." A soft voice called out to Bruce, bringing him back from the depths of sleep. Bruce rose from his bed, rubbing his eyes. An empty scotch bottle lay beside him.

Hearing voices now Bruce?

"Daddy." Bruce lifted his head up from its resting place in the palm of his hands. The door to his quarters was open. Soft footsteps echoed down the hall. Rising to his feet, Bruce quickly followed. He peered into the main hall; it was empty.

Wow Bruce, it finally got the better of you this time, didn't it.

It wasn't a sound that now caught his attention. A flickering green glow appeared at the far end of the hallway, radiating from the cargo bay. It disappeared as fast as it had appeared.

Bruce ran down the hallway as quietly as he could. Whatever it was he didn't want it to know he was following. Approaching the entrance to the upper deck of the cargo bay, he heard the footsteps on the stairs, going down. Bruce was halfway down the stairs when he saw it again. This time it came from inside engineering.

Am I hearing things? Deep down he knew it was real. The melody of a child's laughter echoed in the room. It was familiar to him; it had haunted his dreams each night for the last two years. Stepping into engineering, Bruce knew who it was before he saw them. The glow rose from the behind the bench like a sunrise. Moving carefully around the bench, Bruce saw a little girl on the floor. She wore a white dress with a floral pattern. Bruce's legs gave way and he crumbled to his knees beside her.

"Daddy."

It can't be. You're dead. As if reading his thoughts she responded, "No Daddy… I am here." Her voice was as tender as he remembered. Tears flowed down his cheek as her hand stroked his arm, leaving a wet glisten in its wake. Memories invaded his mind, replaying like a home movie. Days with her on the beach, the day she held his hand as they launched into orbit. These visions blinded him to the truth, to the flickering static form of his daughter. To him she was real, and nothing was going to change that.

Martin also heard the footsteps. He saw Captain Sampson walking down the stairs and followed him from a distance. The captain was out of place, dressed in his flight pants and white singlet. Martin was the ship's grunt, the muscle. He had been a soldier for the last eight years and had served under Sampson during his command on earth, but still could not call him by his first name like the others. Too much military blood flowed through his veins. This was Martin's first mission with Sampson since he had left the service; he had been assigned to the crew at the request of Sampson himself. It was a posting Martin was more than willing to follow; however, since arriving on board, he had sensed that Sampson was no longer the man he had once served. Now the captain had demons of his own, which he drowned in an amber ocean.

Was Sampson still fit for command?

Martin paused on the upper cargo deck landing, giving Sampson time to move away from the stairs so he could descend unnoticed. He wanted to give his old commander the benefit of the doubt. Throughout all the battles and conflict, he found the only thing he could trust was his instincts, and his instincts were telling him something dark was afoot. It wasn't the strange behaviour of Sampson that chilled him but something else. His hand brushed past the knife strapped to his leg as he grabbed the steel rail. Maybe this was just the way Sampson dealt with his loss. While Sampson had never mentioned it, Martin had heard that the Captain had lost his daughter on a mission.

Don't know how I would deal with that sort of loss. He continued down the stairs, careful not to make a sound. During an exploration of a potential colony world, Sampson's daughter, Chelsea, who was only seven years old, was killed en route back to Discovery. It wasn't normal protocol to take children under the age of 10, but somehow the Captain had convinced command to let her aboard. Needless to say, the Captain bore the weight of his decision.

There had been an accident. A minor explosion had rocked the engineering bay. Three crew members were injured, one fatally. It was Chelsea, her body bombarded with shrapnel. Her wounds were horrific. She died in her father's arms. The investigation team found no cause of the explosion, no signs of sabotage, nothing. When they salvaged and reviewed the engineering computer records, the logs all said the same thing: "All systems operational."

It's no wonder he drinks.

The cargo bay was empty. The overhead lights were on

standby and only emitted a dull glow, showing the room but leaving enough shadows to keep his hand close to his weapon. Engineering was to the left of the cargo bay, out of sight behind a movable tool bench. Drawing close he could hear quick breaths. The sound was the same as someone crying or, at least, trying not to cry. It came from the other side of the bench; as he silently moved around he found Sampson sitting on the floor, rocking and mumbling to himself. Martin could only pick up broken sentences. "Say you won't… No… I can't lose her… No… Away…" Martin approached slowly, letting him know he was there but not a threat. His hand left the safety of his blade and reached out, resting on Sampson's shoulder.

"Captain?"

"Don't take it," Bruce whispered.

"Take what, Captain?" Martin's eyes scanned the scene.

"She said it was for me." Moving around from behind him, Martin could see the Captain was holding something tightly to his chest.

"I won't take it," Martin said, trying to reassure him. "Can I see it?" Martin moved in front of the Captain, kneeling down. The Captain continued to rock, shaking his head from side to side. On the Captain's bare right shoulder were four long red marks that went down only a couple of inches. On the other shoulder was the same, four red marks, like small fingers. As he watched, the red marks appeared to be pressing into Sampson's skin; he could see the indents.

"Ok… Ok…" murmured the Captain. He had stopped rocking. Martin didn't know if he was talking to him, himself or someone else entirely. Bruce slowly brought his hands away from his chest, holding them out to Martin. Bruce's eyes were bloodshot from tears. There was something else in his eyes, though, a tiny green shimmer. Looking down at Bruce's closed hands, Martin realised the shimmer in his eyes had come from a small, green sphere that lay in his hands. The sphere was semi-transparent, the size of a ball bearing, with the shimmer dancing around it as though it was alive. It reminded him of the nucleus of the fusion reactor. Before he realised it, Martin found himself reaching to touch it. Bruce retracted it immediately, clutching his hands to his chest.

"She was right." Bruce's voice had tone and purpose now, it was no longer the frail, and there was anger behind it. "She said you would take it."

"Who?" Martin's heart began to race; sweat beaded on his forehead. There was a long pause; Bruce stared directly into Martin's eyes.

"Chelsea," Bruce finally whispered.

"Chelsea is dead, sir," Martin responded. Bruce, still staring, shook his head gently. Like static, a little girl appeared from nowhere, standing behind the captain, her hands resting on his shoulders. Martin jolted backward with surprise. Her form shimmered like the sphere, and the green haze that was outside the ship. Her long blonde hair flowed behind her back and her crystal blue eyes watched his every movement.

But how? Her gaze was enchanting, but it seemed to have a purpose. It was as if his body was violated, as if someone was in his head, scratching at the recesses of his mind. He tried to break the hold, to stop the pain by pushing his palms against his temples. He closed his eyes, trying to concentrate on something else, but all he saw in his mind's eye was the green sphere.

That is not Chelsea. No child could do that. Not even a dead one. Could it? The girl's eyes flashed an electric green, intercepting Martin's thought. Her smile widened; the corners of her mouth began to tear at the flesh as her smile widened further, drops of blood running down from the tears. Crimson invaded the whites of her eyes as they became bloodshot. Deeper and deeper the eyes became as the last of the white disappeared. Red streams began to flow down her cheeks. Martin's legs refused to obey his command to run.

Chelsea moved around from behind her father. Her face looked shredded, the pink flesh of her cheek hanging down.

The floral dress, once white, was now stained red; pieces of torn fabric exposed deep flesh wounds. Finally, Martin's legs obeyed, scrambling backwards as the walking corpse approached. He was moving towards the stairs to raise the alarm when his legs were pulled from under him. The sudden impact of his chest on steel expelled every breath from him. Chelsea stood near his feet, still grinning, still bleeding. Pushing with the heels of his feet, Martin propelled himself backwards. His right knee raked his body with pain as his kneecap returned to its normal position. He walked backwards using the palms of his hands like feet. Martin felt the sharp cool of steel on his back when he reached the far wall of the cargo bay. She was a few metres away; Martin looked for a way to pull himself up, his legs still uneasy. A load tie hook hung just out of reach. Glancing back at his tormentor, he saw she was gone. *Now's my chance.* With his eyes still on the empty cargo bay, Martin reached for the hook. Only a few inches more. Martin stretched with every ounce of his strength, his fingertips feeling the cool, smooth hook. Pulling with his arm, his feet pushing against the floor, he slowly rose off the steel.

Martin paused for breath, his arms tingling. The hairs on his arms rose and fell in waves; a chill ran up his spine. All noise was gone except the erratic beat of his heart.

Beside him Chelsea appeared from nowhere. Her image flickered, semi-transparent. Pain surged at the back of his head as his hair ripped backwards. Chelsea pulled it back farther, leaving his neck exposed. She looked at him, her eyes crimson, soulless.

The last sound Martin heard was shattering bone as Chelsea smashed his face into the steel wall of the cargo bay before dropping his lifeless body to the ground.

Captain Sampson watched from the base of the stairs. Chelsea looked back at her father, her face restored to that of a living girl. She smiled at him; he smiled back. "Goodnight, Chelsea," he whispered. Chelsea smiled again and waved, her image flickered, and she was gone. All that remained in the empty cargo hold was Martin, alone, lying in a pool of scarlet blood, waiting to be found.

Sonya's head was bowed, eyes closed. She was rhythmically rubbing her temples as she sat in the pilot's chair on the flight deck. It was o-seven-hundred, but she had been awake for hours, she couldn't sleep. It had been two days since the encounter, the engines were still offline, Corporal Martin Leeks was dead, and Captain Bruce Sampson was acting strangely. He had barely left his quarters since late yesterday, hardly speaking to anyone, and the few times she had spoken with him she had the distinct impression he was hiding something. They had not heard anything from UAV Discovery since lunch yesterday, and they were still no closer to finding what the shimmering green haze surrounding the ship was. The crew were looking to her for answers but she had none. Raising her head, Sonya gazed out into the void, not focusing on anything particular. Each star shone brightly, pulsating their light to their beat. For a moment, the weight of questions was eased, and she felt at peace. She welcomed it, even if it was but a short reprieve.

As she gazed, immersed in the scene, logic began to break down the door to her sanctuary and for the first time since sitting down, she became aware that the cosmic view was uninterrupted. The green haze was gone. She waited. Watching, desperately trying to keep from blinking. Nothing. *How long had it been gone? Why did I not notice it earlier?* Sonya ran from the flight deck, past the captain's cabin towards the gallery. She didn't see the point in telling the captain. The man had his own personal issues going on; besides she wanted to confirm it first.

"Take 2." Dee slid the card across the table. She stopped abruptly, looking up towards the stairwell. "Someone's coming," she whispered to Darius. They reached for their sidearms. Since the discovery of Corporal Leeks's body they were both on edge. The Captain's strange behaviour since also disturbed them. The approaching footsteps were fast; they were coming from the stairwell to the main hall. Darius slid his chair out, slowly standing up, unclipping his holster. Sonya appeared in the stairwell. She was puffed from running.

"What is it, Lieutenant?"

"The haze." Sonya took a breath. "When was the last time anyone saw it?" Darius and Dee turned and looked at each other. Darius answered.

"Probably last night before we found Martin? Though I can't be sure, I wasn't checking the view after what happened…"

"It's gone."

"What? How do you mean it's gone?"

"I just noticed it myself, just then on the flight deck. There is no shimmer." Sonya breathed. "Gone." Darius watched her; she was telling the truth. He had no reason to doubt her. They were all about to return to the flight deck when Sonya jolted backward as the room jerked softly. Darius felt the gentle hum of the engines through his legs. He knew instantly what it was. It was a welcome feeling, but his stomach sank.

"You fixed the engines Darius." Sonya smiled. Darius felt the warmth drain from his face. Her smiled disappeared.

"What is it, Darius?"

"I didn't." His response was simple, direct, and it scared the hell out of her. As soon as the words left his lips the two of them ran for the ladder. Sonya felt as if she was running in slow motion, the thud of her boots hitting the grilled floor of the main hall, each step pulsating up her legs leaving a feeling of numbness. She was in the lead, Darius and the remaining crew following closely behind. Entering onto the cargo bay's upper deck Sonya drew her sidearm before ascending the stairs. She felt the absence of Martin, of the unconscious protective sense she felt around him. He was a soldier, christened in the violence of battle. Yes, she was in the service, but Sonya was a pilot first, soldier second. She had never seen the conflict. Holding the pistol, she gripped it tightly with two hands. Feeling them tremble, she gripped the gun harder. Her knuckles were white.

The hum of the engine grew louder as she approached the engine room. Darius was behind her, followed closely by Dee, both with their guns drawn. Sonya stepped carefully, her footsteps making no sound as the rubber soles kissed steel. The room glowed electric blue from the fusion reactor. As Sonya and Darius stepped into the room, their bodies became tinted with the same blue glow. Darius was about to command the lights to turn on before Sonya grabbed his wrist, shaking her head and signalling to him to cover the left flank. He nodded. Sonya took the right.

The room was bare except for workstations built out from the walls on the opposite side of the room. In its centre rose two steel pillars, breaking at waist height to triple reinforced glass that continued to the engine room. The pillars were the source of the blue glow that bathed the room as they housed the twin fusion reactors: incandescent orbs of electric blue, in the centre a nucleus of dazzling white. Around the orbs, three purple moons spun quickly orbit it.

The room, despite the gentle hum of the engines, had an unnerving presence about it. Hairs on the back of her neck rose as if someone was gently breathing on them. They looked in every hiding place the room had to offer, which were few. At last, meeting opposite the entrance, they stood before the door to the Gravitic Drive. Through the observation window in the door, Sonya surveyed the room. Lights danced in the dark. Sonya was about to unlock the door when Darius held her hand.

"There is no way anyone could be in the Grav Room if the engines are on, not without the maintenance suit… We would be cleaning them off the walls." Slowly moving her hand away from the lock, Sonya commanded the ship.

"Careus - Engine Room Lights." The room exploded into light, the shadows disappeared. Surveying the room quickly,

Sonya returned her gaze to the observation window. The drive room, now bathed in white light, was void of shadows. Its walls were patterned with large round magnets, dark silver against the black panelled wall. The entire room was curved, and in the centre hung a large black ball with the same pattern of magnets. It spun slowly as three large rings rotated around it in opposing directions. Each ring was lined with a series of lights, the ones Sonya had seen in the dark.

Sonya reluctantly holstered her sidearm. Deep down she knew her eyes were lying to her, but the engine room was empty. She looked to Darius, who was now busy at one of the workstations, interrogating the engine's main computer system. "Status Report," she commanded, her voice more confident than she felt.

"I don't understand it, Lieutenant, it's like she was never offline."

"What about the log reports of the last two days?"

"Nothing Lieutenant."

"Nothing? No log reports?" Sonya walked over to the workstation Darius was working on, leaning over to see the screen.

"The log reports are there, ma'am…"

"Then what?"

"See for yourself." He stood up and moved over so Sonya could see. Her eyes swept from left to right, scrolling down until she reached the last status log. Her gaze met his, sharing his confusion.

"Each log says the same thing…" Her voiced trailed off, turning to look over at the Gravitic Drive room. Finally, she finished her sentence, her soft voice trailing off with bewilderment:

"Engines Operational."

Footsteps stirred in the stairwell; the group turned. Sonya was the first to have her gun pointed at the figure that approached. "Holster that weapon Lieutenant." It was Captain Sampson, fully dressed in his flight suit with command stripes. Sonya complied.

"I hear the engines are now functional, good work Darius." His tone was military.

"Don't thank me, Captain, they started by themselves."

"Nevertheless, thank you." Sonya waited to give her report, but the captain never asked for it. She still was taken by his tone, authoritarian, a stark comparison since the last time Sonya had spoken to him that day. Too structured. Something had happened. Maybe communications from Discovery. "Return to your stations." The remaining crew looked to Sonya to speak.

"Captain…" Her tone was overly direct, trying to disguise the nervousness in her voice. She wanted to express her concerns: the strange nature of the engines, the log file's bizarre report.

"We will speak Lieutenant, shortly." He didn't want to hear whatever it was she had to say. The group dispersed, Sonya following the captain down the stairs to the cargo bay. Her hands were sweaty; she wiped them on the side of her flight pants, working up the nerve to speak again.

How the hell do I say this, I can't explain it. By now Darius was walking back to the engine room. Dee was the only person still in the cargo bay with them. Sonya breathed in; the words were on the tip of her tongue. The Captain began climbing the stairs back to the flight deck. She cleared her throat. The Captain stopped but did not face her.

"Yes, Lieutenant?" There was still the authoritarian undertone, but he seemed slightly gentler than earlier. She didn't speak; her mouth was open, but the report she had been rehearsing in her mind disappeared. Her vision shifted past the Captain to the ship's hull behind the stairs. What she saw seeping through the cracks of the entrance hatch to the Forward Maintenance Shaft sent a chill through her. Then it was gone.

"Did anyone else see that?" Dee's voice broke the silence.

"I saw nothing Dee." The Captain was the first to respond. Dee's eyes darted from the Captain to Sonya's.

"Tell me you saw that Sonya?" Her eyes fixed on the shaft's steel entrance hatch. "A faint green glow." She walked to the hatch, looking through the gaps surrounding the door frame. "It was like a full light was coming from behind here." Sonya came closer, also studying the gaps. The Forward Maintenance Hatch opened up to a shaft that ran all the way up to the flight deck. Mid-way down, the shaft split in three directions, the right side leading to the captain's quarters, the left side to the lieutenant's quarters, each side finishing at the ship's inner hull wall. The shaft was used to reach the left and right cross-stating axial stabilisers, and the main nav-com system below the flight deck. The maintenance shaft could occasionally be seen through the main hall's grated floor, and could be accessed through both quarters. These entrances usually were barricaded. Dee was about to open the hatch when the Captain said, "It was nothing. Dee assume your post."

"Permission to investigate the maintenance shaft?"

"Denied. It was nothing."

"Sir, I saw it also," Sonya said. The two women looked at each other, acknowledging what the other had seen.

"I said it was nothing, Lieutenant. That's an order." The Captain's voice was starting to rise; there was almost a note of desperation.

"Captain, given the strange occurrences that have taken place over the last few days..."

"Strange occurrences? What strange occurrences?" The tone of his voice brought Darius down from the engine room. Sonya's cheeks flushed.

Had he forgotten that Martin got killed last night?

"Well, where do I start, sir..." She was direct. Whatever he was at war with inside his mind, it now put them at risk. "The engines suddenly dying for no reason, all logs stating that they were operational, the static voice we heard while reporting the situation back to Discovery. That green haze that suddenly disappeared and the fact that Martin is dead." She knew that she should have stopped, but she couldn't. "I don't know what the hell is wrong with you at the moment Bruce, but you're diving deeper and deeper into that bottle. You're no longer fit for command, sir." She took a breath. Never had she thought she would need to do this, but she had to, for the good of them all.

"Captain Bruce Sampson, under section 9 of the Core code of conduct, I am relieving you of command." He didn't react, he just stood there, looking at her. "Darius, take the Captain's sidearm and confirm the removal of the Captain's authorisation." Bruce remained still, lifting his arm, revealing his weapon still in its holster.

"Careus, Under section 9 I authorise the rejection of Captain Bruce Sampson's ship access and assume command of this vessel."

"Secondary confirmation required." The computer's electronic voice boomed over the loudspeakers.

"Careus, under section 9 I second the rejection of Captain Bruce Sampson's ship access," Darius confirmed. He removed the weapon, all the while maintaining eye contact with the lieutenant.

"Request confirmed."

Darius handed Sonya the weapon. Bruce began to smile; it was something she rarely saw but, this time, it was unnerving.

"Glad to see you finally had the courage to take control for once Lieutenant." His smile broadened. "Hope you are ready to deal with the consequences."

"You've risked the lives of your crew... Are you?" Their eyes silently battled for authority. Putting the final nail into the coffin of his command, Sonya overrode his last order.

"Dee, permission to investigate the Maintenance Shaft granted, but I want you harnessed."

"Yes ma'am."

"Darius, cuff the Captain to the stairs."

"Yes, Lieutenant." Darius walked over to the Captain, who nodded and began walking towards the stairs to the upper level. He sat down on the third step, holding up his wrists, one on each side of the handrail. Clicking the final restraint into place Darius slowly backed away, an uneasy feeling coming over him, but he couldn't pinpoint it. Was it the change of command or the broadening smile of the captain? Either way, something wasn't right.

Dee could hardly feel the cold steel of the shaft walls through her leather gloves. She looked down the dark square tunnel, the light from her headlamp lighting the way she needed to go. Dee climbed in. Feeling a hand on her shoulder, Dee turned around.

"Dee set your com to auto; I want to hear you each step of the way. Darius will feed you the rope. If you get into any trouble, yell out or pull twice, and he will bring you back."

"Yes Lieutenant."

"And Dee, don't be a hero. If you see anything strange get your ass back here." While Sonya knew Dee could handle herself in almost any situation, she also knew Dee had a habit of taking on harder battles than she should; must have been the Gaelic in her. Sonya stepped back, giving Dee room to climb in. She gave her a couple of minutes before she spoke.

"Com check Dee, you read me?"

"Yes ma'am, all clear so far." Leaning down, she could see the faint silhouette as Dee crawled farther in. "Coming to the first junction soon." Sonya took a step back, hearing a faint snicker behind her. She marched over to the Captain on the stairs, his head bowed. "You knew it wasn't nothing didn't you?" Silence. "What the hell are you hiding Bruce?" Finally, he lifted his head and raised his eyes, a green shimmer passing over them. Sonya staggered back, unsure whether it was just in her head. Bruce spoke softly, articulating each word as if each had a deeper meaning. A shiver went through Sonya, stinging her body all the way to the bone.

"You will find out soon enough."

Tight spaces never scared Dee, which was a good thing as the shaft was only big enough for her to crawl through on her hands and knees. Each step sent a shiver through her knees. She finally reached the junction: ahead lay the shaft to the flight deck, to the right was the tunnel below the Captain's quarters. The left tunnel ran under the Lieutenants quarters. She was unsure which way to go, but she felt drawn to the right. Maybe it was the Captain's behaviour that made her feel that way; deep down she had suspicions he knew more about Martin's death than he was saying. As much as she thought Martin was a dumb grunt, even she had to admit she missed his protective presence. If the Captain had something to do with his death, he would pay. Dee stuck a glow disc on the tunnel wall, giving a faint yellow glow to the surrounding tunnel. Glow discs were used to mark areas in the ship during maintenance and had a temporary life span. "I'm at the junction, going right first."

"Roger that Dee," the radio crackled a response. She had taken only one step when she saw the sparkling green light at the far end of the tunnel.

"I see something, it's at the far end near the turn to the stabilisers. It's a green light."

"You mean like the haze?"

"Similar but different, it doesn't seem to shimmer in and out of view. Moving forward."

"Roger, be careful." Dee didn't want to say but it was more like the haze than she wanted to admit. There had to be a logical answer. She passed other junctions, each leading to other maintenance points on the ship. Dee had rarely come down here except when helping Darius, but she knew enough to get around and know where she was. The light became brighter as she drew close; she was only a couple of feet away now. It was a ball, radiating an eerie green colour that seemed to dance along the walls of the shaft. It looked like the shape was changing, but it remained the same. The ball had to be some energy sphere like that of the fusion reactor, but she had never seen anything like it before.

"I've reached its source, it is some energy sphere but can't say for certain."

"Is it safe?"

"If it's not, it's a bit late for me Lieutenant. I'll place it in my glove."

"Ok, report back."

"Roger, on my way." Having nothing else, she took off her right glove, placing the sphere in it before clipping the glove to her belt. Dee then began the slow crawl backwards to the main tunnel junction.

***

Dee gave a sigh of relief as she approached the cargo bay. She was glad to see the end of the maintenance shaft. Her knees were sore, and her gloveless right hand was starting to stiffen from the cold of the steel. Sonya waited for her at the exit. Dee was impressed that Sonya had stood up for the crew against her mentor. She liked Sonya, who was always fair but did take a step back when there was a conflict with the Captain; instead of expressing her views she silently acknowledged he was right. It was Dee's second mission serving under Bruce and even she could see the shift in his personality, and smell the alcohol on his breath. Though she questioned some of his decisions, she never felt at risk under his command, until now. In the back of her mind something still wasn't right; there was something else wrong with this picture. She welcomed the light as she finally came to the entrance hatch.

Dee stretched her sore back when she could stand up straight, handing Sonya the glove. Sonya had brought over a mobile maintenance bench, and quickly emptied the glove's contents onto it. The sphere glowed.

Dee heard that noise again, closer this time. The sound had a meaning; it was not the sound of random shifts in the ship's steel structure but instead acted purposefully. She turned to the source: the maintenance shaft she had just emerged from. Intrigue got the best of her, and she moved closer. The sound grew clearer as the excited chatter of the crew faded into the background. Pausing for a moment at the stairs as if fighting the urge to continue, Dee stepped past the Captain. He had an arrogant smile; with each step it became more unnerving; a million tiny hairs stood up along her back. Dee struggled to shut him out as she continued her investigation; she kept her gaze firmly on the hatch, but she could still see him out of the corner of her eye, still watching, still grinning.

"Once you see…" His voice was soft and solemn, capturing her unaware. "You can never un-see." Dee fought back the urge to look at him. *Just trying to scare you, Dee, that's all.* She didn't want to give him the satisfaction of rattling her.

"Goodbye Dymphna, I always did like you." She paused. He honestly sounded sincere, which left her uncertain.

Colds drops of sweat began to bead on her forehead. Only a few feet away from the dark opening of the shaft, taking a breath Dee bent over and looked in; the yellow glow of the glow disc was faint. The sound echoed again, faster than earlier, like someone or something was scurrying about in there, just out of sight. A hunched-over shadow darted past the remaining Night-Caps, casting silhouettes through their faint yellow haze. Dee stumbled backwards, turning to Sonya and Darius, who were still in deep conversation speculating as to the origins of the sphere.

"There is someone in there." Dee's voice broke through the intense discussion, catching the others unaware. Sonya turned, dropping the handheld scanner she was using to analyse the sphere. Dee picked up the headlamp from the other mainte-nance trolley, before turning back to the shaft.

"Dee. Stop!" Sonya shouted. Darius was already running

towards her as she positioned the headlamp.

Goddamn it Dee, just wait. Sonya found herself running towards them; she only heard the sound of her own breath. "Rope Up!" Darius had the same thoughts as Sonya, grabbing a rope as he passed the trolley. He arrived at the shaft hatch just in time to see Dee's boots slip into darkness. Reaching into the shadows he grabbed her boot, pulling her backwards.

"Wait."

"Darius. Let Go." Dee turned around, the headlamp blinding Darius for a moment.

"Don't rush it, you don't know what it is." He held up the rope. She nodded, taking the rope and clipping it to her maintenance harness, before disappearing into the black. Sonya watched the exchange as she approached. She stopped next to the Captain. Between breaths she glanced at him. He was smiling.

"What the hell is going on Bruce?" Sonya demanded, but he just looked at her, his eyes keeping their secret. "Who is it?" His lips pressed together, stretching further in the corners. Smug bastard! Sonya's cheeks flashed with a searing heat, her fist clenched at her side, the skin on her knuckle tightened, turning the skin white. She couldn't hold back any longer. She punched him. Hard. The blow connected with the side of his jaw. He was knocked over, hands pulled above his head by the cuffs. Slowly he pulled himself up, returning to his seat on the stairs. Where's your smug smile now, Bruce? They both remained silent. He lifted his head up to his hands, looking back at his assailant; he licked the corner of his mouth where a single drop of blood started to spill. "What are you hiding?" It was a question that almost bordered on a plea. He paused, looking at her, looking through her before quietly speaking a word that made Sonya's blood run cold.

"Soon."

As she approached the junction, Dee slowed, moving softly. The shadow had darted from left to right, down the tunnel where she had discovered the sphere. Edging closer, she peered around the corner, half expecting the intruder to be there. The light from her headlamp reflected two crystal blue eyes staring back at her. They belonged to a young girl. Dee touched the comm, bringing the mic closer to her lips. "Lieutenant…" She paused, not sure how to explain the situation. "Lieutenant, it's a young girl."

Waiting outside the hatch, Sonya stared down the dark tunnel, only able to see Dee's silhouette against the moving glow of her headlamp. It took a moment for Dee's statement to sink in. She pulled her comm closer. "Repeat that Dee?"

"It's a little girl, approximately seven to eight years old. Blonde hair, blue eyes."

Sonya turned to face the Captain. He lifted his cold steel eyes to hers, exchanging a silent conversation. An invisible breeze sent ripples of goosebumps across her skin. Sonya's stomach sank. She ran back to the hatch, grabbing at the comms pinned to her collar.

"Dee get out!"

Dee shifted closer to the girl, who was sitting with her feet crossed at her ankles, holding her knees to her chest. The white of her floral dress was crisp and unblemished, out of place in the dirty tunnel. Her blonde hair reflected the light like liquid sunshine, standing out in stark contrast to her pale skin. Her head buried in her knees.

Is she crying?

"Hello." Dee used the softest tone she could manage, scaring the child was the last thing Dee wanted to do. Her blonde hair swayed as she turned her head to face Dee, her eyes like diamonds sparkling in the night. "I'm Dee, what's your name?" There was something vaguely familiar about her that she couldn't put her finger on. Maybe she saw her once on the Discovery. The girl looked at Dee, her expression anxious, yet she kept eye contact.

"Chelsea." Her voice was soft and tender. That name was so

familiar. Dee slid closer. Her comm crackled with static; she could hear Sonya's voice but couldn't make out what she was saying. Chelsea flinched from the static noise that echoed through the tunnel. Dee didn't respond; she needed to be present with the scared child.

"Have you been hiding since we left the Discovery?" She didn't answer. Instead, she sat twisting the hem of her dress in her fingers; she took a breath.

"Are you going to kill me?" Her voice was so innocent. What would make her say something like that?

"No hun, of course not," Dee said in an attempt to reassure her. "Why would you say that Chelsea?" The child looked down at her twisted hem before responding.

"Because…" Chelsea paused, and the headlamp flickered, plunging the tunnel into darkness. Dee felt Chelsea's small hand touch hers, resting on her fingers. Her soft voice seemed to cut the darkness. "Because… They all do." The headlamp erupted the tunnel back into the light. Dee was relieved the light had returned, but her heart raced as Chelsea's words swirled in her mind. What the hell does she mean? Chelsea was now kneeling, leaning forward. As Dee looked the child up and down, she noticed a dark spot on the side of her otherwise unblemished floral dress; with each passing second it grew. Dee was about to speak when she saw another dark pool, though it wasn't on the dress, but under Chelsea's knees. Dee's eyes darted back to the child's face, and Dee's cheeks became cold as the steel flooring. Chelsea's crystal blue eyes had become polluted with crimson darkness, swirling in the light. Her tender face was now a multitude of deep cuts and flesh tears. Blood flowed from each wound, dripping down her mangled cheek. Dee tried to move but Chelsea gripped her hand with a force well beyond that of any child, her nails sinking deep. Dee could feel each nail like tiny knives piercing the skin; trickles of warmth ran down the back of her hand. Despite the pain Dee couldn't scream out for help, her voice lost in the darkness of those eyes.

It was the exaggerated, unnatural smile that finally did it. Curled up at the sides, tearing at the corners on a path up towards the child's ears. Dee finally screamed. It was all she could do as she watched the smile: blood-coated teeth, lips dripping blood. Her tiny hand reaching up, fingers walking along Dee's face, the nails cutting the skin before reaching around behind her head, gripping the hair and pulling with force. One hand pulling her hand, one her head, Dee was being drawn into the disfigured child, closer and closer to the blood stained smile, jaws now widening in anticipation. Another scream. The tunnel went dark.

Dee's scream echoed through the tunnel, filling the cargo bay with ricocheting terror. Sonya fell backwards. "Darius pull!" He began to pull the rope's slack when the second scream echoed out into the bay. The rope retracted back into the darkness with speed, running through Darius's bare hands before he had a chance to tighten his grip. Searing heat burnt his palms as he managed to slow the take of the rope. As quickly as it had begun, the rope fell slack to the floor. Darius gripped the rope tightly, pulling it back out into the light. He feared the worst for Dee. The rope had weight, but it wasn't heavy enough to be Dee. He hoped she was moving with it, but in the back of his mind he knew that wasn't the case. His stomach turned. Dee was a tough woman, one of the toughest he ever met.

For her to scream like that. Darius shook his head, trying to dislodge the thought before it could take hold.

Sonya waited anxiously near the hatch, sidearm drawn. Each length of rope Darius retracted from the darkness made her heart beat faster, half expecting someone or something to jump out.

Was it a little girl? If it was, who was it? She glanced over at the Captain.

He knew all along what was going on, and he said nothing.

The mere thought of her mentor's involvement with Martin's death sent a shot of boiling blood through her body, washing a flush of red over her cheeks; she gripped the sidearm tighter. The sound of scraping brought Sonya's attention back to the hatch, just in time to see Dee's boots emerge from the darkness. They weren't moving. Her stomach sank. Sonya holstered her sidearm, pulling at the boots. The lack of weight was unexpected, and Sonya stumbled backwards. Landing on her back, she felt the impact of the boots on her chest. Winded, Sonya struggled to sit upright, the weight on her chest hindering the effort. Behind her came the sound of dry retching as she slowly sat up. Her vision moved from the black soles of the boots and up the legs that owned them. A splattering of crimson stains increased in size and number with each passing inch until they merged with blood soaked cloth. Her eyes finally reached Dee's maintenance belt. Above it, there was no more, no head, no arms, no torso, nothing. Sonya pushed the severed remains off her, scrambling towards the safety of Darius. Light-headed she quickly stood up, fumbling for her sidearm. Her stomach turned, all warmth drained from her face and body; coldness burnt her skin as she saw the blood-stained trail flowing from the hatch to the corpse. Blood everywhere.

It cannot be happening. It echoed in Sonya's mind as she tried to control her breathing and remain calm, but all that seemed to do was boil her blood instead. The shakes in her hands stopped, and she gripped the sidearm. She turned and faced the Captain. Darius knew what was coming but was too slow; she reached him before Darius could intervene, her hand raised, steady and purposeful, the barrel pointed straight at the Captain's head.

"You have five seconds to tell me what the fuck just happened Bruce." Her voice raised, deep and forceful. Darius didn't doubt she would pull the trigger; this was a pure rage.

"They shouldn't have taken it." His tone was calm despite

having the barrel of a standard issue sidearm pointing directly at his face, held by a woman who not only knew how to use it but also had the will.

"Taken what…" Sonya was about to demand clarification, but then it dawned on her. The sphere. Sonya stormed over to the maintenance trolley, picking up the sphere with her bare hand. "You mean that this," holding up the sphere, its green glow captivating his eyes, "is what got Martin and Dee killed?"

"It's mine," he hissed. "She gave it to me." Beads of sweat began to form on his brow, eyes darting back and forth from her stern gaze to the sphere and back again. The smug grin was gone, replaced by desperation.

Oh my god Bruce, what has happened? Sonya watched for a moment, speechless as to the turn of events which had led to her mentor's fall into madness. His fingers scratched at the handcuffs like an eternal itch; it was only then she noticed the scarlet scratches around his wrists. Is this all connected? Dee's thoughts ran rampant. The haze, the sphere, the Captain's madness, Martin and Dee's death. It has to be. The look in his eyes was like that of a hungry animal, consumed with the sphere. Taking a step backwards, she closed her eyes, trying to focus her thoughts. Trying to piece it all together.

"What are you thinking Sonya?" Sonya looked up, her eyes meeting Darius's.

"First there was the haze." Sonya's thought pattern became vocal. "Then Martin was killed." Sonya began to pace. "The haze was gone, for how long we don't know. It could have been before or after Martin was killed. I didn't notice it was gone when I went to the cockpit after we found the body. Then there is the Captain's behaviour. When did the Captain start acting strange?" Sonya looked up at Darius, hoping he could shed more light.

"I had seen him before we found Martin, he seemed preoccupied, but I put it down to the engines issue," Darius responded.

"Ok so he might have killed Martin, but I'm not sure. We

know he didn't kill Dee, we were with him, he was in handcuffs."

"Something killed Dee, in the shaft, and it wasn't human. Her torso was torn or bitten off. It's not a clean wound that you would expect from a weapon or mechanical accident.'

"Dee said it was a little girl in there. There were no stowaways on board; sensors would have alerted us. It's all got to do with the haze and the sphere. It's too much a coincidence that when the haze vanished, the sphere appeared." Sonya looked down at the glowing sphere.

This thing causes death. Her mind began to scream at her. *Destroy it.* Sonya knew she needed to get rid of it for all their sakes, but there was something else not right. She looked up at Darius. "There is something missing."

"She's coming." Both of them turned to the Captain; trickles of blood ran down his wrists over his blood-smeared fingers. He was smiling in some insane anticipation that sent an unsettling wave over the two of them. "What did you say?" Sonya asked.

"Turn around Lieutenant."

Sonya and Darius both turned. The lights to the engineering bay went dark, and the rest of the cargo bay soon followed, plunging them all into darkness. Darius always kept a few glow discs on him for times when he needed to investigate the maintenance shafts. He tossed two onto the ground, giving a yellow glow to the stairs where they were standing. Sonya was about to speak when she heard a familiar sound of faint steps. It was just like she heard before being captivated by the haze. The footsteps grew louder. A flash of a green dispelled from behind the workbench, quickly followed by darkness again. The footsteps kept coming, as did the flashes, except the glow lasted longer each time. Sonya squinted, trying to see what was approaching. It was close. A cold wave washed over Sonya, chilling her to her very core.

"Did it just get really cold in here," Darius said. Sonya didn't turn her gaze, her sidearm hanging by her side. She could see something moving in the shadows. It was small. Taking its time, before entering into the light. The eyes came into view first; they cut through the darkness like crystals reflecting the light. As it approached the darkness washed away from its face revealing a young girl.

"Chelsea," Sonya whispered under her breath. She knew who it was straight away. Sonya turned back to Bruce; he sat smiling like a doting father watching his daughter perform. As she came into full view, she stopped. It was her dress that left Sonya with a dread. The flowers were bright and colourful; it was all too vivid. Too perfect. Sonya took a step back; a bright green shock wave rippled over Chelsea. The missing piece. Not Chelsea. She now began to piece the puzzle together. It wasn't the Captain who had killed Martin and Dee, it was this creature. This creature had come from the haze somehow. Chelsea looked Sonya up and down before its eyes settled on the sphere that she held. Its eyes darted back to hers, and Chelsea's eyes began to darken.

Have to act. Have to get this sphere off the ship. Now. Or we are all dead. The child's dress began to tear; stains began to appear. Sonya stepped backwards until she was standing next to Darius.

"Darius, we have to get rid of it." He didn't respond. "Darius." Still no response. "Darius!" she whispered sternly. He turned towards her. "We have to jettison the sphere into space."

"How… Oh my God." Darius's question was stonewalled by what he was witnessing. The child's face began to rip open. Her mouth widening, tearing at the corners, exposing blood stained teeth. Taking a step forward, it spoke in a high pitched hissing tone.

"Feed me Daddy." She heard next to her Bruce pulling at the handcuffs, his movements erratic.

"It's ok honey. Soon." Sonya wanted to hit him again. She began to take a step towards him; the creature hissed. Was it trying to protect him? Sonya had an idea.

"Where is the closest outer-shoot?"

"Umm… the engineering bay. Below the bench."

"I'll be the decoy, you run. Send it into orbit."

"But Sonya…"

"That's an order, Darius." He looked at her and nodded. She handed him the sphere, and immediately the creature's gaze turned on Darius. "On my mark." Sonya took another step towards Bruce, and Chelsea hissed again, crouching down, its mangled dress hanging low to the floor. "Now!" Sonya ran over to Bruce, punching him in the face; Chelsea screamed, running towards Sonya, her image flashing with green static like a damaged monitor. Darius darted to the left, side stepping Chelsea's attack and running towards the engineering bay.

Sonya felt the impact and slid across the floor before smashing into the wall below the maintenance hatch. She lay on the ground winded. Chelsea had rammed into her, and now she had turned her attention to Darius, moving to intercept him. Her dress dripped blood onto the floor with each step. Darius neared the stairs to the engine room. "Kill him! He has the orb," Bruce shouted. Watching from her sprawled out position on the floor, Sonya noticed a glimmer coming from one of the child's wounds. Chelsea stopped, reached down and gripped the object, pulling it from her body: a piece of scrap piping like those that impaled her all those years ago. Chelsea threw the piping like it was a toy, hurling it across the room and hitting Darius in the back, expelling all the air from his lungs. Darius fell to the floor. The orb flew out of his hands and rolled away. He lay motionless as the disfigured child continued her menacing approach towards him.

She could see Bruce's eyes sparkling with madness as Chelsea drew near to his beloved orb. She slowly rose to feet, her body stiff, her leg unsteadily obeying her will in holding firm. The child was wielding another piece of scrap metal, dripping with crimson. Have to stop her before she reaches him. Sonya pulled her sidearm and fired at the girl, bullets exploding puffs of red as the flesh tore open, leaving more horrific wounds in their wake. Still she moved closer to him, as if the ammo were nothing but insect bites. Sonya's mind filled with a multitude of thoughts, each fighting to be heard; her mind went quiet; all became clear.

Raising the weapon, she brought it up to the Captain's temple. The barrel's cold steel returned his attention to his lieutenant. "Chelsea!" Her shout echoed, catching the corpse child's attention. "Move and Daddy dies." Bruce's face lost its madness as if the threat to his mortality had brought sanity back within reach. The child paused, watching her, judging the sincerity of her threat. "You want Daddy? Come and get him." Chelsea ran towards her father and Sonya began to move to her left.

"Don't Chelsea… She wants the…" The impact of the butt of Sonya's sidearm knocked him out cold before he could finish. Rage flew over the child and she bared her blood stained teeth with a hiss. Sonya spun the sidearm around, pointing it once again at the limp body of the Captain.

"Calm down or he dies." Sonya spoke with a calm authority like a teacher to a misbehaving student. Chelsea stopped instantly. Sonya saw the child's blood stained torn dress mend, her flesh healing. The crimson faded from her eyes, revealing the crystal blue of the innocent child Chelsea had once been. She began her advance again, this time slowly, a walking pace. Sonya, in turn, stepped away from her father's body.

Darius still lay motionless, the sphere just out of arm's reach.

This is it. Sonya ran, giving Chelsea a wide berth as she passed; the child didn't flinch, still believing the earlier threat. Despite her need to see if Darius was alive, Sonya ignored her instinct and picked up the sphere, resisting the urge inside her to look upon its glow for more than a few seconds, though she did feel a sense of submission. Sonya glanced back at Chelsea, hoping the child had fallen for the trick; she had. Chelsea stood next to the limp body of her unconscious father. Her blue eyes were gone; only sockets remained. Instead of eyes, they housed a radiating green glow; like a smoky haze it flowed, trickling out of the sockets.

Sonya's hand began to tingle as though a million tiny creatures were crawling over it. The sensation spread over her fingers and up her wrist like a wave. *Move dammit.* Finally, her body complied, the sensation fighting each inch along her arm, the sense of submission growing in intensity. The thought of giving herself to Chelsea came into her mind, but Sonya shook her head to dispel the thought.

Maybe this is what happened with Bruce, he submitted. With another shake of her head, Sonya returned to the moment.

Airlock. Now. Sonya's free hand gripped the rail leading to the engine room. Each step hurt her body, each step she felt the fingers of submission claw at her, pulling her back to the vengeful child.

Reaching the top step, Sonya glanced back. Chelsea was at the base of the stair, her face distorted, mouth torn at the corners, scarlet droplets running from her lips. Her mouth opened wide, wider than a human could ever do. The child let out a banshee scream that shook Sonya's body, her ear screaming back in pain. The child began its advance at a rapid pace.

Skidding to a halt in front of the airlock, Sonya tapped the its hub screen. The hub was positioned to the left of the airlock's door, out of reach of the doorway. Punching the keys she tapped in the maintenance pin and the airlock hissed, sliding open to reveal a large chamber with the second hatch on the floor that led out into the nothingness of space. Behind her, loud footsteps made her turn. Chelsea stood on the final step, her dress torn, hanging fabric stained with blood giving way to mangled flesh and exposed organs. Her mouth strung wide like the old Cheshire cat from Alice in Wonderland; teeth just visible through the scarlet stains, broken and jiggered. Tilting her head back, her tiny hand entered her mouth, drawing a large serrated blade of scrap steel. Returning her gaze to Sonya, she brandished the blade like a knife, thin streams of blood flowing over her fingers.

"Chelsea." Sonya made her voice as sincere and unthreatening as she could. She had to let instinct play out and not think of her plan; she had to disguise her thoughts from the child. Standing next to the airlock she continued, "I'm sorry I took your sphere." Keeping a watchful eye on the approaching monster, she placed the sphere on the floor. "Here it is, it's yours." Gently she pushed the sphere with her foot and it rolled like a ball into the airlock, stopping against the far wall. Chelsea's head turned as she watched it roll; her steps were slow and cautious. Her gaze shifted from the sphere to Sonya, then back to her precious sphere. Sonya slowly gave her space, stepping away from the airlock, keeping distance between the two of them. Sonya arrived at the opposite side of the room; the fusion reactor stood between them, its flickering electric blue glow illuminating her young face. She paused, watching the sphere, then Sonya. There were only a few metres between her and the entrance to the airlock. Chelsea launched herself forward, running for the sphere; Sonya ran too, hurling herself towards the hub. Chelsea entered the airlock, quickly picking up the sphere just in time to look up and see the doors slide shut as Sonya pushed the hatch button.

The child's screams muffled as Sonya peered through the airlock's window. A small fist was beating against the door, her other hand gripping one of the handrails. 3. 2. 1. Sonya failed to follow normal protocol; she failed to pressurise the airlock first. The child had to go. The hatch flew; one second she was there the next she was gone. It was over.

Sonya navigated through the landing bay, finally securing the Careus onto the UAV Discovery's docks. Her hands were still shaking but at least they were home. She couldn't wait to get off the ship. The journey back saw her anxiously waiting on the flight deck, guiding the ship from her new position on the captain's chair. She drifted off to sleep once or twice before quickly awakening, remaining on alert for any more signs of Chelsea or the haze. There were none. Darius relieved her on occasion, but her sleep was fractured, full of memories of Chelsea as she was jettisoned from the ship.

It wasn't a child. The words kept repeating in her mind, yet still she felt as though she had killed a child.

During her waking moments, Sonya completed her report for command. She must have re-done it, at least, three times before she finally gave up on it. There was no way to sugar coat it for command; they were going to think she was suffering from Deep Space Disorder. She had sent it still. Fuck Em. She and Darius knew the truth; Bruce probably wouldn't admit it. It didn't matter now; they were home, and that was all that mattered.

The ship shuddered as it docked with Discovery. Sonya still hadn't heard anything back from command yet; maybe silence was a good thing. Classed as a Certified Contract Vessel, Careus had an assigned docking bay which meant they could come and go as they pleased without the check-in. She was expecting some response from Discovery, but she was glad of the silence of the comms.

Rising from the control chair, Sonya took a deep breath and left the flight deck. Bruce met her in the main hallway, handcuffed with Darius behind him. He was the battered man who finally lost what little he had left. *Was it all his fault?* Sonya fought the idea, reminding herself that two of her crewmates were dead, killed while he sat there smiling. He would go down for this. Her cheeks burned, and a bitter lump grew in her throat. Sonya swallowed the anger down. *Let Command judge him as they see fit.* She didn't care if she never saw the smiling bastard again.

"Good work Lieutenant, we are home in one piece." How dare he talk to her. Her fist clenched, knuckles cracking, and before she could control herself she had punched him in the jaw. Luckily Darius was holding the handcuffs. Otherwise, Bruce would have been on the floor when the hatch slid open. Sonya turned, expecting to see the guards at the hatch waiting to take the Captain to the brig, but there was no one.

"Where the hell is everyone?" She was in no mood for this. "Bring him, I'll drag him to the hole myself if I have to". The three of them left the Careus and ventured down the corridor of Discovery towards the Town Centre. It was too quiet.

Empty. The Town Centre lay deserted. Darius and Bruce stood waiting in the entrance as Sonya stepped out into the centre, her steps echoing through the empty hall. Normally there would be over a hundred people walking the halls of the Centre, each carrying out their assigned duties or mingling. It was a hot spot of human interaction, 24 hours a day. It was how they lived; this was not possible. There were no signs of riot, violence, anything.

"What the hell is going on?" Her question echoed through-out the Centre as if answering it with emptiness. Sonya turned towards Darius and Bruce.

"Don't ask me," Darius responded to Sonya's pleading eyes. At first the footsteps were distant and steady like the beat of a metronome. Sonya turned back towards the Centre, looking around for the source of the sound. She had heard that sound before. Soft and faint, then quickening. A child's soft laugh ricocheted off the steel walls, hiding its source with confusion.

"Let him go Darius," Sonya ordered over her shoulder. Sonya heard the click of the metal handcuffs as they were removed, followed by heavy footsteps approaching her from behind; Bruce took up a position beside her. "She's here isn't she?" Sonya questioned him softly.

"What do you think?" replied Bruce, smiling again. He began to walk towards the middle of the town centre. "Leave while you can Sonya."

"What are you going to do Bruce?" Sonya called out to him. From the far side of the town centre, she saw a familiar green glow, followed by the sound of footsteps. The green glow flickered into view; it was the little girl. Disappearing, she appeared again as if she was still walking the same path. Her form flickered one last time before she appeared again beside Bruce. Sonya called out again.

"Bruce, what are you going to do?"

Bruce smiled as he looked down at the image of his lost daughter. He crouched down to eye level, looking the young girl in the eyes, exchanging words without lips moving.

"I'm going to give her what every daughter needs… a father," Bruce finally answered. Standing up, he reached out his hand, the little girl took it, and together they began to walk away. Their image began to flicker as she had once done. Then they were gone. Sonya looked around the empty centre, silence encroaching them. Sonya felt that now, they were truly alone.

TO BE THE SURGEON

By Michelle Mullins

Authors' Note: *This story originated from thoughts of the Imagi-Nation and those left behind and a series of extremely lucky roles in a tabletop roleplaying game. Ending up with super competent assassins and hackers, I decided it would make an interesting story. When the Typhon expanse project started I had the last element to write To Be The Surgeon.*

The air cars moved through the brightly lit upper storeys like schools of silvery fish. The light from Hermes's three moons created shifting colours on the sprawling cityscape. Like the bottom of the ocean, little light filtered to the city floor, where the base of the towering buildings was dark and bare. The concrete, though only a few years old, was grimy and covered in graffiti, illuminated by harsh fluorescent lights. Even during the day, little sunlight penetrated down to the ground.

Short buildings, only a few storeys high, clustered around the feet of giant skyscrapers, squeezed into the gaps between them. The lower floors, crowded with cube farms and maintenance areas, bore almost no resemblance to the upper levels that belonged to the elite.

Moving away from the centre skyscrapers—formed on the back of massive colony ships—the city floor remained cramped as the taller buildings dwindled. Near the edge of the inner city there was a rough redbrick fence, enclosing a large building and a barren concrete courtyard, edged by brown weeds and bare dirt. The sign on the front of the building said, "The Hermes Foundling Home."

Inside, painfully clean children, from toddlers to teens, moved around under the watch of stern adults. Lunch was just finishing and across the intercom an authoritative voice rang.

"Lunch is over, assembly in main hall in five minutes."

All the children headed into the building. Even the most rebellious knew some commands must be obeyed immediately.

Like the other children, Hitomi's mother had been forcibly selected for colonisation of Hermes, in this case simply for being in a relationship with a man who turned out to be involved in things he shouldn't have. While in transit she had found out she was pregnant and Hitomi was born on the colony ship UAV Angelia, which was in one of the later waves headed to the planet Hermes. Not long after arriving she had gotten ill and Hitomi's mother couldn't afford not to work. It didn't take long for the illness to develop into something more serious and by then it was too late. Hitomi was too young to send out to the farms, so she, like so many others, was sent into the orphanage system with her mother's few belongings of no monetary worth. The children at the foundling homes were meant to be moulded into proper citizens of the Union, but mistreatment and cruelty were served up next to the education and propaganda they were fed.

Hitomi supposed she had been lucky to avoid being shipped straight out to the farms, to work from dawn to dusk for the rest of her life. Were the orphanages better, though? Especially when their visitors were, at best, rich couples looking for a toy. More likely, companies looking for cheap workers.

Today it was a pair of… Hitomi thought they were men. The one who wasn't talking was unusual: hair covering their face. What she could see of their face leant more towards woman than man, but their form was most definitely male. Regardless, they were almost certainly looking for some cube slaves, so Hitomi ducked out of sight.

She left the main rooms, aiming for the alley between the building and fence. It was a path she had taken many times. Getting out of sight of the adults was a difficult task, but the inventiveness of several dozen children over many years did the trick. Hitomi leant against the rough wall and closed her eyes. For several minutes she enjoyed what passed for fresh air here, then tensed as she heard the door creak.

In a quick moment, Hitomi was surrounded by a group of older children, and a sickening chill crawled down her spine when she recognised their leader, Hal. Bullying and beatings from teachers and other children were common in the orphanage, but every girl and some of the younger boys knew this group.

"Well look who we have here," Hal said with a leer.

Hitomi wondered if all bullies worked at their *clichéd* dialogue, but suspected lack of imagination was the cause. She slid her hand into the pocket of her uniform, closing her fingers around a small blade that she had spent hours honing. As her fingers touched the weapon the older child swung his fist towards her. Stepping into the blow Hitomi jerked the blade from her hiding place aiming to do as much damage as she could.

"Stop." Though the voice was calm, Hitomi froze, her crude blade pressed against her attacker's neck. She turned her head and saw a figure leaning against the wall, watching the scene. It was the strange man from before, one eye still concealed by hair and the other cold and hard. They surveyed the scene then jerked their head towards the door.

"I think you boys have other places to be don't you?" came a cool, deep voice from the delicate frame. "Maybe you should get to them while I might still forget this scene."

There was a moment of silence before the children fled, leaving Hitomi alone with the intruder.

"So are you going to take me to the administrators?" she asked, an edge of defiance in her voice.

"Should I?" the man asked with bland curiosity. "That was an impressive draw, but what were you intending to do with it?"

Hitomi looked down at the crude blade in her hand. "I'm not sure," she said. "I suppose I would have just sliced him a bit. You see I'm just sick of the way those idiots treat people. It's not like the adults care. Might been worth killing him. That way I at least will have done something."

"Hmm." The man looked at her then nodded, pulling a card out of his pockets and writing something on the back.

"I can respect that sort of viewpoint and so I won't be reporting this." He handed her a card. "My organisation would have a place for someone like you. If you want it."

Hitomi read the card. "Black Lotus Security Solutions" and an address on the back.

"You're offering me a job, just because of this? Do you think I'm stupid? You could be a pimp or just looking for someone to do your scut work."

"And the opportunities here are better? I could be offering you something better." he shrugged. "It's your choice what you believe, but keep the card," he said as he walked away. When he reached the door he paused and looked back.

"Do you really want to be stuck here, with no future? Think about it."

Hitomi staggered down the dark alley, using the wall for balance and leaving a smear of blood. She paused at the intersection, turning her head painfully. She glanced at the street sign to get her bearings. After a few seconds she moved out into the light, doing her best to hurry while looking at the building signs with swollen eyes. She stopped in front of a plain but scrupulously clean building signed with Lotus Relaxation Centre.

Walking up to the frosted glass door, she saw a sign.

Open 24 hours a day, No hawkers.

With steady hands the bloodied girl pushed open the door. She could feel the stares of the few people in the waiting room as she walked to the desk.

"Can I help you?" the receptionist said calmly, as if badly beaten and bloody people came to his desk every day.

"Yeah," said Hitomi hoarsely, dropping a tattered business card on the counter, "I was told if I came here with this card I could get a job."

"I see," he said with a composed visage. "What is your name then?

"Hitomi Sayre."

The room she was escorted to was painted in soothing greens. Hitomi lay back on the plain but comfortable bed and closed her swollen eyes.

"Well you've definitely done a good one on yourself, haven't you? I hope at least that the other side got it worse?" Opening her eyes, Hitomi saw the man who had spoken to her at the orphanage.

"I'm not sure, they were definitely bleeding when I left though," she replied, trying for a light tone, but pain blurred the words.

"Ah well you can't be expected to be perfect all the time," he replied with a slight smile, but his eyes showed concern.

"You never told me what your name was."

"Really? Kaira at your service," he said with a slight bow.

"My service? Really. What do you want me for? A possibly unstable teen, certainly violent considering how you met me."

"Being able to act under stressful situations is a rare trait. It can be trained but natural talent shouldn't be wasted, don't you think?"

"And what sort of organisation needs that sort of person?"

"As the card I gave you said. Black Lotus Security Solutions. We do security systems, even body guarding occasionally."

"I can tell that isn't all of it. It never is."

"Clever," he murmured, "and cynical, but perhaps you are entitled. Yes I suppose we do more than the 'typical' security

firm. Hacking, assassination and plain theft come into it sometimes too."

"And you want me. What makes you think I would do any
of that?"

"You wouldn't be required to, and we don't take job that
comes to us. Sometimes to fix a wound, you need to remove the
rotted flesh. We are that doctor, the surgeon with the scalpel."

Hitomi mused over that for a while.

"Such heroes," she said dryly, but she nodded. "What are the
terms?"

"We give you an education and you agree to work for us for
five years when you reach your majority."

"What about the foundling home?"

"Easy enough to deal with, they don't want to draw attention
to themselves after all."

Another period of silence as Hitomi absorbed this.

"Before I agree, tell me why you are here. Such charity usually
has a price. So what do you pay?"

"I can indulge your curiosity," he said, "but it is hard to know
where to start."

"Does it have to do with why you're covering your face?"

"I suppose it does," he said tucking his hair behind an ear.

Hitomi blinked, surprised at the revealed face. It was delicate
for a man's but the surprising thing was the glittering silver
lines spreading across it and the iris of his eye.

"That's my cost and my ticket out of a dead end life."

Hitomi gave him a sceptical look, but nodded at Kaira so he
would continue.

"I grew up on Hestia, my parents had managed to work their
way out of servitude, at least official servitude, pretty typical
really. Anyway I was working at one of the local processing
plants and as you can expect I got a lot of shit from people,
mostly due to my appearance. Most of the time it was just
minor stuff but one day things escalated."

"I don't know if they were trying to kill me but I got tripped and fell into one of the chemical mixers. The mixing blades damaged one of my arms, a leg and side. I managed to pull myself out a bit so I only got chemical burns on part of my body. Well the machine jammed and my co-workers managed to get me to the hospital. I lost my arm just below the shoulder, a leg above the knee, my eye, and I had extensive nerve and skin damage."

"While I was recovering, as much as I could, I had a visitor. A woman, who made me an offer. There was some experimental tech they had access to but they needed a volunteer to do the final tests."

"Why did they want you?"

"I suppose I had nothing else to lose at that point. I had also done martial arts training. I was pretty good and they wanted someone fit and skilled to test the new limbs and nerves properly. Well I obviously accepted and after a few years I was almost as good as new. They did have to take more of my arm because of the joint, which could have been bad if the cybernetics failed in a big way but as you can see it didn't."

Hitomi looked at Kaira for a long moment, thinking. What was that phrase her mother had used? 'From the frying pan into the fire.' Not much choice now though and who knows, maybe things would work out. She said nothing, just gave a nod and lay back.

Almost a year after she arrived, Hitomi sat on a bench in a small garden, looking at the blue-green of the sky, so focused that she jumped to her feet when another person sat next to her.

She sank back down.

"Nice day out," Kaira said.

"It is," Hitomi said, wondering why he was here. He had helped her adjust to this place, so different from the foundling home. He was her mentor she supposed and occasionally he came out with sage advice. Irritating as that could be she had to admit Kaira was usually right.

"As nice a day as it is, I am surprised you aren't spending time with the other children."

Hitomi shrugged, not wanting to admit she felt uncomfortable around the others—she just couldn't seem to relax around them.

"Didn't feel like it I suppose," she said.

"Really? It seems you rarely do," Kaira said. "When was the last time you let yourself really care about anyone? Or had a friend?"

"I like you."

"I meant a friendship with someone of the same age." Kaira let out a sigh and shrugged. "I understand your reluctance somewhat. Orphanages such as the one you were in don't encourage long term relationships."

Hitomi looked at the grass, lips tight. Kaira glanced at her face.

"Friends, relationships and our connections to others are important, especially in this line of work."

"Why?" Hitomi said, feeling the stirring of stubborn defiance.

"Hitomi, in our tasks we can do horrible things, paying our way with service to the bloated leeches at the top. This job allows us to do what good we can, but being honest with ourselves is important. There will always be situations that need to be dealt, and the dealing will not be clean. Someone has to do it." He looked at the sky, his face sad. "And when we can, we levy justice."

"What gives us the right? To maim, or kill? To stand in judgement?"

Kaira looked at Hitomi. "If not us then who?" He moved from the bench to crouch in front of her.

"My young student, out there are people who will countenance any evil, allow any inequity, so long as they stay in power. This should be opposed."

Hitomi shrugged and looked unhappy.

"Hitomi, we have been given great gifts, and have had those gifts trained to the highest degree. If we were not to use these gifts, that would be a wrong, I think."

"But why us in particular? What we do seems…"

"Useless? Pointless against the mass of history. The smallest rock can start an avalanche. Our actions are leading to a result. And in the meantime, we help the helpless." He smiled. "You must be patient."

"So we spend time learning about history and philosophy?"

They sat in silence for a long moment and Kaira sighed. "I suppose my point is that this sharing of history and belief helps create a community. We come from all over after all. We need the balance of others so we don't go off the deep end and lose ourselves. The Black Lotus could become something terrible."

Hitomi rubbed her eyebrow in thought. Kaira was right—there were a lot of different kids in her group. There was a sort of unspoken rule that no one asked why anyone was there, but it was obvious that troubled pasts were common, no matter their previous social standing. However, Hitomi had not formed close bonds with any of the other children and even she could not deny fear had a lot to do with it.

A head poked around the corner: Devlyn, a kid near her age. He waved at Hitomi before noticing Kaira and dropping his hand. The blonde teen was slightly younger than Hitomi and often tried to involve her in activities.

"Oh sorry didn't realise you were busy. Just wanted to see if Hitomi wanted to—"

"It's fine, we were done," Kaira said getting to his feet. Hitomi looked at Kaira in confusion.

"You have to start somewhere," was all he said before leaving the garden.

Sweat dripped down Hitomi's neck, where a wooden practice sword rested.

"Again," Kaira said, eyes calm as she staggered to her feet.

They had been at this for over an hour, bout after bout. Fighting had become a focus of Hitomi's education as soon as she agreed to be part of the more violent operations of the Black Lotus, a decision she was allowed to make on her 16th birthday. Guns, stealth and infiltration were all included. Blade training, which seemed to be an excuse for Kaira to kick her around the practice room, was on the menu today.

Now 18, she had moved into her last growth spurt. She would always be someone of average height, but she was well muscled and lean, the result of three years of martial art training. Her furtive nature she had acquired in the orphanage was replaced by confidence in herself and her training. Which of course did not mean she wasn't in for a beating.

He circled her again, darting out with blows Hitomi could barely block. Kaira kept up his punishing pace, real and artificial muscles moving in sync. A blur of chrome, flesh and black cloth. All the while advising, cajoling and mocking her.

"You have to focus. I don't care if you're tired or angry or in pain. Focus!" he said, breathing hard. "We are not barbarians flailing around with great swords. Precision is key. You will only have one shot, so make it a good one. Like the surgeon, if you mess up, people who rely on you will die." All this while launching a savage series of strikes aimed towards her head.

Hitomi tried to bring her thoughts into order, to move her tired body, responding to the continuous attacks with rapid parries and evasions. Then Kaira suddenly struck low. The old Hitomi, from several year ago would have taken the blow in the stomach, but almost without thought, she dropped her blade to parry the strike and made a rapid riposte at Kaia's head. With a smile he dodged it.

"That's enough for the day," Kaira said. "You did well. Do your cool down. I will see you later."

Kaira quickly did his cool down and clean up and left as Hitomi stretched her aching limbs, then sat, leaning into the wall. As she was considering rising to her feet, Hitomi was joined by Devlyn. He often visited, even though his focus was on computers and electronics instead of fighting. The other teen looked at her with a grin, seeming disgustingly fresh and comfortable.

"Looks like Kaira kicked your ass," he said, passing over a cold bottle of water.

"I might be tired but I can still kick you round the salle if I have to." Hitomi's words were tart but she accepted the bottle with a nod of thanks.

"I must decline, my poor tired warrior. As a keyboard warrior I have done my necessary self-defence training. If it comes to a fight I will have to hide my skinny body behind tough fighters such as you."

Hitomi snorted into the water bottle.

"Laziness," was all she said, continuing to drink. The conversation lapsed, but the silence between the two was companionable.

"Come on, time to raise those weary bones," Devlyn said, breaking the silence and standing up from the wall, "or you will miss out on dinner."

Hitomi groaned but stood, following the other teen. What a difference time makes, Hitomi thought.

***

She stood in shock as people moved around like ants in a disturbed nest, crowding around several figures who had been carried in only moments before. The floor was streaked with bright red blood, some with an oily sheen, mixed with the fluids from artificial limbs. Hitomi's shock was broken when someone ordered the room cleared. She followed the others into the common room, silent in the worried chatter.

The head of the building, Daiyu Liu, an older woman, dark of skin and eyes, called for silence.

"You have all heard of an incident. However this particular attack was during a meeting known to few. This was caused by a betrayal of trust, and we do not stand for this. We will find the person or people who did this and deal with them. Several of you will be given tasks in relation to this. Remember that you must remain focused."

After Liu left Hitomi sat staring at the floor, listening to the murmurs of the people around her. She didn't know how long she sat before someone spoke to her. Devlyn, once again. For someone dedicated to tinkering with computers he could be remarkably stealthy.

"Hey, just got out of the security centre. Tracking what on Terra happened tonight," he said, rubbing at tired eyes.

"What have you heard?"

Devlyn hesitated at the intensity of her voice.

"All I know is the meeting was called for by the head of Symes Technology. Unusual for certain, but we have worked with the company before."

"So they are almost certain to be involved," Hitomi said, clasping her hands so tightly together the knuckles were white.

"We don't know anything yet," Devlyn said with a worried look in his eyes. "And even if we did going in guns blazing won't solve anything."

Hitomi nodded jerkily before returning her eyes to the floor. They both sat in silence letting the noise of the room flow over them. They both knew that no matter the culprit there would be blood for this.

The trio of bright moons illuminated a grey clad figure lying flat on a small grassy ridge near a farming warehouse, one of the many that dotted Hermes's landscape. Hitomi rose to her elbows with her night-vision binoculars in hand and checked her earpiece. There was an uneasy feeling in Hitomi's stomach, replacing the centred calm she had cultivated and maintained for other missions. Then again this wasn't just any mission. This was retribution. Hitomi's dark thoughts were interrupted by a voice in her ear.

"Primus team about to enter target building. Over-watch group maintain observation."

Hitomi took a deep breath bringing the binoculars up to her eyes, watching the area. The warehouse was dark with only dim safety lights on, wind rippling through the grass. No one ever saw the Black Lotus coming, not even their own. It was unlikely that much would cross her sights. As that thought crossed her mind Hitomi's eyes widened in shock. A dark form moved out of a side door. She zoomed in and her breath hissed through clenched teeth as she saw the figure's face. Even from this distance and with the distortion of night vision she knew who it was. Samuel Symes, the treacherous bastard they were here for. Hitomi's hand rose then paused, her mind flashing to memories of Kaira's wounds, images of blood, raw flesh and exposed circuitry, the electronic guts of a robotic limb. It didn't matter that he had survived when others didn't, as it so easily could have been different. Her hands clenched, her eyes glued to the skulking figure. He turned away from her, fleeing, and Hitomi sprang into action, footsteps muffled by the grass and brisk wind.

Hitomi rapidly made ground on Symes, who never even looked behind him. Soon she was within striking distance, surging forward, grabbing her mono-filament blade from her thigh sheath and driving her shoulder into his back, sending them both tumbling. She landed on top with him face down, but instead of driving her blade home, Hitomi turned Symes over, wanting to see him face to face before she killed him. His face was a rictus of fear, his surprise and Hitomi's weight confining him. She raised her blade, heart beating rapidly, a snarl on her covered face. Then another memory of Kaira intruded.

"Focus, detachment and calm. Never get emotionally involved when on a mission, put it away for later. Anything else will kill you or a comrade or send you down the path of evil. Revenge is a bitter pill."

Her mind went cold looking down at the cringing figure

beneath her. Hitomi took a slow deep breath before raising her hand.

"Primus? Over-watch 6 here. A rat escaped the net. Got him trapped."

There was a deep silence from the other end then a crisp voice responded.

"Acknowledged Over-watch 6. Finishing building sweep. Secure the target and go to meeting point." Devlyn's voice was emotionless and steady.

As she bound the cringing man, Hitomi felt calm. Justice was for everyone and in the Black Lotus they made their own.

JELENA
by Stephen Ryan

Author's Note: Jelena started out life as a robotic cyborg. After many years interacting with humans, she eventually became sentient. She chose the hermaphrodite model with her new body. Watching the humans interact as they do she didn't want to miss out. Stumbling on information she manages to pass this directly to the King. But deep down she just wanted to slow down and stop and smell the roses.

The driver handed the serf a card. "Here ring this when you're finished. This is only a 60 second parking space. I'll be a couple of minutes away." Closing the door, he looks around. The shop sign flashing in front of him says, "New Bodies: all genders catered for by appointment only." Entering the shop, he finds a receptionist sitting behind the counter. Looking up, she smiles.

"May I be of help sir?" He hands over the documents to the young lady. She takes a quick look, picks up the scanning device and scans the barcode engraved on his chest plate. She looks up and smiles.

"Take a seat sir there will be someone to see you very shortly." Sitting down, he picks up an info pad and starts scrolling through information that's about 10 years old. A door opens and a well-built man dressed in a full-length white coat walks over.

"Good morning sir! My name is Quezz, how should I address you?" Standing up, he shakes the serf's extended hand.

"Jelena."

"Very nice, now please follow me. Today is a big day." As Quezz extended his arm to point Jelena in the right direction they approached a double door that opened automatically, finding two chairs facing the same way looking at the opposite wall. As they sat themselves down the doors closed and the chairs started moving down the long hallway.

"Now you realise that you've picked a female name?"

"Yes I have."

"I was just making sure. That means we can bypass the male models. Now what you are about to see are some full size models of body types that we can supply. Don't worry about the blank faces as that is something you will decide on how you look.

These versions are female, ranging from muscle bound down to our average models. Also today you're in luck as this is the first of the new models; this is what we call a Hermaphrodite. This model as you can see comes with or without accessories." As the chair stopped Jelena was looking at the last two models. He thought for a few moments.

"I like the model without the accessories please."

Quezz raised an eyebrow. "Very well now follow me. We need to work out the fine details on how things look before we start the exchange." They sat down in another two chairs, each with its own built in view pad. A full size three-dimensional image appeared in front of them, turning around.

"Right Jelena, now looking at the screen we start with hair colour."

"I like the brunette colour."

Quezz entered the details. "Now with hair length I recommend having a short cut style until you are used to the idea of having and looking after hair. Remember this hair will grow so you can change the cut if you wish." On the screen about a hundred styles of short hair appeared. Jelena chose the simple straight style that would just cover the back of the neck.

"Now we have eyes. Again the first 15 are normal colour eyes that you will see on everyday people; however if you wish you can choose basically any colour you like." Jelena checked the first 15. "The green appeals to me."

"Very well, now the eyebrows." They looked at the screen. "Will the hair on the eyebrows grow like the hair?" Jelena asked.

"Yes it will, but not to the extent it does on the head. You will still have to trim the eyebrows. These are general shapes they come in. They also can come in different colours."

"For now I'll choose this shape and keep the colour the same as my hair."

"Now the shape of your face. On screen you can see that we have up to 300 basic shapes. All I want you to do is to delete the ones that don't appeal to you. When we get it down to ten then we can show the 3D image."

Jelena deleted the face shapes. "Okay let's put what we have on the 3D image so we can see what we have." As the image flickered for a moment in front of them, slowly turning around in circles, an image of a face with the hair, eyes and brows appeared.

"Jelena just touch on your screen the next one until you find the one that appeals to you." As she flicked through the face shapes, she stopped on one that she liked. It had a strong jaw line.

"Now time for the nose. Again, same as before, just flick through. It will appear on the image as you touch each shape." Jelena stopped on the one he liked, not overly big, but it had an inward curve and seemed to set the eyes just right.

"You are very sure in what you want Jelena. Now we choose the lips." As before, Jelena flicked through the images until he was happy.

"Okay let's refine the image and see how we look, shall we." Quezz adjusted the image.

"So Quezz how do I look?"

"Let's just say if I saw that face in a shopping complex it would certainly make me look more than twice. Now to the main body shape. How about you let me give you an idea." Jelena indicated it was okay. The body shape appeared under the image of the head. "I like that one."

"I thought you would. Now with the breasts, again just flick through until you find the ones you like. Starting with small and working up to a full D-cup. Now Jelena if you would allow me one little indulgence they just need to be positioned a little more to the left and up." Quezz moved the image. "Now how does that look?"

"It does seem to look more appealing."

"Down to the lower area. Now that you have the accessory it can when it's cold shrink down to this small, but when aroused we can limit it to a size that won't be to off putting. Allow me to show you." The image of the appendage increased. "I think Quezz that at the moment it is just a little too big."

"Good I just wanted to make sure you understood what you were going to use. How about we just do a little adjustment." The appendage reduced in size.

"I like that size."

"It is a little larger than average but well within acceptable limits. Now about pubic hair. With or without?"

"I would like it without the hair thank you."

"Oh one last thing. We nearly forgot about the tongue. We basically have one size fits all but we have three different lengths that it can stretch to."

Jelena looked at the pad. "I'll take that one."

"I thought you would." Quezz adjusted the final 3D image.

"So Quezz as a male like yourself how do I look?" Quezz looked at the screen. "Breast about right size for the body curves and not overdone. Let's just say you can practically wear anything and you are going to look hot."

"Good, that is what I was hoping for."

"Now come sit down in front of this screen, as I need you

to pay very close attention. There are two ways we can do this transfer. Each has it pros and cons. The first method, as you can see on the screen, is we place you in this full incubator and after two hours you will walk out looking like you what see on the 3D image. However, as you are still in your metal frame you won't be able to eat or drink as technically your body is still in a serf form and you will need to plug yourself in and you will need to come in about once a month to be reinjected with amino food to keep the organic body viable. This is not cheap and the government will not pay for it. The other method is a bio-body. You'll still have a metal skeletal frame, but your muscles and organs will be organic. You'll have a heart that will beat, sweat, feel pain and pleasure like any other human. Your brain will be what we call a memory gel. We take out your central memory component from your brain, then enclose it in the gel. This is as close as we can get to a human brain; it will act and respond like any other brain.

"Can I go back into my body if I can't adjust?"

Quezz thought for a moment. "If you can't adjust and you want to convert back, then it will be at your expense. The government will not pay for that. If you had an accident that caused massive injury to your body, providing the main memory component hasn't been damaged we can put you back into a serf body in an emergency. We find that when that has happened people find it very hard to go back, so we make a new body."

"Should that happen, could I change my new body?"

Quezz shook his head. "We have to put you back in the same body you ordered. If you want anything changed it will be at your expense, but we can cross that bridge when we come to it."

"So what happens to my old body?"

"By law we have to crush it for recycling." Jelena stood up and walked around the 3D image. "To be or not to be, that is the final question."

"So you have done a lot of reading then. If I take this form how long will I take to adjust?"

Quezz thought for a moment. "It's hard to say; everyone is different. But I strongly recommend that you stay away from any form of alcohol for the next year cycle because that will do serious damage to your brain and once it's damaged there's no fixing it. You could end up in a mental institution for the rest of your life and those places are not fun to be in."

"Will I be able to enjoy sex?"

"Yes, that is a part of being human, which also includes feeling pain. I will give you a phone number to a support group for people like yourself, who are going or have gone through this process. I strongly recommend it. Feeling all alone can be very detrimental to your full development."

"I think I'll take the second option. How long will it take?"

"About an hour. Your body and the specifications you asked for will be nearly done. We just have to take you to the lab to get the process started." Quezz directed Jelena to another set of double doors. As they entered the room she found a massive metal table with what looked like locking mechanisms. Lots of technicians were walking around with info-pads.

"Now don't be alarmed. We need to secure you in this just in case you somehow override your internal defence systems. It is only a precaution, that's all." As Jelena positioned herself into the table it was locked down. A female technician came up to the control panel.

"Hi Jelena, this won't take long. I'm going to open your main cranial plate so I can remove your main central memory component. Then we'll place it into the memory gel. With a very small charge we'll activate the gel synapses. They will connect to your memory component. It's hard to explain; all I can say is just try to relax and let the process do its thing. Within the hour you should be fully integrated with your new body."

She opened the main cranial plate. "Right Jelena, what I need you to do is to shut down your internal defence systems. I am now putting in the main protocols telling your computer that this is a system upgrade." As Jelena shut off his defence system he suddenly felt his arms and legs being disconnected.

"What is happening? Why can't I feel my arms and legs?"

She smiled. "It is just a safety precaution that is all."

Jelena watched as the technicians wheeled in a large acrylic canister with her new body submerged in a jelly-like substance. It appeared to be breathing through a facemask as they wheeled it alongside.

"Okay Jelena. I just need you to shut down. I can activate the memory component once I have set it in the memory gel. Now this is your final chance to back out."

"No. There will be no backing out." She checked with everyone around her.

"Okay Jelena, in about an hour we will see you in your new body." The technician removed the memory component and placed it in the gel, closing the cranial plate then placing a small constant charge into the gel.

At first Jelena sensed nothing. Suddenly she woke, feeling little charges of energy attaching themselves to her. She started exploring the neural pathways. The synapses seemed to get excited as her memory component adjusted. Suddenly sitting up in shock, she looked around, eyes wide open. Ripping off the facemask, she took a deep breath and after a few moments she finally registered that someone was talking.

"It's alright Jelena, you have just transferred into your new body. Don't try to stand yet, just let yourself catch up."

She now realised that she was completely naked. She tried to cover herself up.

"Relax Jelena, all the males have already left. It's just us girls now." As she relaxed a little, she could feel a strange feeling of blood rushing to her head and turning red.

"That feeling is called embarrassment. You are doing well now that the jelly has been drained out. We are going to stand the tank up and we will assist you to the showers. Then a few quick tests to make sure you are functioning okay." As another female assistant came alongside and took her hand, she took her first steps, a little unsure whether her legs would hold or not. After a few steps the body started working.

"Would you like an assistant to come and teach you how to wash?"

"No thank you, I have been studying those instruction downloads on the galactic net."

"Very well, don't be too long."

After a short time Jelena came out dressed in a white bathrobe, drying her hair with a towel.

"Oh it was so good. I could have stayed there all day."

"Wait until you have a bath with scents mixed in with the water."

After completing lots of small tests, Jelena was allowed to dress for the first time. When she walked out to reception and picked up her documents, the receptionist handed her a framed part of her old chest plate with the barcode in full view.

"That's just a little something to remind you how much you have achieved."

"Thank you. Very much appreciated. Can I use your phone? I need to phone my ride." The receptionist handed over the phone and Jelena held her card up against the glass front. In moments the phone started ringing.

"Good to see you finished. I will be there in about two minutes. My undercar number is Gov-0800. When you see just wave to me. I'll find you easier that way."

She walked out onto the street, looking up and watching all the hover cars flying overhead. She realised for the first time that she was not entering what she saw into a memory chip. In fact she was just letting it all go by as though each moment was not important to her situation. Seeing the plate, she raised her hands and started waving. The driver gently landed and slid the door open and Jelena eased herself in.

"Whoa, I would not have recognised you if you hadn't

waved." As he was taking off and trying to operate the hover car, he kept looking at Jelena.

"If you don't have an accident I need you to take me to this address. I have to get an outfit for tomorrow night's function."

He made the necessary adjustment on the on board computer and the vehicle headed across the city, finding a park in a street close by.

Jelena walked to the complex still feeling a little awkward. As she entered the shop her eyes filled with rows of clothing. She looked around, very confused, as this was the first time she had to make a choice. A shop assistant came over. "You look a little overwhelmed, can I help you?"

Jelena handed over the document. "Oh we've been expecting you. I'm Shoal."

"Well Shoal, you can call me Jelena."

"Good, now let's see how you look in this. Just go into the change room and if you get stuck just let me know." After a few minutes Jelena came out and looked in the mirror. Shoal entered the change room. "Right then let's take a look at you." She slowly turned around. Shoal's eyebrow raise when she noticed a bulge down below the belt. "Err what is that?"

Jelena looked down at what she was pointing at. "Oh I went for the hermaphrodite model, is this a problem?"

"In this dress, yes. Hang on, I'll get you a new outfit." In a few moments a new outfit was on and Jelena was admiring herself in the mirror.

"Now that looks a lot better and for tomorrow night's awards ball it will be perfect. Now for shoes, high heels always look good but I seriously recommend these types of heels, that way you won't break an ankle." After looking at all the accessories and a few more outfits for everyday wear, Jelena walked out, with some help from the staff, to the waiting government car. She loaded up the car.

"Right where to next?" asked the driver.

"Home please, I've had enough excitement for one day and

for some reason I feel this emptiness in my stomach and I'm feeling a little tired."

"Welcome to being human. When you unload at home that small corner coffee house will help you out."

She entered her apartment and offloaded everything onto the lounge suite. Opening the fridge, she found nothing in it. *I should do something about that*, she thought to herself. Picking up her handbag and leaving the apartment, Jelena entered the coffee shop, looking at what was on display in the virtual display case.

"Can I help you Miss?"

"Yes, I 've never eaten before and I've got no idea what I like."

After a few moments of looking a little confused, the waitress asked, "What do you mean you've never eaten before?"

Jelena looked up. "I'm sorry I should have told you, this morning I was a serf but now I have been given this new body. I'm getting used to all these new things."

"So you're telling me you have become sentient and you live here?"

"Sure do. Just up the road."

"I tell you what. You sit down and I will bring a small piece of most of the food and you can have a taste test, so then next time when you come in you will have some idea."

After a few minutes the waitress returned with coffee and a plate full of various foods. "Now the coffee is hot so just take a small sip." Tasting the coffee, she felt a little shock as the hot liquid went down the back of her throat.

"I suppose it will be something I could get used to?"

"Trust me, it won't take long if you are in a high stress job. Now this is what we call the mother of all chocolate. It's triple with a coffee icing."

Jelena placed it in her mouth and the thick chocolate filled her taste buds. "This should be classed as an addictive substance. I could eat this all day."

"Careful, too much of this stuff will go straight to the hips.

Then you have to work three times longer in burning it all off. It should only be eaten on special occasions." Jelena finished the coffee and the rest of the plate. "I did not realise all this food could taste so good."

"Well, that one was on us. Next time you will have to pay, and just keep in mind this type of food isn't three times a day. You need other types of food as well."

"How will I know which food to buy? There are so many choices."

"Look, tomorrow I don't start work until 12 O'clock. Why don't you meet me here and I'll take you to the shopping complex and help you out."

"But I don't even know your name?"

"I'm Zelda."

"Pleased to meet you Zelda. I'm Jelena."

"Great. Meet me here tomorrow, just after 9 O'clock."

Leaving the shop and entering her apartment, Jelena closed the door and checked the time on her watch. Still a few hours to go before she needed to be ready. Going to the spare room, she opened a small box and picked up her info panel. Turning the panel on, she entered her password and selected 'stand alone' mode, making sure it was not going to connect to the galactic net. She inserted some info chips to check that she had the correct ones for the night. Then she took out the chips and turned off the info pad, placing the chips in her handbag.

Entering the bathroom, she, for the first time took a good look in the mirror, moving her head from side to side and doing facial expressions. Soon the clothes were off as she checked out her new body. After leaving the shower and drying off, Jelena lay out her outfit for the night. Brushing her hair and keeping the makeup simple, she chose the cherry lipstick and just a light liner around the eyes. Applying nail polish and allowing her nails to dry, she finally slipped on the dress, adjusting the outfit and the chest area, ensuring the chest was sitting just right. Happy with the way she looked, she picked up the handbag and invitation and walked out of the apartment. As she left the building, she found a government hover car waiting for her.

"Miss Jelena?"

"Yes." As the driver opened the door for her she slid into the back seat. Looking up at the driver, she realised that he was really checking her out. Closing the door, he settled into the driver seat and started the stretch hover car.

"So how do I look?" The driver looked up in the rear view screen. "Let's just say you nailed it for the night. I have no doubt you will be the centre of attention."

"Good. For the first time it will be a strange feeling being the centre of attention instead of being ignored." The stretch limousine positioned itself in a long line at the rooftop venue. Jelena watched the flashing lights from all the cameras. The venue was all lighted up, showing off the enormous acrylic dome covering the whole entertainment area, including all the tables in the dining area already full of people. As the limo parked itself onto the platform, the door opened and she was assisted out of the car within nanoseconds. She was bathed in flashlights from the media.

"Miss Jelena, how does it feel to be human?" She thought for a moment. "You know I think us humans have been thinking about that question since the dawn of time." She smiled and continued to walk down the steps. At the end of the steps a well-dressed man held out his arm. As she took it they started walking towards the doors of the dome.

"Evening Miss Jelena, I'm your escort for the night. I'm Rodezz. I am just here to help you out should any difficulties pop up. I will introduce you to people and explain how you should address them if it is required." Entering the double doors Jelena, handed over her invitation. As a gong was sounded the doorman, dressed in black, addressed the party. "Miss Jelena and escort Rodezz." As everyone went back to what they were doing, Jelena and Rodezz walked down the stairs. A serf came up to them with a tray of drinks.

"No alcohol. Can you bring me a water or fruit juice please?" Rodezz took a glass of wine as the serf went away. They started to mingle with the other people.

"So Rodezz, is it true that the high King will be here tonight for the presentations?"

"Yes, won't be hard to spot. He'll be the one in the expensive suit with a gold or silver tie and about six bodyguards hanging around him."

"I take it you work in the special services?"

"If I told you that I would have to kill you." He smiled. The gong sounded and everyone paused as the next person was announced. The serf appeared with several choices of fruit juice on a silver tray. Jelena chose one and the serf disappeared. Other serfs were carrying around trays of food as Jelena and Rodezz helped themselves.

"Well Jelena, how are you finding the food?"

"Still getting the hang of all these choices I now have. I tried a triple chocolate with ice coffee and they should class it as an addictive substance."

"Yes Miss Jelena, if we ban the good stuff like that we would have the biggest black market in the known universe." One of the staff walked around hitting a small gong.

"Come, it's time we found our place at our table." Everyone was making their way over. Finding their table, they were joined by two couples and exchanged pleasant smiles. They made themselves comfortable. The serf came around, poured drinks, and Jelena found hers to be another kind of fruit juice.

"Ahh excuse me serf, what type of fruit juice is this?"

"Is something wrong with it Miss Jelena?"

"No it's really good, I just don't know what it is?"

"That's pineapple juice."

"How many fruit juices do you have tonight?"

"Miss Jelena, we have up to 15 different types."

"Well when my glass is empty can you give me a different one please?"

"As you wish Miss Jelena." The serf continued to serve the rest of the guests. Everyone settled down with drinks.

"Miss Jelena, please allow me to introduce you to the guests on your left. We have Knight landed Mr Tony Greyezz and his wife Mrs Sina Greyezz."

"Pleasure to meet you Miss Jelena, but please call me Tony. It's an informal occasion and we prefer to relax and enjoy the night."

"Thank you Tony I will."

"Now on my right we have Knight errant Mr Makis Oke and fiancée Miss Jarita Eshe."

"Pleasure to meet you. I must say you are the first serf I've met that has become sentient and looking very attractive." Makis felt a hard kick under the table from his girlfriend.

"Thank you Makis, but don't let this look surprise you, I am full of lots of little surprises."

"May I ask where did you work?" Turning to face Tony she said, "I still work in the defence space craft assembly. I was mainly working on the superstructure welding, even though they do change us around, so I did get to learn quite a large aspect of the manufacturing process of the craft we were making."

"So did that help make or start to make you sentient?"

She took a sip of juice. "No, the most likely cause was a human I was working with a lot. This man was the weirdest I've ever had the pleasure to work with. Everyone called him crazy but his problem was he couldn't stop thinking. It was like both sides of his brain were working over time. Hardly ever slept. They ended up giving him his own workshop. This is where they sent me to help him build new prototypes."

The MC for the evening walked from behind the curtain on the stage and tapped the microphone to make sure it was on. "Ladies and gentleman, please be upstanding for the High King, his Royal Highness King Thordis."

Everyone stood up and faced the large double doors. The

planet's national anthem started playing as the door opened. Everyone made a slight bow as the King entered, dressed in black suit and gold tie with his six bodyguards escorting him. When he went to his table and sat down everyone else followed suit. As the conversation level started to rise again, everyone relaxed once more.

"So Miss Jelena. As we were just discussing, what started making you sentient?"

Jelena tilted her head for a moment. "Probably the most likely cause was when we were building the prototype. He had me doing designs on a standalone computer with graphics programs already installed."

Tony looked a little confused. "Couldn't you just upload the specs?"

"Yes that would be the normal thing to do, but he was, as I said, a little crazy and wouldn't have it. He was always thinking that someone was always trying to steal his ideas, so if they were not connected to the galactic net then they would be safe."

The first course was placed in front them. As Jelena was about to pick up her knife and fork, Rodezz placed his hand on hers. "It is proper protocol to wait for the king to start eating first, then we follow."

"Sorry, it just looks so good."

As the evening continued and the final course was taken away, the MC entered the stage. The lights dimmed down on the main dining area as everyone went quiet.

"King Thordis, distinguished guests and ladies and gentle-man. Tonight on this special occasion we honour those who have achieved, shown acts of bravery and compassion. Tonight we are especially honoured as King Thordis has personally asked to present these awards. So now if King Thordis would like to present himself."

As the King stood up everyone stood up and applauded. Standing behind the podium, he allowed the applause to continue a little longer before indicating for everyone to sit down.

"Thank you for your applause. But tonight for once is not about me." Everyone laughed. "Tonight we show our gratitude as a nation for those who have excelled above what is expected. This is our chance as a nation to recognise those individuals, so without any further waffle let's get this show on the road."

The night was filled with applause and short speeches by the recipients. Rodezz bent over towards Jelena. "You'll be up next." She opened her small hand bag, took out a small compact and gave her face a quick check. As she placed the mirror back in the bag, she cupped the info chips in her hand, holding them between her fingers to give the appearance her hands were empty.

"Now our final award tonight is to someone who broke all protocols, and has even decided to change her whole appearance. Miss Jelena." She stood up and smiled. Everyone applauded as she walked up the stairs to the stage. As King Thordis extended his hand she took it, and the King felt the items in his enclosed hand. Jelena leaned forward for the welcome of touching both cheeks. As she reached the left cheek she whispered, "What is on those chips is very important and you need to know." As she stood back and smiled, King Thordis handed over the gold frame certificate to Jelena. She stood behind the podium and everyone's applause died down.

"Thank you. I find it ironic that people want to become part machines so they can do more things efficiently, and yet the machines they make want to become human so they can experience simple things like touch, taste and sleep. You could say while you humans are speeding up to keep up with technology I'm slowing down to stop and smell the flowers."

She held up the gold frame certificate and everyone applauded. When she sat back down at her table, Rodezz leaned over to whisper in her ear. "That was very smooth."

She looked surprised. "Would anyone else see it?"

Rodezz thought for a moment. "Only those in security. Most

of the people here wouldn't know. I just hope whatever information you handed over doesn't get you killed. I must leave you now Jelena. Enjoy the night,"

A young gentleman came up and took Jelena's hand. "May I have this dance?"

She smiled. "Only if you hold me close."

He smiled as they found their place on the dance floor, holding each other close for the slow dancing. "Miss Jelena, allow me to introduce myself. My name is... Err what is that?"

"Oh sorry but I chose the hermaphrodite model." As the look of discomfort appeared on his face, he stood back, trying not to look embarassed. "Err I think I need a drink."

Jelena smiled as she watched him disappear into crowd.

Saying goodnight to the few people she met, she walked to the platform to a waiting hover taxi. When she closed the door the taxi driver looked over his shoulder. "Where to, Miss?"

"To sector six, to the Sunset Building complex on Warp Street, please." Suddenly all the doors locked. The taxi driver started looking scared and confused as the instruments would not respond to his action.

"What the fuck! Something's taking control and it's not me." Picking up his radio mike, he hit the emergency frequency. The taxi took off at fast speed, flying above the approved routes. Screaming into the mike, the taxi driver was doing everything to gain control. Suddenly, out of nowhere, military hover jets surrounded the taxi. Jelena looked out the window and realised that there were no markings on the craft. The taxi driver looked around, pulling out a laser pistol. As he turned around, Jelena hit the security screen button. The screen shot up within a fraction of a second, trapping the man's hand to the ceiling. He dropped his gun, screaming in pain. She picked up the pistol and placed it back on safe. She sat back. Heading up into the mountains, the taxi was guided to the base. The driver was still yelling curses.

The landing pad was being surrounded by armed men in full battle regalia as the taxi landed. The hover jets stayed up and flew around in formation, patrolling the area. As the taxi shut down the doors unlocked and the screen came down. The driver nursed his wrist. The door was flung open with weapons drawn. The taxi driver was still yelling abuse and was dragged out and taken away. Jelena put her hands up.

A masked figure approached her. When he took off his mask she found it was Rodezz. She smiled. "There's a face I didn't expect to see again."

Rodezz smiled. "I could say the same. Please allow me to assist you out."

As she was guided into the complex, she walked down a long hallway, passing doors with only numbers above, passing what seemed endless passage ways. Rodezz opened a door to a fully furnished room with a very stylish interior.

"Please, Miss Jelena, take a seat." Sitting down in a comfortable chair, Rodezz walked over to a small fridge and took out a bottle of water, placing ice in the glass and pouring the water. He then handed it to her, sitting down himself in the chair opposite.

"Miss Jelena I don't know what was on those chips you handed over to the king, but whatever it was, it has certainly raised a lot of ruckus. Already arrests are being made and the King has scrambled each planet's armadas on full alert just as a precaution. Now I'll be leaving you here. The next lot of people are the kind of people you don't lie to. When they ask a question you better have a straight answer. If they feel or see that you are lying you will be questioned until they are fully satisfied."

"How do I know that those who are questioning me aren't the corrupt ones?"

"Fair question. All I can say is you won't know, but if the King fully trusts these people it will be in your best interest."

Rodezz stood up. "Jelena, you started this and now you have to see it through. With any luck you will come through this unscathed."

Rodezz left the room. Jelena took a mouthful of water. After what seemed like hours the door opened. Three men entered, all dressed in expensive suits. The one who sat directly in front of her was bald, well built and didn't take his eyes off her for a moment. The other two sat on either side, holding onto info pads, and were too busy looking at their screens and paid no attention to her.

"Let me introduce myself. My name is Otto. The other two you don't need to concern yourself with. You just need to answer my questions."

"Ask then. I can only answer what I know."

"Good. Let me put your mind at some form of ease. I answer to the King directly. No matter how bad whatever information I give him, he must always be in the know. I have a direct line that is never ignored. When I use this phone the in joke is when I call the King he answers to me, so to speak. So my first question is: why wait so long to hand this information in?"

"Because corruption always comes from the highest levels. If I tried to alert any form of authorities I would have an unfortunate accident that would never be fully investigated and give the ones with power a chance to cover their tracks or destroy any vital information. By giving it to the King I knew he would have to act this way. The ones involved in this corruption wouldn't see it coming." Otto sat back in his chair with his legs crossed and his arms resting on the arms of the chair, making a triangle with his hands. "Why did you sit on this information for so long?"

"I didn't know I was sitting on the information while I was a serf, nor did I realise that the individuals concerned were talking code in plain English. As I started becoming sentient I was intrigued with puzzles and games and codes. By chance I found this old tattered book at the local markets. It was in very bad condition, but as I read the book things slowly fell into place. It didn't click until I overheard a conversation with the same individuals that I made the connection."

Otto sat there not moving, staring right through her. The suit on his left showed Otto something on his info pad. Otto took a moment to look at it and gave a little nod. The suit turned the info pad screen towards Jelena.

"Is the book you're talking about the one we found in your apartment?"

She looked at the screen. "You're searching my apartment?"

"As we speak. Just to let you know, when you go home you won't find any evidence that we have been there. However we are taking the book. If you want us to reimburse you we can arrange that."

"No that won't be necessary, but I can be compensated in other ways." Otto's look changed yet he still gave no hint. His stare just seemed to turned to ice. "You are not yet in that position, Miss Jelena."

"True. So am I under arrest or free to go?"

"You can go when I am satisfied. Until then you just have to be patient." The other suit showed Otto what was on his info pad. Otto gave a look like he expected the result. "Well Miss Jelena, looks like I have no further questions for you, so just out of interest, what was your price?"

"It's a two part price actually."

"I'm listening."

"We know war is coming. You know where I work and who I work with. I believe, like most people, he does have a loose wire. He has come up with a prototype weapon, which I believe will win us the main battle. All I ask is that you send people down who can think outside the box. The second part is, next week I will apply for military pilot school. Now I may not get in as they are very choosey, but I'm sure with your contacts you could pull a few strings in my favour."

Otto sat there. His stare went through her. "Very well. I have one question. If I should get your name through what happens if you fail?"

"Then I will have failed and I will find another form of employment."

Otto let the thought sit for a moment. "Very well. I'll see what I can do, but I will not promise anything. However, I will send down a team of my most trusted advisors to your company within the week. Just make sure you and your friend are prepared. You will now be escorted back to the landing pad. The taxi you came in will be waiting with the driver. He has been well compensated for the trouble we put him through and we have already informed his company what has happened."

Jelena stood up and walked to the door. She stopped and turn. "Just one more thing Otto. If you guys want to talk to me next time please just come to my door and knock without all the theatrics of a hit team at 4 O'clock in the morning."

Otto smiled. "I make no promises Miss Jelena."

She smiled and opened the door to find two heavily armed men waiting for her. She sat back in the hover taxi and closed the door. "Sorry about all that."

The driver started up the craft and took off fast. "Sorry about pulling the gun on you. I thought you were trying to rob me."

They sat in silence when they arrived at her home. "How much do I owe you?"

"No need to pay miss, I was very well compensated."

She opened the door to her apartment to find nothing out of place. It was like no one had been there. Too tired to think anymore, she lay on her bed and went to sleep.

Next morning, waking up late, she showered and dressed. She arrived at the coffee shop just as Zelda was getting there.

"And here I thought I was going to be late."

"So I heard. I was watching the uplink cast last night. Must admit I really liked what you said. Anyway time to get shopping. Hope you remembered your credit card."

Jelena pulled it out of her handbag. "No woman would leave home without it."

Zelda smiled. They walked down the street towards the shopping complex. Zelda placed her finger just under her left ear and tuned into the news report. "Security forces have been busy last night and this morning they are arresting a lot of the Nobles, especially from the old houses, who were kicked out centuries ago from the Union."

Jelena looked a little confused. "So what does that have to do with our shopping?"

"Good point. It's just that those guys always seem to squirm their way out of anything, but this time it looks like it's not going to go well for them." Entering the shopping complex, Zelda led Jelena to a coffee shop.

"I thought we were shopping."

"Relax girl. First rule: never go shopping on an empty stomach. You have to try these muffins with hot chocolate. Find us a table and I'll place the order."

Jelena chose the table so she could have a good view of the shoppers walking past. Zelda sat down. "It won't be long. Service here is good. So what type of food do you like?"

Jelena thought for a moment. "It's not so much the food I like or don't, it's just if I cook something and eat it, how do I know it's the way it should taste?"

Zelda thought for a moment. "Well if it is very bad you will know, but don't get too hung up about it. You can invite me for dinner tonight and I'll give you a hand with some of my mum's recipes."

The hot chocolate and muffins arrived. As Jelena took her first bite of the muffin her eyes went wide. She swallowed and let it go all the way down. "What is this?"

Zelda smiled. "A peach muffin. Now try the chocolate."

As Jelena took a small drink of the hot brew she tried hard not to go cross-eyed. "That is awesome."

"They use a rare chocolate and it takes three days to prepare."

As they finished up Zelda directed her to the centre of the open area. "Right now this is how I shop. If I want good quality cleaning products or high sugar content products then this is the place to go. Now if you want good quality fruit and vegies follow me."

They left the complex and walked around to the back. As they rounded the corner they found a large space full of shade tents and produce of all kinds on makeshift tables full of fresh food. "Now if you want the best home grown organic hydroponic fruit and vegetables this is where you go."

"But Zelda what's wrong with the fresh produce in the complex?"

"One, Jelena, it's not fresh. Two, you don't want to know what they do to that food just to preserve it."

Jelena and Zelda entered her apartment with bags full of fruit and vegies. After they placed it all on the kitchen bench they sat down, taking a deep breath.

"I feel like my arms have stretched and are touching the floor."

"Well I thought you might have overdone it buying all this food, but soon you get in routine and buy your stuff during the week in smaller quantities."

Packing everything away, Jelena made some coffee, sitting down on the lounge with Zelda.

"Anyway Jelena, are you looking for a boyfriend or girlfriend?"

She thought for a moment. "Actually I'm leaving that thought open for a while."

"Why wait? You should be out there finding out." Zelda took a sip of coffee.

"Well I'm going to apply for the space force. I'd like to be a pilot."

"Are you nuts? Do you have any idea the crap they put you through?"

"Hey remember I was a serf once, so I have a good idea what crap is all about."

Zelda thought for a few moments. "Well why not get on the net now and I'll help you fill out the application? But don't hold your breath as they don't just let anyone in."

Jelena went to her computer, logged on and found the appropriate site. After a few hours of laughing and making fun of some of the questions she hit the submit icon. A message came up explaining the time frame for an official reply would be in the next 72 hours.

"Well Jelena it is getting late and I'm on the afternoon shift, so I'll catch up with you later."

Fixing a light dinner and reading her book pad, Jelena went to bed early.

***

Next morning, she woke up, fixed breakfast and readied for work. Arriving at the foundry, Jelena walked up to the gate and swiped her identification card, giving a cheeky smile to the security guard. Entering the complex, she went to the change rooms. Finding her new locker, she opened it to discover a set of specialised coveralls with boots, gloves, hardhat and glasses.

"Hey you must be the new girl?"

Jelena looked up to find one of the what they called Ruff girls. "You could say that."

"Hey bitch if you want to get smart I'll show how smart hurts."

A crowd started gathering around the change area, expecting a fight. Standing close, staring the Ruff girl in the eye, Jelena just smiled and with a quick kick just under the kneecap caused the Ruff girl to scream in pain. Jelena bent down and grabbed her knee. Then with a swift right upper cut, she knocked her flat on her back. Looking down at the Ruff girl, Jelena picked up her hard hat and put on her safety glasses. She stopped as she was about to step past her. "You have now been told once.

If there is a second time I won't play so nice."

As she left the change room there was a lot of cheering.

Jelena followed the well-marked safety lanes. Machinery worked to full capacity, making parts above convenor belts. Frames of aircraft moved slowly overhead at the far end of the complex.

She entered the lift, swiped her card and pushed the button for level 12. The doors opened. Jelena entered the large underground workshop. Suddenly automatic guns rose out of the floor and with infrared lasers homed in on her. She took a deep breath but remained still.

"Who are you."

"Good morning to you too Tarak."

"How do you know my name?"

"Because I worked with you for the last 10 years as your serf. Remember, I told you I was getting a body upgrade." Suddenly he appeared from behind one of the cabinets, hair all over the place like it hadn't been combed within a good month.

"Well if that is true you certainly did not spare the small change did you." As he was looking her up and down, his eyes went wide.

"You can close that jaw of yours if you like Tarak."

As he regained his composure he said, "So how do I know it is you? Anyone could come down here and say that." Jelena took a deep breath. "You keep all of your information on an old stand alone computer which you hide under the desk and you place the fake computer in the safe in case they try and steal all your work. You do all the technical drawings by hand as you don't trust our bosses, who you are convinced will sell any information for the right price. Finally you have been bringing in the same lunch every day, which is a wrap containing sliced ham, grated carrot and cheese and occasionally you might have chicken instead of ham or both."

Tarak tilted his head for moment. "Have you heard all of my war stories then I take it?"

"Yes I have and if you start again I'll change all your work into a foreign language and I'll let you sit there and work out how to change it back." Tarak lowered his weapon and switched off the security system, retracting the automatic weapons back into the floor.

"So now young lady, what do you call yourself now?"

"The name is Jelena."

"Nice name, really suits you. Anyway you are not due to start work for another two days, so what brings you back to my humble abode?"

"Good news actually. To keep a long story short I have managed to bypass the company bureaucracy and sometime this week we will have some very high ranking people looking over your work."

"Finally I will be able to have my work recognised."

"Well that's why I'm here: to make sure we are ready. Because these are the kind of people who don't like wasting time."

Flicking a switch, Tarak pointed to covers. As they lifted Jelena's eyes widened. "What have you done? It looks like it's dressed to kill."

"Yes it does. I found out how to get the protective coating to fuse with the metal."

"So what's the trick?"

"A combination of just the right temperature with the right sound vibration and an electrical current going through the metal," he said with a look of pride written all over his face.

"Good to see you kept it simple then."

"As always. Now down to work. We have too much to do and very little time to do it in."

For the next two days Jelena and Tarak worked on the ship and their presentation. Going over and over the test runs and slide shows, they made sure all the specifications were presented well and looked professional.

"Well Tarak, I think we've got it all covered."

"Yeah that's the part that narks me." He paced around his

workbench, looking around the workshop for any more thoughts on the prototype they may have forgotten.

"Well I'm going to the canteen for something to eat and a shower to change into clean clothes."

"Good ideas. A break out of here for a while will help clear the head."

Jelena opened the lift door and turned around to see Tarak turning on the security systems. The lift stopped on the sixth level. Another woman walked in. She turned to Jelena. "Were you the one who punched out that Ruff girl the other day?" She just smiled and shook her head.

"Well my name is Jaya and I'm just giving you the heads up. She trashed your locker."

Jelena raised an eyebrow. "Tell me who operates the machine compressor on ground level?"

"That should be Kit. He really hates that bitch so if you ask nicely for whatever your planning, it shouldn't be a problem."

"Is she still here?"

"No her shift ended hours ago. She should be due back in another two hours." As the lift door opened they both walked out.

"Well first things first I'm hungry. I'll worry about her later." As Jelena entered the canteen there was a great cheer. She smiled, stood up on a chair and gave everyone the hands up for quiet. "Okay, I've just been told my locker has been trashed. Who would like to see me escalate this to the next level?" Everyone cheered. "Right, which one of you is Kit?"

He put up his hand. "Over here."

"Okay Kit, can you compress her locker down so it can still fit in the locker space it is in now?"

"It shouldn't be a problem."

"Good. Who here is in stores?" A couple of hands went up. "Okay what I need is a new locker and another set of safety outfits. Can you do that?"

The older one put his hand up. "The locker won't be a

problem but I need you to come in and sign some paperwork for the clothing. That stuff is not cheap and the bosses upstairs will want to know why."

"Okay then, I'll see you soon after I have something to eat." As everyone settled down Jelena went and picked up her tray for the food. As it was served out she seemed to have larger portions than everyone else. Finding a table, she sat down and ate the meal, her first canteen meal, and found it not so great. Eating what she could, she took her tray back to the wash sink. Walking to the stores area, Jelena saw across the workshop a locker being transported on a two-wheel trolley towards the compressor. She approached the stores counter.

"Hi Jelena, you didn't take long." Looking at his name on his security pass card, she said, "Well Skeeter I have lots to do and really have no time for people who think they are better than everyone else."

Skeeter pulled out an electronic pad. Ensuring he had the correct page, he gave it to Jelena. "Just sign the bottom and I'll get you your new kit." She read the document and signed the bottom. Skeeter arrived with all of her new clothing and placed it on the counter. "Now this can't keep happening every day so whatever is going on, get it over with quickly, for if this happens again there will be an investigation and usually somebody's going to loose their job."

"Don't worry I have a good feeling this will be over soon." Picking up her gear, she walked back to the change room, placing her clothing in her new locker. The ruff girl locker was back in the same spot but now only six centimetres high. She smiled, took a quick shower and changed into her clean clothes.

As she was walking out of the change room, a message over the workshop communication system requested Jelena report to the main office immediately. She approached the receptionist. "Hi, I'm Jelena. I've been asked to report here."

The young girl looked up. "Into the conference room over

there." She went back to her work.

Jelena walked across the foyer and opened the door to the conference room to find about a dozen men and women, all in extremely expensive suits, all looking like they fell out of a clothing catalogue, all carrying briefcases and electronic clipboards.

"Good morning Jelena, can you please tell us why these people decided to pay us a visit today without any warning?"

Jelena stared her boss in the eye as he sat at the far end of the long table. He was not looking very happy; his smile wasn't fooling anyone.

"They are here to check out the new prototype that Tarak and I have been working on."

"And why wasn't I informed through normal channels?" His voice had a slight hardness to it.

"Tarak fully believes that you would have sold that information to the highest bidder and these ladies and gentlemen would not be the ones sitting here now."

A woman said, "That's one of the reasons why we are here to check out these allegations."

Instantly the boss lost all colour in his face and started sweating. "Well I'm afraid I can't allow this to take place without prior warning and approval process. I'm sorry to waste your time ladies and gentlemen, so if there is nothing more I ask you to leave."

Within a fraction of a second the one closest to the boss produced a document.

"This is our authorisation. Any attempt to block us will be considered as an obstruction in our duty. Let's say if you want to follow this up you better lawyer up real fast and they better be very expensive."

The boss slumped back in his chair and swallowed hard.

"Okay ladies and gentlemen if you would like to follow me," the man said. Everyone left the conference room and followed Jelena to another room where they put on safety clothing.

Jelena said, "Now before we go I'm going to do a slight detour. All I need you lot to do is just give that look."

"Err Miss Jelena, what type of look?"

"Oh you'll know when the situation comes out. Now remember when we are in the factory stick to the safety lanes."

They followed Jelena into the factory and she directed them to the change rooms. As they were getting closer they could hear a lot of yelling from one very pissed off ruff woman. Jelena rounded the corner of the change room and found herself standing behind the ruff girl as the rest gathered behind her. The ruff girl turned around to find Jelena and all these suits standing with her, just looking through her.

"One, who the fuck are they bitch?"

Jelena kept a straight face. "These people are investigating allegations of personnel selling company secrets. Apparently the boss is now squealing like a little girl and your name has been mentioned quite a few times."

The ruff girl went silent. All colour drained from her face. She looked at the suits behind her and they gave that cold hard look.

"Fuck," was all she said as she ran for the closest exit. Jelena turned around to the suits. "Thanks for that. Now just follow me and we can get started."

Entering the lift, she swiped her card. "Now listen very carefully, you are about to meet Tarak. He is a bit of an oddball so to speak and really doesn't care for the likes of you lot, so if he is very abrupt and starts going on about conspiracy theories just keep quiet until he settles down. When we enter his workshop, if his security system is turned on, don't move." As the lift stopped and the doors opened they entered the workshop. Tarak came into view with a clean work coveralls and some attempt at his hair to make it look like he'd actually put a comb through it.

"Afternoon ladies and gentlemen, please come in." Jelena gave Tarak a look saying: you bastard. He just gave her a slight smile. Gathering everyone around in the open space, Tarak turned his attention to the suits. "Right what I'm going to do is show you the prototype. First look it over, go inside, check it out. All the armaments on this prototype are certified dummies so they can't fire no matter what you do. After about 20 minutes I'll take you through the specifications."

Directing their attention to the covers, Jelena pushed the button. The covers lifted off, showing the prototype. She watched as all their jaws seemed to drop. Within seconds they were all over the prototype like little kids at an amusement park.

"I thought you were going to put on your nutty professor routine."

"That is only for you. Start warming up the display screen and loading up the 3D image. We want to keep these kids entertained, otherwise they lose interest and go home."

After about 20 minutes they gathered around in the open area with the 3D image slowly turning around. Everyone sat down on chairs around the image and watched it.

"Well judging by your first look, you lot were impressed. Now let's get to what this craft can do. Please feel free to ask questions at any time. I call it the Black Knight. When fully fuelled and armed it has enough energy to go to the other side of the galaxy and back. When warmed up and placed in standby mode it can move into light speed from a standing start within a heartbeat."

One of the engineers stood up and walked around the 3D image. Tarak could see he was crunching the numbers. "You have a question sir?"

Without looking up at Tarak, the engineer asked, "It's Zane. Are you nuts? Going into light speed within a heartbeat sounds good but if you don't check the way is clear, when you run into something you're not going to have a nice day."

"That is a good point. Allow me to clarify just a little. The idea of the light speed jump is not so much to go to the other side of the galaxy. It's for only a short distance, just enough to get out of range of what they have just attacked. Also if it is coming out of light speed into a hot zone it can adjust position by a couple of degrees so if the enemy is waiting this should mean the initial first enemy shots should miss."

"Won't that put the craft and crew under a lot of physical strain?"

"True. But I'm talking of a glancing blow to the craft, not a direct hit. This craft has the capacity to take several direct hits from the energy weapons when the deflecting shields are fully operational. It's just those few moments coming out of light speed before those systems are up and running. Not to mention the protective coating on the craft should absorb the energy with very little if not superficial damage to the craft."

"That's fine, but you need a lot of these craft. What is that going to cost?"

Tarak smiled. "Then I ask you two questions. One: how much does it cost to build one fully operational heavy cruiser?"

"A hell of a lot."

"How many non essential personnel on that same heavy cruiser when it is in combat?"

"Around about one thousand personnel."

"Well for the same price of the heavy cruiser you could make one hundred thousand of these attack craft and those one thousand personal are now flying those craft."

"That's good, but if they are attacking a full battle group we are going to take a hell of a lot of losses."

Tarak walked around the 3D image for a few moments, deep in thought. He pointed to a part of the Black Knight with his laser pointer. "This craft is fitted with a Gravity Grail gun with six rounds, which can be fired in single round fire all within 1.2 seconds. This craft will be capable of holding its own in any dogfight with other fighters. But it's best strength is to get in behind a heavy cruiser and fire those rounds at close range into the engines. That cruiser will be crippled. The only thing left to that ship still working will be basic life support. The Black Knight fires all it missiles and the two nukes into that ship then light jumps outa there. They will be able to turn around and watch the fire show."

One of the female engineers spoke up. "One of these crafts is not going to put a heavy cruiser out of action with the shields in place around the engine area. Even with Gravity Grail guns they will only weaken the energy of the shields."

"Your name is?"

"Erica."

"Well Erica. You are right. Now think: you have one hundred thousand of these craft lying in ambush. Because they can reach high velocity from a standing start they would have worked out their targets as they approached. When they attack coming from behind, each group will be a dozen ships. The first three or four's main job is to hit those shields simultaneously as they fly on through the battle group, hitting light speed and firing their missiles. The rest are right behind them, firing on those same engines. Once those shields fail whatever gets through is going to make one hell of mess. If the ambush goes well the enemy will have been lucky to get a shot fired."

"Well Tarak what you have seems very impressive on paper. Should we proceed with the manufacturing? How long will it take to convert the assembly lines?"

Tarak smiled. "80% of Black Knight parts and systems are all straight off the shelf. It shouldn't take more than a month for the conversion. I have already detailed what is required in the reports I will be giving you."

"In the actual aircraft, who controls what?" someone asked.

Tarak pointed the laser pointer to the large screen, clicking on an icon. A detailed picture appeared on screen showing the craft. "This is a five crew ship. With duel control craft you have your pilot and co pilot. The other three control shields and weapons."

"What if the craft is put out of action and looks like it will be captured?"

"Good question. The crew do have a choice of being taken as prisoners of war, which is not a good option. Or they can initiate the final protocol. If they still have any nukes on board then they will activate them to make sure there is nothing left to salvage."

"Will the crew also have access to this protocol?"

"Yes they will, and the necessary safe guards will be in place."

"So how does the craft reload?"

Tarak again pointed at the screen as the display showed up. "When the craft comes to the predetermined location they simply detach the capsule, then position themselves within the next frame, connect, make sure systems are operational and continue on."

"How long will that take?"

Tarak thought for a moment. "For a well trained crew I believe they could have it down to about 15 seconds, maybe less."

"As a tactician I like the idea of the hit and run. If this plan worked and everything went according to the plan we could reduce their effectiveness by at least 60 to 70%."

Tarak went to the console and switched it off. "I won't bore you with any further details. If I have convinced you all enough on what you have seen and heard today, then I'll hand out the info chips that include variations for the other two planets' weapons and the simulators for training."

"What if we don't take this idea and shelve it?"

"Yes you could do that, but when they come, if you fight their way, we will lose. Oh have no doubt, we will put up a good fight, but once they have won they will lay waste to everything that we have built and they will not lose any sleep over it or the innocent casualties they are responsible for. So if you want that on your conscience then look your loved ones in the eye tonight and ask yourself is it worth it." Tarak let it hang for few moments as they all stood there thinking about it. Tarak felt relieved. He had sold the concept of his work. Now he had to let it go and let the process take its course.

A suit stepped out and hit a button on the device. The face briefly went out of focus before them. Otto stood in front of Tarak and Jelena. Tarak wasn't sure what to make of this.

"I'll take those specs thank you." Tarak started seeing red, thinking that he had been had.

"Relax Tarak, this one we can trust," said Jelena. "Allow me to introduce Otto, the King's right hand man. If you can convince him you can convince the King."

Tarak smiled, picking up a small electronic container. Placing the info chip inside and closing the lid, he handed it to Otto. "It will need your thumb print and a code so only you can open it."

Otto was inputting the code.

"Take good care of it Otto, that is the only one. There are no other copies on any other data bank." Otto looked up at Tarak, placing the device into his suit pocket. "Can I borrow Miss Jelena for a few moments?"

"Actually you can borrow her a couple of days if you like. She now has some time off to get some sleep like me."

Otto motioned her towards the lift as the doors closed.

"Okay Otto what do you want?"

"I have some good news. It might pay you to check your messages when we are topside, and I'd pay a visit to the pay clerk. Also listen to the news tonight. What happen is because of what you did and somebody very high up is very thankful."

Jelena led the suits back to the lift. Otto had his info board out and was flicking through the screens, checking up on what had been going on. The lift doors opened and Jelena led them back through the factory, receiving cheers from the workers. Jelena turned to Otto. "Are you behind this?"

Otto looked up from his info pad. "I think you'll find that the news has been leaked and I believe your picture and name were in the leak."

Taking off her safety equipment, Jelena watched her boss being taken away by the authorities. Even the ruff girl was being dragged away kicking and screaming. She smiled watching the ruff girl fighting hard, trying not to be put in the hover van.

As the suits left Jelena checked her emails to find her application for the space force had been accepted. She needed to sign in at the recruitment centre in the city in three weeks. She went to the administration and placed her notice for termination of employment. Leaving the factory complex, Jelena opened the door to a waiting hover taxi. "Sector six, Sunset building complex on Warp Street thanks." As the taxi took off the driver put the taxi in autopilot and turned around and look at Jelena.

"Excuse me for asking, you are that woman aren't you?"

Jelena smiled. "You have to give me a little more clarification." The driver pushed a couple of buttons on his console. A screen on the back seat that was displaying advertising turned to the news channel, with her picture in the top right hand corner as the news presenter was recapping on today's news. Jelena turned up the volume.

"Just recapping this very good news which happened only hours ago. Our King Thordis scrambled the armadas from each planet, apparently acting on news he received from a surprise source. Our forces ran across a fleet from the Terran Union, which were heading directly towards us. They confronted the fleet from three different sides and apparently our commander gave them the option to either withdraw back home or surrender. The order was given to the three armadas to fire warning shots over the fleet. The Moshi made sure they were direct hits, catching the fleet with their pants down, which then caused our commander to join in, leaving the fleet, after short fight, a very reduced Teran Union fleet. Latest reports indicate that the ships that did manage to escape are very badly damaged. The Moshi are ensuring that they are not turning back and are hot on their heels. This information came from one young lady whose picture is showing up on the screen. We have confirmed that her name is Jelena, a serf who only became sentient a short time ago.

"Yes that's me. I bet I'll have a lot of news reporters outside my building waiting for me to come home."

"I don't doubt that for a second."

"Driver, can you please take me to the little coffee shop just down the road from my building." The driver nodded. Flying over her building, Jelena could see news crews everywhere. The taxi landed next to the coffee shop around the corner so she was out of view from the news crews. Jelena was about to pay.

"Not this time Miss Jelena, this one is on me."

"Are you sure?"

"Wait till I tell the guys at work I drove you home in my cab. The guys will be making me coffee for the next month."

"Well thank you. I have your number and I'll keep it in mind so next time I'll give you a good tip."

Jelena walked into the coffee shop and was pleased to see it was empty. Zelda looked up from behind the counter. Her eyes lighted up as she walked around the counter.

"Having trouble getting home?"

"I don't think I'll be able to walk down that street until the next big news event."

"Would you like to stay at my place for a couple of days?"

"Could I!"

"It's a one bedroom apartment so if you don't mind sharing a double bed. Or you could sleep on a very uncomfortable lounge."

THE CHASE
By Terry Mullins

Author's note: The Chase is a short story with a mix of themes; the evil that men do, escape from oppression and a bit on artificial intelligence. The story is told from three perspectives, Margaret, nick named the Wicked Witch, and her AI friend Primey, Lieutenant Fuller, the man tasked with arresting her and lastly Two, a gynoid sent by Margaret to distract her pursuers. The story is an action piece in general, with some discussion of wider themes by some of the characters. It is also an introduction to characters I hope to use again. Enjoy.

The Special Forces team moved up to the doors of the small farm. It was a quiet night on the northern continent of the planet Circe, its two moons lighting the sky.

The Lieutenant in charge examined his readouts, showing the collected intelligence for the raid. All was well. A thermo scan showed the target sitting in a kitchen, using a computer. All entrances were secured. Grenade launchers covered every window. The raiders were ready, night vision on.

'Ok team, nice and easy. This radical is not getting away. Remember we want her alive for interrogation' the lieutenant's voice whispered through the team's ear pieces. This was a major op, higher-ups were watching, so the lieutenant wanted no screw-ups. They had been hunting this one for some time, but the priority on her capture had just gone up.

He wondered what she had done to earn that. Still capturing her, then sending her to a colony dirt farm for the rest of her life would be satisfying. The lieutenant had little time for radicals who upset the system. *This little op is not going to hurt my resume when promotions are due.* He smiled.

He had decided squad one should enter via the back door, as it was closer to the target. Squad two would enter from the front, but that was simply to seal the deal. Squad three would fire the grenade launchers, filling the house with tear gas, and then maintain the perimeter. According to intel, it was a simple home. A kitchen, living room, two bedrooms, inherited on her parent's death five years ago.

The squads paused, placing a breaching charges on the doors. Then they stood clear.

'Good to go sir/ ready here sir/ we are set sir.' The three squad commanders reported.

'Excellent. Go in three, two, one. GO!'

The grenade launchers fired as one, smashing through the windows or flying through the open ones. Inside came the noise of detonations as the tear gas and flash bangs went off. The charges on the back and front doors were nearly drowned out by the attack. Squads one and two burst into the building before the detonations had ceased.

The rear team stormed the kitchen, shotguns in hand screaming 'Terran Security Corp, get on the floor'. One of them slammed the staggering figure down. It was at this point everything started to go wrong. Very wrong.

As disaster unfolded the lieutenant's first thought was *this is not going to look good on my resume.*

In a crevice, a kilometre away, the target of the raid - one Margaret Hamilton aka the Wicked Witch (her online name) - was watched the assault on her laptop. Beside her crouched three figures, still in the darkness.

'Damn Ticks!' she said, using the popular name for the Terran Security Corp. With a vicious smile she pressed an execute function on her computer.

'That's why I'm called the Wicked Witch. Give them hell, Number Three.'

With this, her counter attack unleashed. Three, the life model android pinned to the kitchen floor suddenly spun her head a hundred and eighty degrees, startling the officers.

'You're no longer in Kansas boys!' Three cackled.

With that twenty 10000 candle flares detonated in the kitchen and living room, releasing an incredible blast of light. At the same time, another ten on the roof went off, launching into the air on rockets, adding to the spectacle. Flares like these normally were used to signal air or spacecraft many kilometres away. In such close concentration it was an explosion without the Kaboom. Fires started throughout the house as the two squads reeled from the onslaught. In the house's hidden basement, the same command caused the computer server there to start transmitting the events onto the net.

Margaret could see the blast, and hear the screams, from where she sat. Setting the house's home server to self-destruct as soon as someone breeched the basement, she stood. A small amount of explosive attached to each hard drive and no one was getting anything off them. They would keep transmitting until then to the net. 'Come everyone, let's go. We have an appointment to keep' and with that she shut her laptop. Even in the twenty second century, battery life was limited.

Margaret was of a tall and slim build, with short, auburn hair and sharp features. She was wearing worn jeans, hiking boots, a backpack and a rifle over her shoulder. The woods of Circe could be dangerous, as much of the planet was still an untamed wilderness in many ways. Three others stood with her. These figures looked identical to Margaret, but something about them was...off. Perhaps it was the expressionless faces. They started to walk quickly through the field into the nearby woods

As they walked one of the figures asked 'Why did you do that to the TSC? That volume of light will have caused permanent eye damage, and possible unconsciousness. In combination with the flares incendiary effects some may be killed.'

Margaret considered her answer carefully. 'Several reasons Primey. First this will aid our escape, as the ticks reorganise and recover. Those losers are…were, our immediate pursuers. Second the house will burn down, but the signal coming from the basement will keep going so they will hopefully think I'm hold up down there, delaying them further. And third…' Margaret's savage smile emerged again. 'They deserve it. Those animals…captured Icepick and then "questioned him" to find out about me. Let them burn!'

'This is not a good human emotion.' Primey observed.

'No it's not' Margaret sighed. 'It's not. You are not seeing me at my best.'

The lieutenant moved around the chaos the Wicked Witch had left, the house burning merrily behind him. Off the twenty-four men in the assault group, ten were still unconscious, another ten were blinded and many had burns. Only the lieutenant and his technicians avoided the damage as their screens had burned out before the blast affected them. After the incident he and the technicians raced to the house and pulled out the blinded or unconscious troops before the fire consumed them. He looked up, hearing the approach of several grav vehicles.

That bitch! If she's still alive I will gouge out her eyes for this. That a radical could inflict such mayhem on prepared troops was unnerving, and panic and then fury. What a wreck! How am I going to explain this to command? When I find that witch I'll…

The Lieutenant's internal monologue paused when someone spoke to him.

'Lieutenant Fuller, we have something.' One of the remaining techs was holding a tablet in his hand. He flinched at the look he got in return. He turned to face him; his first impulse to lash out. All he felt at the moment was anger. But he bottled it up, took a deep breath and said 'well, what!'

'Um, this situation is being transmitted, live onto the net' He held out the tablet.

'What?' He grabbed the proffered tablet and looked at it. On it he saw a multiple camera view on the tablet, showing his men lying on the grass, and himself with the tech.

'Shit! Get this feed off the net.' His mind whirled. *Oh my god, this is going to ruin my career.* 'Where is it been transmitted from?'

'A basement substructure sir.'

'Close it down. Now!'

At this the first grav cars landed; ambulances and rein-forcements. And a black uniformed individual stepped off, with four others in the same attire, all armed. The lieutenant looked at the new arrival and froze, an icicle of fear spearing his thoughts. *No, not him.* Personnel bustled about, attending to the injured and the new figure examined the situation, ignoring the panicking lieutenant.

Not now, not the Dagger. The Dagger was the local head of the Special Intelligence Directorate, the branch of the service dedicated to overseeing the rest, and completing "special jobs". They had a reputation for ruthless efficiency, and the Dagger was the worst of the lot. The lieutenant unconsciously straight-ened up as the man approached.

'Lieutenant Fuller, what is the situation?' The Dagger's voice was mild, even gentle.

'Uh, Commissioner' Fuller swallowed. 'The radical set unan-ticipated booby traps sir. I'm still evaluating the situation.' *Oh God! What are you doing here?*

The Dagger gave him a wintery smile and said 'Well be about it then. I'm just observing, right now'.

'Yes sir' Lieutenant Fuller headed off to his techs. 'Quickly, what have you got?'

'Sir! We haven't being able to stop the feed.'

'Why not?' the lieutenant snarled at him.

The technician paled. 'It has an underground link to a Wi-Fi transmitter, and we haven't located it sir. It could be kilometres away. Breaching the basement would be the quickest method to shut it down.'

Fuller looked at the cowering technician with cold blue eyes, and said 'then be about it!'

Squad three's commander, Sergeant Chou, came up and saluted. Fuller turned his gaze on the Sergeant, flicked a return salute, and said 'yes?'

Chou, a tall Chinese man with a scar on one cheek, was a veteran of the service, and weathered the baleful glare. Face blank he stated 'I have reformed what's left of the unit into a squad sir. Orders?'

The lieutenant forced himself not to lose it, as he fought the combination of fury and fear surging through his mind. 'We need to penetrate into the basement. A computer signal there needs to be halted, and we can drain the memory cores for information. Let's see.' Fuller pulled out his tablet and looked at the house plans. The Sergeant moved to see the map. 'Two entrances, one inside and one out. Move your men up to here.' Fuller indicated on the image. 'Enter, but watch for traps. Wait a second.' He turned to the nearby technician. 'Could she be down there?'

'Um, it is unlikely sir. But possibly.'

'Ok.' Turning to the waiting Sergeant he said 'take that into account. If she is there, we really want her alive.'

'Sir.' Chou moved off, already talking to his men.

In the background, the Dagger watched as order replaced chaos in the operation. And stayed silent.

After walking about three kilometres into the woods, Margaret paused. In front of her was a concrete circle, flat to the ground, a hatch in the middle of it.

'Here we are.' She opened her laptop and watched the ticks operation for a moment, then closed it. 'Looks like we're about to lose transmission. It's taken them long enough. Time for us to vanish even further. 'Number Four, Primey, could you open the hatch.'

'Yes Margaret', they both replied. The hatch was nearly 200 kilograms, and was weathered shut, but the two gynoids made short work of it. As they finished Margaret looked at the last one. 'Number Two, you are up. Wait until we are down, then close the hatch. Try to conceal the entrance, then head north, and draw their attention. When they get close, you know what to do.' She hesitated a moment and said 'If you can, evade after that. Head to the old hunting cabin. If possible I'll meet you there. Good luck'. She handed her the rifle, and a pouch of spare clips. 'I won't be needing this from now.'

'Thank you Margaret'. Number Two said as she took the rifle.

Margaret and the other two descended a metal ladder. After they were gone, Number Two shut the hatch with an ominous clang, and dragged branches and leaves to cover the concrete. Then she headed away. She had a task.

The others climbed down about 10 metres, and entered a dark room. Margaret had a flash light out, once her feet were on the ground she looked about. 'Hmm, where is that switch. Ah.'

With a click the room is revealed. A table with several chairs surrounding it was in its centre, and a battery pack was against one wall. On the table was a box, and several maps.

Two doors adorned opposite sides of the room. Margaret opened her pack and removed the laptop, plugging it into the battery pack.

Primey looked around the room with interest, while Number Four starred vacantly. 'What is this place, Margaret?'

'Its's an old civil defence centre, mothballed now. When the colony was established, the Terran Union was at war with, well, quite a few people. Some of them had spaceships. So the colony constructed these'. Margaret gestured about the room. 'A series of underground bases, linked by a monorail net, so they could resist invaders. Ha!' She sat down on one of the chairs. 'I don't know much about war, but I don't think these would have been very effective if it came down to it. In fact, I think it was a way for an interstellar corporation to make scads of cash.' She pointed and said 'Through that door are bunks, a kitchen, an armoury and a storeroom. These were supposed to be fully stocked up, but someone looted them and sold every-thing after it was decommissioned'. She opened the box, and removed its contents. 'It was shut down, just after the Moshi War and was quietly forgotten. I found this place about two years ago. And it is now part of my escape plan'. She paused. 'Our escape plan'.

'I see'. Primey sat in one of the other chairs. 'So what now?'

Margaret had emptied the box on the table. There were ration packs, water bottles, an electronics tool kit and a small pistol and holster, with several clips of ammunition. A smaller box, bore a label saying Shock Grenades. Setting aside a water bottle and ration pack, she put the supplies in her pack, and took out four grenades from the small box, and stored them in packets on the pack. Then she stood and put the pistol on her belt.

'Well, I eat and the laptop charges. Then we head through there' she said, pointing at one of the doors. 'That leads to the monorail net'.

'It is functional?'

Margaret laughed. 'No. But the tunnel leads to our destina-tion, and hopefully help'. And with that, she sat and started eating.

With a loud crash the outside door to the basement blew apart. Once the smoke had cleared, a drone floated into the stair, its antigrav unit humming. Sensors examined the stair and the door at its end, and saw no obvious traps. Outside, Sergeant Chou and a technician watched its video feed on a tablet.

'Try a sonic sweep, Mal' Chou ordered.

'Yes sergeant.' The technician sent the order to the probe, which swept its surroundings. Nothing reacted, and the scope was still clear.

'Ok, focus on the door. Check the lock.'

A more focused probe examined the lock. 'Ah, double dead locked, with an electronic key system. A good lock. Very up market' the technician said. 'Shall I breach it?'

'Get ready to, but hold for my signal' Chou saw the lieutenant walking over to him.

The aftermath of the raid was now much calmer. The wounded had been shuttled away, and more squads had arrived. Fuller had just had an annoying conversation with his immediate superior, Captain Marstein, who was not impressed with the situation thus far. As he walked over to Sergeant Chou, he glanced at the Dagger and his personnel, who were seated near their vehicle.

'Well sergeant?' he said.

'We have discovered no new devices sir. We're about to enter the basement.'

Fuller smiled. Well something was going right. 'Be about it then.'

'Sir' the Sergeant responded, and turned. 'Execute, Mal.'

The technician tapped his tablet and there was another small explosion, followed by several more. 'What?' More smoke poured out into the night.

'Sir, the transmission has ceased,' another technician announced.

Chou and Fuller exchanged glances. The big Sergeant turned to Mal and said 'Send in the drone.'

With Fuller and Chou looking over his shoulders, the technician ordered the probe forward. The image revealed a computer server, and several subsidiary systems, all showing extensive damage.

'Mal, could the charge the drone set have done that?'

'No sergeant. It was too small. They must have been set to

blow upon entry.'

'Well done anyway. Scan and report, then send the squad in if it is clear.' Chou moved away gesturing for the lieutenant to follow. 'Sir we should start an air search pattern for the fugitive. She has been on the run for nearly two hours.'

'Yes, set it up.' Fuller looked up as he saw the Commissioner approaching, and sighed. 'Chou, set it in motion. I think I have to talk to someone.' He walked over to the Dagger. 'Sir,' he said without expression.

'Lieutenant. Is your superior concerned with your performance?'

Fuller looked at the Dagger. 'You know?'

The Dagger nodded. 'I have been fully accessing your comm net for some time. For some months. You intend an air search?'

Fuller nodded, unwilling to say anything. *They were spying on him*? That though was terrifying. He had heard stories about internal security, and unpleasant hearing they were. The Dagger looked at him with some amusement. 'You don't seem over joyed, lieutenant.'

'Candidly sir, no.'

'Don't let it worry you, we do not consider you a security risk.' Unspoken was the word "yet", Fuller noted. 'Ah do not be concerned with the good captain. It is best you simply do your best. So what is the situation, as you see it?'

'The fugitive anticipated our assault sir, and has already left the area. She left a decoy and booby trapped the house. We believe she has not gone far, so I have instituting an aerial search.'

'Very well. Continue Lieutenant!'

Lieutenant Fuller spoke through his comm, and several grav vehicles took off, beginning a spiral search as they gained altitude. Then he turned to the Dagger.

'Can I show you to my command post, Commissioner? It's just this way.' The Dagger nodded and Fuller led the way. All the while thinking hard. *This will either make my career, or break it. I must be careful.*

Number Two moved quickly through the forest, alert to pursuit. Although she could move much faster at need, she kept to a pace that a healthy human could go. She never looked back, but she could hear the distant whine of grav vehicles. Soon they would track the heat spoor she was intentionally leaving. Although she was a highly advanced model for her type, she never questioned her role or orders. Never concerned herself as to her fate. Never even questioned that she was a she, not an it. Margaret had made that instruction plain.

Then, nearly a kilometre above, she heard a grav chopper pass, then turn to circle her. She smiled, although she wasn't happy, it was an automated response. But she was satisfied in a way. The program was proceeding according to plan. She took the rifle off her back without losing pace. Soon.

Within minutes another two vehicles had joined the first, and two others swept past her. She sensed the sound of the landing. The Terran Security squads would be setting an ambush. Yes, all was going to plan.

'Sir, we are tracking a target on foot, moving north, north west towards the Pelicar Range.' A technician breathlessly announced.

'How certain is that report?' Fuller asked. It had been a stressful half hour, with the Dagger breathing down his neck. But at the moment the Commissioner was taking a call, talking to his men.

'Confidence is high sir.'

'Launch the reaction force. Have them go past her. Time to show this wicked witch that we can set traps too.' He activated his comm. 'Sergeant Chou! I am downloading our information to you. We are going to land you in front of the target, and track her in, so you should be able to choose your ground. We want her alive, sergeant.'

The Sergeant voice was distorted by the sound of the grav choppers engines. 'Yes sir, we are on it.'

'Good. And good hunting.'

Chou checked his head up display, and nodded to himself. He had 12 operatives, including himself, wearing combat armour and well-armed. It was an ad hoc unit, but the Terran Security Corp was used to this due to the varied tasks it carried out. And Chou was a veteran of these sort of operations. He cued his comm. 'Now, ladies and gentlemen, we have the drop on the target, but she is a tricky sort so chopper two will remain airborne as a reserve. If all goes well, we'll only need squad one, but if things don't go well, chopper two can still react to take her.' He pauses a moment then continues. 'She is armed, we believe, and we have been ordered to take her alive. So stun rifles and electro batons only.'

'Yes sir', the others replied.

The pitch changed as the grav chopper dusted down, and Chou yelled 'Go!'

Squad one bailed out and the chopper rose into the sky, to orbit the area with chopper two. Chou consulted the map his suit flashed up on his heads up display, still tracking their target. He then examined their surroundings. 'There should be a good spot ahead.'

They had landed in a clearing, just before the trail rose into the foot hills of the Pelicar Range. The moons, dowsed the area in a soft silver light. Deep shadows lay beneath the trees. From his map, the target was following the trail. Smart move, Chou mused. Going off the trail in the dark would have been very dangerous.

Moving forward, the squad found an area with good cover, and spread out, using shadows to hide their positions. Chou touch his comm and said 'Command, we are set. The target is heading straight towards us. Should be over in a couple of minutes.'

'Confirmed sergeant'
Now they just had to wait.

Two saw the grav chopper ascend through the trees in the distance. She could see quite well with her night-vision optimised eyes. The wicked witch never stinted with her "girls" upgrades. Two's computer brain saw 12 targets in different areas of concealment when she shifted to thermal vision, still not altering her stride. She would probably have a 70 percent chance of taking out the forces ahead of her, but that was not the plan. She deactivated the heat she was generating to simulate a human, flushing herself with her heatsinks. Once done she changed course ninety degrees. She reasoned she had a forty five to fifty percent change of destruction, but only if Terran Security strafed and bombed her immediately. But if they would do that was beyond her power to predict.

Chou saw the target's heat image suddenly flare, then drop to extinction. His eyes widened as his brain sought an answer. 'Shit, it's an LMD. Go, go, go before it evades!' If they could capture it, they could at least raid its memory for Intel. But the squad took several seconds to move from waiting in ambush to charging in pursuit. By the time they reached Two's last position, she was gone. She had stopped mimicking human speeds and shot away.

Chou said, 'Support, chopper two, the target was last detected heading east at high speed. The target is a life model decoy. Try to track any electrical activity. It may also have a heat trace, but not at human levels. Chopper two, if you can drop on the target, do so. Chopper one, come pick us up.' His orders clipped out precisely and quickly. He and the rest of squad one turned and trotted back to the clearing they landed at. 'Control, the primary target is not here, repeat not here. She must have gone to ground elsewhere.'
'Control Confirm. Bring chopper one back here, let chopper

two and scout one and two continue pursuit. Scout three and four also return, and orbit control for now.' The disappointment was palpable over the emotionless voice of the control technician.

Chou grimaced. This was not going well.

Margaret, Primey and Four were walking down a long tunnel, in near darkness. Primey and Four could see quite well, and Margaret was wearing head gear that gave her the same edge. It had being a quiet walk, except one time when they encountered some crawlers, a savage dog sized burrower. One grenade and a few shots later and the problem was solved. After that they had been walking and talking for a few hours, and were nearing their destination.

'So yes, I think that maybe Icepick may have given them information to find me, and possibly you, Primey.'

'And, as an artificial intelligence, I must be destroyed. That makes sense, I guess.'

'They're still thinking in an old paradigm, that AI would supplant humanity. Rubbish, really. The so called super AI is impossible. You are certainly much better laterally, able to think more rapidly and in many independent streams, but humans can be upgraded to the same capability. I think they have other reasons, to do with maintaining their power and position.'

'Ah, I see.' Primey looked at Four. 'And she has the same potential?'

Margaret sighed. 'Potential yes. Actuality? Probably not. No one knows why one system develops self-awareness, and another doesn't. Even in the Sword Kingdom they don't know why, and from what I gather they are the best cyberneticists in existence. Well, that we know of.'

She smiled and patted Four on the shoulder. 'But I hope.'

Four responded 'I am sorry I have not met up to your expectations, Margaret.'

Margaret laughed. 'You have Four. You have completed your work to my expectations and total satisfaction. I just hope, one day, you may want more.'

She looked ahead, seeing a mark on the wall. 'Ah, we are here. Just a second.' She activates her comm, setting it to low power and directional. 'I come seeking insight and release' she said and waited.

A voice spoke through her ear piece. 'The wise seek both, for the world is transitory.' Then the circuit died. A figure faded into sight in front of them, more a silhouette than a figure. 'Welcome Wicked Witch. We of the Lotus have been waiting. Come. Transport to safety is nearby.'

'Not a good result, lieutenant' Captain Marstein said, sitting behind his desk idly toying with a letter opener. 'Not good at all.' Standing beside the Captain was the Dagger, not smiling for once, but quiet and still.

'Yes sir' the lieutenant replied. The chase for the LMD had been a long one, and they had gotten close, he was certain, but in the end it slipped away. In the process it had disabled one of the scouts that flew too low, and three of his men had been wounded. Considering the accuracy of its rifle fire, the last had been intentional.

'Well, it has been a bad day all round. We think we had a security leak, which is how Ms Hamilton was ready for you.' He activated a console and a holographic display lit up. 'That same security leak led to another breech, a major one. It appears that a prisoner has escaped. The same prisoner from whom we gained the intelligence to launch your raid. Icepick I believe he was called.' Captain Marstein grimaced as he considered the situation. 'There was a systems crash that caused all security systems to fail, and when they went back up, he was gone. He was still "recovering" from the interrogation, and couldn't walk on his own. So he had help. A lot of help.

Despite himself, Fuller asked 'But wouldn't the cellblock lock down in that circumstance?'

'It did. But he got out anyway.' The captain put down the letter opener and shook his head. 'Circe is full of potential rebels and traitors. So this cannot be broadcast. So the raid was a success, and there was no breakout. The net transmission is an obvious fake.'

Fuller sense something different. Something had changed, or was going to change. The Captain was never like this. 'Yes sir. What if she resurfaces?'

'Then that person is an imposter.' The Dagger interjected. 'But I feel she won't turn up soon. A problem for another day.'

'Yes sir' He hesitated a second, then asked 'So what happens now?'

The Dagger smiled. 'As you know, you have been under surveillance. But I can now assure you, not because we questioned your loyalty. Quite the opposite really. We were evaluating you.' He moved around the desk, and sat in the chair next to the lieutenant. He looked at the Captain and said 'Captain Marstein?'

The captain sat back in his chair. 'Let me explain lieutenant. You may not know, but we have been in a state of war for a short time. A new human polity, calling itself the "Kingdom of Swords" has destroyed a liberty squadron. The Fleet is assembling as we speak, and will deal with them, I am sure. But we believe that this "Kingdom" has infiltrated the planets in this region, and is associated with hostile aliens.' He leaned forward, fixing Fuller with his gaze. 'So security is now most important. To that aim, the lieutenant governor has appointed me as head of security for the planet.'

'Uh, congratulations sir'

The captain waved it away. 'But we need a replacement for me. And so we return to you. You are to be promoted, and take my old position.'

Fuller sat silently for a second, processing what he had heard. 'But I failed.'

The Dagger said 'Yes you did. But not through any fault of yours, and I consider you performed well. You can learn a lot about someone when they're in an impossible situation.' He gestured in the air vaguely. 'Besides, now it is a victory. Your men will know the real story of course, and why we are doing this.' He settled back. 'Besides, "Captain", truth is illusory, and subject to reinterpretation. So do you accept?'

Fuller did not hesitate. 'Yes Sir.'

Margaret came to. She was in a container. Inside a small, grey, room. On the wall near her was an oxygen supply, and a plastic water tank. A second container holding a man was opposite her. Everything was fuzzy.

'Stay still, Margaret. The coldsleep drugs take a little while to fully clear your system.' The talker came into view. It was Primey. Four was near the wall, powered down.

Gathering her scattered thoughts, she tried to speak, but her mouth was dry.

'Let me hydrate you.' Primey held a bottle, with a straw. Margaret drank from it, and cold water tasted like the most marvellous of drinks. Her arm had a drip inserted.

'Where are we?' she managed eventually.

'We are in the capsule the Black Lotus placed us in. We have been picked up by a space vessel. As planned. We are safe, I think.'

'Oh. Good.' Her thoughts began to order themselves. 'Who's that?'

'Icepick. The Black Lotus saved him, as well.'

At that a series of clicks echoed through the capsule, and the end of it opened. Several people entered, some in white coats, one in black, with a red trim. On the breast of that one's tunic was a set of crossed swords, over a sunburst. He looked at her and smiled.

'Hello, I am Knight Lieutenant Cameron Faye. Welcome, Wicked Witch. You are on the Sword Kingdom Vessel "Granite".

Welcome to safe haven.'

'We made it?' Hope filled her cracking voice.

The knight Lieutenant smiled. 'Well we still need to slip out of Union space, but yes. You are safe, as are your two friends.'

Margaret smiled. As the medical personnel started to work on her and Icepick she thought *Safe haven indeed. For me and Primey.* Then her smile faltered. Both Two and Three had given their existence for her and Primey's escape. Although they were only sophisticated machines, they both had had the potential to be greater. Three was gone, and Two may also be. She resolved that one day, she would return and see if Two survived. She looked at Primey, and saw the AI starring back at her. Sensing what she was thinking, Primey squeezed her hand. 'One day, we will find my lost sister.'

Margaret's smile returned. 'Yes we will.'

In mountains, far away, Two arrived at the hunting lodge. She was damaged, with one arm hit by an errant round, but she had evaded pursuit. No one was tracking her now. She slipped into the cellar, and used the workshop there to repair her arm. She considered her options. She set an alarm, in case any should trespass, and then sat in a chair, facing a computer. She typed in a function to awake her if a signal came in, and settled herself. Her task was done, and well. There was nothing left to do. That there was anything else she could do was beyond her. She would wait for Margaret. She took one last look around the room.

Then she powered down.

TIMELINE

1969 Man walks on the moon

2001 Twin towers attack in New York. The start of the War on Terror

2017 The China Seas conflict. The war lasts six months, with fighting across the southern china sea, northern Vietnam and in Korea. The result of the war was the collapse of North Korea (eventually unifying with South Korea), and the destruction of much of the Chinese fleet. The war ends in a treaty, with no side really happy.

2018 Fusion technology is invented in Germany. This advance required the invention of Gravitic systems to allow the manipulation of gravity required to create the pressures needed.

2020 Gravitic technology, developed, for fusion power, leads to the invention of the Gravitic drive, allowing cheap and easy space travel. This also changed military hardware. Due to the expense of the new equipment, richer nations up arm first, and so maintain dominance.

2021 Inner Station, earth's first orbital spaceport, is constructed. Clearing of space junk around earth commences.

2022 lunar base established, Mars landing.

2023 First orbital habitat is created, population 5000

2025 orbital population reaches 20000. Jovian expedition. Mars settlement founded.

2026 Commercial mining of the asteroid belt starts. Funding allows many private contractors to fund ships to mine and support asteroid settlements. Earth space ports created at Woomera, Cape York, Heathrow, Cape Town, Cairo, Beijing, Tokyo, New York, Los Angeles, Moscow, Warsaw, Berlin, Paris, and Rio. More are planned.

2029 The orbital population reaches 200000. Orbital farms produce enough food so world hunger is alleviated. (***Sunraysia***) (***Ghost of the past***)

2030 The Apocalypse Attack. Extremists of differing types, Muslim, fundamentalist Christians and other various religious terror groups, undertake a worldwide strike, using nuclear and chemical attacks to devastate many cities across every continent.

Attacks were foiled on other cities, or were less successful. An attack on Inner Station was stopped when the suicide bomber was killed at the Woomera space port. Israel launches nuclear counter strikes on perceived threats in Syria and Iran. Iran retaliates with nerve gas and biological attacks. The death toll is immense (some 300 million worldwide)

The USA, Russia, China and The European Union form the Terran Union government, dissolving the United Nations, with an aim to end the threat of terror attacks once and for all. Nations refusing to cooperate are attacked and occupied. Terrorist cannot hide in populations now as those populations are destroyed if they do so and the locals do not reveal them. Many nations fall into ruin.

2036 The last nation opposing the Terran Union falls, but terror attacks continue, from time to time. The defeated nations are either occupied or placed under strict rule or, if devastated by weapons of mass destruction, simple are abandomed. The final death toll of the war is over a billion. Pandemics still cross the world, killing many.

Due to the threat of disease and other health effects resulting from the war, medicine advances greatly. During this time life extension medical practices become possible, but are restricted to elites.

2037 The Terran union is now established as world government, the only organisation allowed an armed force. All nations are reduced to police forces, as autonomous zones. Occupied areas are ruled directly by the Union, and abandoned zones are secured.

The last pandemic is ended late this year.

2038 Flux drive developed. Orbital population is now 41 million, Mars 1 million, the moon 20 million, the asteroids 10 million. This is the result of large scale immigration due to the fighting, and that not one Terror attack has succeeded in space. Space industry has rapidly expanded in this time, with asteroid mining expanding as well.

2040 First manned vessel (the Enterprise) is sent to another star, Tau Ceti. There is shock upon its return when it reports the discovery of a habitable planet. The Union quickly claims the planet and colonisation commences quickly. The new world is called Prometheus. Colonies, mostly for mining and research spring up across the solar system. Notable bases are on Europa, Ceres, Vesta, and Titan and in orbit around Venus. Terraforming of Venus starts, expected to finish in 150 to 200 years.

2046 Union policies on earth and in space over the last ten years have produced discontent, with large corporations moving in on colonies, small scale miners and freight companies. The Union has not relaxed security laws despite the wars ending ten years before. Laws are passed supporting the corporations, and despite words of support for small companies or individuals, the Union government does not act to curb the problems. This is where international corporations turn into transtellar corporations.

Off planet population is now 70 million and growing rapidly. This includes 1 million settlers in other systems.

2049 (*The Queen of Mars*) Agitation for independence grows on Mars (population now 25 million), with strikes and protests. This grows due to perceived sweet heart deals favouring corporations over local companies.

2050 The Union occupies the Mars colony, claiming to prevent a terrorist attack when an explosion occurs at its spaceport (later shown to be a tragic accident). Corporations move in quickly to "support the local economy". This causes a violent backlash, starting the Outer System War. The population off planet is now 200 million

2050 to 2058 The Outer System War consists of many minor skirmishes. Initially the "outies" depend upon converted merchant vessels and semi fixed defences, while the Union depended upon police vessels. As the war continued the Union's industrial might takes hold, and it constructs the first pure warships. Then it systematically began to capture or destroy their opposition. By 2054 the Outies realised the war was lost, and switched to a delaying action, while evacuating to other star systems. It is estimated that over 20 million flee the system. The last strongholds of the outies were Triton and Galatea, around Neptune. The defending squadron fled once the bases fell, leaving the system. Although individual ships continued to fight for some years, major hostilities ended.

During the war, restrictions on public dissent were reinforced, and many were imprisoned. Great orbital "gulags" were constructed and these prisoners were kept there, ostensibly for trial for sedition or the like. Some were actual agitators, but others were free thinkers, writers, philosophers and the like. Many scientists were also held, due to perceived Outer system sympathy. One significant group was writers, fans of "escapist fiction" as it was called. Decried as a useless waste of time, of unrealistic escapism, the proponents of it were forced to give it up under great social pressure, or were arrested. Many were considered to be mentally unfit. All were deposited in the orbital gulags.

The Terran Union Aero/Space Corp and the Terran Union Marines were formed during the war. Also the Terran Union Security Corp was created to counter dissent.

2055 The rise of the ImagiNation, an activist group devoted to exposing the sordid activities of the elites of the union, an online group. During the war it opposed the imprisonment of the freethinkers with protests, net blockages, and finally online sabotage. Most were captured or killed by 2060. Those who were captured were sent to the orbital gulags. The population of the gulags by the wars end was approaching 50 million. Off planet population was nearly 400 million due to this and people leaving the solar system to escape the fighting.

During this time, environmental damage on earth are becoming obvious, with weather events adding to the destruction, and many species dying off or under great stress. The

The Typhon Expanse

Union institutes a plan to move 90% of all industry off world, a process that was already starting, and sponsored the creation of both fusion reactors and solar energy for power supplies.

2060 After the war, the question as to what to do with the imprisoned free thinkers comes up. Trials would be costly, and divisive. It was decided to use the gulag's population as forced colonists, to open up new worlds for honest citizens. This is the start of the Union's colonial expansion policy, the export of "radicals, the useless and the criminal" to work for the betterment of the union.

Elsewhere, the Moshi home world is visited by outie refugees. Ethnically Asian, they introduce Buddhism, which takes off like wildfire. Within 10 years most Moshi are Buddhist. Unfortunately, after ten years, the humans suffered a disease, that killed and sterilised the survivors. The last died during the Moshi Suppression Wars.

On Mars, and later on Titan, alien ruins were discovered. This race is called the Ancients. The ruins are dated to 12000 to 13000 BCE. These are the first of many found throughout this part of the galaxy.

2062 The first large colony ships are sent to surveyed worlds, before only smaller vessels had been sent. Forced colonists were sent first, followed by volunteers.

2064 In a coup of extraordinary inventiveness and courage, a senior head in the Terran Security Corp (nick named Jubilee), secretly an ImagiNation activist, arranges for many free thinkers in the gulags to be transported to one colony. When they arrive, the ships were seized by his underlings. The crews and guards who were not part of his conspiracy are deposited on the prospective colony world, the rest are sent on an escape route. Jubilee with a few small warships, stay over the colony, faking its existence. More forced settlers are recovered as they arrive, and were sent on. He saves some twenty million people, before escaping himself.

This group flees Union space, and after a journey of over two years, discovers the Excalibur system, near the Typhon expanse. This is the beginning of the Kingdom of Swords. (***The Dawn of Change***)

2070 Union discovers the planet Saati. They are shocked to find that these aliens are humanlike, and have genetically links to mankind. The Saati culture is peaceful, but extremely religious, and they have fought religious wars in the past. The Union government sees them as a potential threat, and occupies the system to "liberate them from a non-democratic government" (***The Alien Integration Act***)

This sets the mode for dealing with potential threats to the union, i.e. all other alien races. The genetic linkage is thought to be created but the Ancients.

2076 (*Grey Matter*)

2088 The expanding Moshi Confederacy is encountered by Union Fleet Scouts.

2090 to 2096 The Moshi suppression war starts. This is the first time the Terran Union has encountered a multisystem opponent, and also one which had been warned of it. The Union navy suffers several defeats before it concentrates enough force to crush the Moshi. Even then, the resistance is savage and persistent. Finally, a large attack strikes the Moshi home world, succeeding due to the use of kinetic bombardment of the planet.

2091 The Union settles several worlds near the Typhon expanse, creating a new governorship. Worlds settled were named after Greek gods or heroes. These include Hermes, Hestia and Zeus. During this time was the loss of the UAV Discovery a survey vessel. It is sighted several times over the next century, becoming a space version of the Flying Dutchman. (***The Echo of Nothing***)

By this time over 1 million people a week depart earth to settle other worlds, either voluntarily of forced. Earth population has stabilized at this point, at 9 billion.

2093 Circe is settled. Ancient ruins discovered. The University of Circe is founded.

2098 Moshi refugees reach the sword kingdom. The kingdom gives them rights to two worlds they have surveyed, establishing a protectorate over them. Within twenty years, the Moshi are given full control, and start raiding the Union.

Also the Union occupy Bastet at this time. An arctic world, it is used for mining and hunting, the prize beast is a catlike creature called a Sekhmet.

2100 A scientific study on earth has shown that global warming has stopped, but was still overly high (+3 degrees centigrade on 20th century levels). This is the result of shifting most industry into orbit, asteroid mining replacing most mining on earth, and the transfer from fossil fuels to solar and fusion power.

2105 The Sekhmet prove to be sentient, but this information is suppressed due the profitability of the hunting trade.

2108 The Sekhmet align with the forced labour colonists and attack the colony. It is soon overrun. The Union decide it is not worth reinvading, so abandons the colony.

2119 The Green Flame War. Civil war between different factions of the Sword Kingdom (Green and technocrat). The war ends when the current high King intervenes, gaining great powers in the process. Once the fighting has ended, he requires that all government members, including himself are to be replaced. Although this is disruptive, peace is restored.

2120 The plasma lance developed and is adopted as the preferred weapon of the Sword Kingdoms nobility.

2121 A sword Kingdom Scout locates the abandoned Bastet colony, and assists the inhabitants. The system is covertly industrialised and the Sekmets move into space.

2122 Defenin first encountered by the Sword Kingdom. Contact is rare, and both polities have little to do with each other at this time due to separation.

2143 to 2165 The War of the Typhon Deeps. This war is between the Sword Kingdom and House Mora, an exiled noble family of the Defenin Imperium. The fighting starts over an argument over the control of a rich mineral site, and raids launched by the Defenin fleet. It ends with a mutually satisfactory treaty. The Defenin in the expanse and elsewhere are very impressed with the Sword Kingdom. The war was characterised by small raids, and ground actions. The obvious psionic power of the Denefin placed the defenders on the back foot at first, but with time and effort (and the help of some newly discovered mystics) the sword kingdom military created defences, and trained their own psi units.

Oddly, trade with the Defenin starts during this time, despite the war. The final treaty reinforced this trade, caused the release of all human captives, and establishing diplomatic contact.

2148 The Sword Kingdom encounter the Sheen, who after

much discussion, agree to trade and teach the Sword Kingdom Psionics. This allows the Kingdom to face the Defenin threat.

2157 Battle of the seventh deep. This was the largest battle of the war, involving about 50 vessels of all types. It ends in

2165 to 2168 Knight Errant Salah and diverse others travels to the Defenin Imperial Court, to initiate friendly contact with the heart of the Imperium. This was a difficult and long trip, involving several battles and duels, but they impressed the Emperor. He declared the Sword Kingdom a brother state deserving of honour, and issued a writ of trade and friendship. Salah became the Sword Kingdoms ambassador. This leads many in the Imperium to regard the Sword Kingdom as their "little siblings".

The Sword Kingdom perfects the use of quantum singularity communication. This will be vital in the upcoming conflict with the Union.

2173 Union destroy Defenin colony on Eros IV, starting war between the Union and the exiles. (***To be the surgeon***) (***Jelana***)

2174 Destruction of Liberty Fleet 210, in the Caliburn system of the Sword Kingdom. This is the start of the Typhon War between the Terran Union and the Kingdom of Swords. (***The Chase***)

2175 Creation of the Outworld Alliance. Against the Terran Union